LORDS OF CORRUPTION

ALSO BY KYLE MILLS

Rising Phoenix

Storming Heaven

Free Fall

Burn Factor

Sphere of Influence

Smoke Screen

Fade

The Second Horseman

Darkness Falls

KYLE MILLS

LORDS OF CORRUPTION

Vanguard Press
A Member of the Perseus Books Group

Published by Vanguard Press
A Member of the Perseus Books Group

Set in 12.5-point Granjon by the Perseus Books Group.

Library of Congress Cataloging-in-Publication Data
Mills, Kyle, 1966–
  Lords of corruption / Kyle Mills.
    p. cm.
  ISBN 978-1-59315-499-8 (alk. paper)
  1. Nonprofit organizations—Fiction. 2. Political corruption—Fiction 3. Volunteers—Fiction. 4. Murder—Investigation—Fiction. 5. Africa—Fiction. I. Title.
  PS3563.I42322L67 2009
  813'.54—dc22

                                                          2008042922

Vanguard Press books are available at special discounts for bulk purchases in the U.S. by corporations, institutions, and other organizations. For more information, please contact the Special Markets Department at the Perseus Books Group, 2300 Chestnut Street, Suite 200, Philadelphia, PA 19103, or call (800) 810-4145, ext. 5000, or e-mail special.markets@ perseusbooks.com.

10 9 8 7 6 5 4 3 2 1

LORDS OF CORRUPTION

PROLOGUE

After four hours of rutted dirt, military roadblocks, and fetid mud bogs, the landscape around Dan Ordman had completely transformed. The jagged, grass-covered hills that made up his world had been replaced by dense jungle rolling into a reddening horizon. Although he'd lived in Africa for almost a year, this was the first time he'd seen the rain forest, smelled the damp rot, listened to the birds and monkeys just out of sight. There was something about it that made him nervous. Probably just the fact that, until now, he'd never been more than twenty miles from the comfortable expatriate community that he'd wrapped himself in. Or maybe it was something more primordial.

"It's going to get dark on us."

Gideon maneuvered the Land Cruiser around a tree that had sprung up in the middle of the road and glanced at Dan. Or more precisely, he aimed his mirrored sunglasses briefly in Dan's direction. Gideon didn't interact with people in the accepted sense of the word. It was always strangely one-sided—what he wanted you to know, what he was willing to do for you, what he had time for. What he cared about.

The first time they'd met, Dan had decided the African looked more like a sculpture by an amateur artist than the product of God or evolution—a little too tall, muscles a little too well-defined, and a slack face with blank eyes. Not the friendly, capable right-hand man Dan had envisioned from his parents' sprawling oceanfront estate. But he'd come here to learn, and his first lesson had been that reality rarely lived up to fantasy. Life was about figuring out how to bridge that gap.

"It's not far," Gideon repeated for probably the tenth time. "And it's cooler at night." There was a stirring behind them, and Dan twisted around to look at the four kids crammed into the vehicle's backseat. The youngest was probably twelve, and his haphazardly nourished frame was dwarfed by the Russian machine gun clutched between his knees. They were all dressed about the same: dirty jeans topped by ragged T-shirts silk-screened with the otherworldly images favored by the local teens. Cartoon characters frolicked, distant sports teams competed, British bands crooned. One had the slogan "I wish these were brains" configured in a way that suggested the shirt had been designed for a well-endowed woman.

Dan settled back in his seat, feeling a dull rush of adrenaline when the sun hit the horizon. Evil spirits came out at night. At least that was what he'd been told, and he had no reason to dispute the idea. Africa changed after sunset. Its normal chaos and dysfunction turned dangerous, malevolent. Wasn't Africa where humans had first developed their fear of the dark?

Gideon jerked the wheel to the right and slammed on the brakes, skidding to a stop in a maneuver typical in this part of the world. Behind the wheel of a car, Africans acted as though everything was a desperate emergency. Out from behind the wheel, they acted as though nothing was.

"What? Don't tell me this is it?" Dan said.

Gideon nodded and stepped from the car, followed by the well-armed children in the back. Their silence had been replaced by excited chattering in the native language that was as incomprehensible to Dan now as it had been the day he'd arrived. Instead of fanning out to look for rebels, as was apparently their function, they milled around the vehicle fiddling with their weapons.

Dan jammed his fist against the stubborn door and jumped out, anxious to do what he had to do and get back behind the concrete walls and iron gates of the compound. Everyone would be hanging around the pool by now, watching the sunset and settling into happy hour.

"You've got to be kidding, Gideon. There's nothing here. Do you have any idea what it would take to clear all this out for farmland?" Dan raised a sweat-drenched arm, pointing to the front of the vehicle where bugs were swaying like smoke in the headlight beams. "And what about those?"

He'd read somewhere that malaria may have killed half the people who had ever lived. Another thing he had no reason to dispute.

"This isn't America," Gideon said. "This is our land. Our home. It is the way it is."

Africans were resigned to the fact that everything on their continent was trying to kill them, but Dan saw no reason to tempt fate. "Look, I didn't mean any offense, okay? But we're already working fourteen hours a day, and we're barely keeping our heads above water as it is."

Gideon started walking, and Dan hurried to keep up. The African seemed to be searching for a break in the jungle, though it was a miracle he could see anything through the shades he never took off.

"What about rebels?" Dan continued. "This area is right on the edge of what the government controls, isn't it? We could get—"

"President Mtiti controls all of his country," Gideon said, a hint of anger audible in his voice. Behind them, Force Peewee went momentarily silent at the name of their fearless leader.

"Of course the president is a great man," Dan said, impressing even himself with the false reverence in his tone. Despite what most of the rest of the world thought, Umboto Mtiti was a world-class scumbag.

The bugs, attracted by light and body heat, began to swarm, and Dan started back toward the Land Cruiser, swatting uselessly at them. "Fine, I've seen it. I'll call tomorrow and see what the hell we're supposed to do with it. But I think we both know this is bullshit."

Gideon didn't respond. He'd never been particularly warm or chatty, but tonight he was verging on creepy. Dan had tried hard to like him, constantly scolding himself for racism whenever Gideon's attitude or personality pissed him off, but tonight he didn't care. Racism or not, he was ready to get the hell back to what passed for civilization.

He pulled open the passenger door and then paused when no one made a move to follow. "Ready?"

Gideon walked around the back and opened the hatch. The kids watched with poorly concealed excitement. Their T-shirts and eyes glowed in what was left of the sun, as did the machete now hanging loosely from Gideon's hand.

Despite his background—a childhood in a neighborhood gated against nothing, prep school, an Ivy League degree—Dan understood immediately what was happening.

There was a gleeful chorus when he ran, quickly drowned out by the wet slapping of leaves against his skin and his own breathing as he entered the jungle.

He'd never been an athlete, but a year working outside in Africa, combined with a volume of adrenaline he'd never known he had, kept him moving forward, ignoring unseen branches as they cut his skin, stumbling over unseen obstacles, and constantly adjusting his trajectory away from the bursts of gunfire that rang out every few seconds.

He had no concept of how long it took, but he finally couldn't get enough air, and the obstructions he had managed to clear before became insurmountable. Soon even fear took too much energy, and his mind fixated on the mundane things that he would never do. He'd never get married, never have children. Never own a home or get the "real job" his father had insisted on.

The side of the tree next to him exploded as a bullet struck, sending wooden shrapnel into his cheek and eye. He slapped a hand to his face, unable to tell the difference between blood and sweat, and felt the fear flare again. He stumbled forward, fatigue and lack of depth perception causing him to hit the ground every few steps. The laughter of children got louder as he vomited, but it didn't seem to be getting closer. Maybe they'd become disoriented by the dense foliage and semidarkness, too.

He could make it. He just had to keep going. The farther he went, the more he would become a needle in thousands of square miles of haystack.

He slowed his pace, moving more carefully than he had before. The pain in his eye continued to intensify, but he ignored it, controlling his breathing and avoiding falling again. He couldn't afford the noise, and a twisted ankle would almost certainly be fatal.

The jungle's edge was completely invisible until he burst across it and found himself standing in the road again. The Land Cruiser's lights were off, but its outline and the outline of Gideon holding his machete were visible in the waning light. The voices of the kids behind him grew louder, and a moment later they appeared, still laughing and chattering, pumping their fists in the air at their success. They'd flushed him into the open like some stupid animal.

There was no way to escape. He could barely put one foot in front of the other, and Gideon had just been standing there, waiting for him. The kids fanned out, creating a corridor that Gideon began walking slowly through.

Dan had never imagined his own death, or even thought about it, really. At twenty-six, it seemed so remote. So theoretical. But now he was overcome by a deep sadness. Tears welled up in his uninjured eye while the other continued to leak blood through the tightly closed lid. What was he doing so far from his own life, from the family he'd never see again? What had he hoped to accomplish? Anything? Or had it all been a game to him?

Gideon was in front of him now, his face erased by the darkness. It didn't matter, though. There wouldn't be anything there to talk to, to plead with. Still, he felt he should say something.

"I thought I could help."

Gideon just raised the machete.

1

The bar was virtually empty, and Josh Hagarty chose a booth far from the windows glowing with the light of what most people would have considered a perfect afternoon. It was the end of finals week, and it would be a few more hours before students celebrating an aced test or wanting to forget a flunked one came flooding in. With a conscientious effort, plenty of time to get commode-hugging drunk.

He watched as the waitress ducked under the bar and started his way, weaving through the empty tables framed by walls hung with sports jerseys and vintage signs. She was too pretty. And the bar was too clean. He should have gone to the other side of the tracks to do his drinking. PBR served by a woman with leather skin and a missing ear—that was where he belonged.

"Nice suit," the girl said, setting a pint of Newcastle on the table and then fingering the creamy silk of his tie. "Things must be going pretty well for you."

He let out a breath that passed for a laugh. "Three months of living on nothing but hot dogs and ramen noodles to pay for it." He poked an Italian leather shoe out from under the table. "And another month and a half for these."

"Well, it doesn't seem like it hurt you any. You look great."

He knew it was true, though he didn't take any pride in it. His genetic luck had been so good it was almost suspicious. He was smart, tall, good-looking, and had been sick probably three days in his life. Maybe that was why everything else in his life was going so soul-crushingly wrong.

He put both hands around the cold glass in front of him and stared at it.

"You okay, Josh?"

"Don't I look okay?"

"Actually, you look like you're about to kill someone. I was thinking about having all the sharp objects removed from the bar."

"That bad?"

"Not far off. What's up?"

He lifted the glass and drained half of it. "The job interviews aren't going as well as I'd hoped, you know?"

He wasn't surprised at the grin that crossed her face. All she saw was that he had an engineering degree, a brand-new MBA, and a 3.94 grade-point average. The truth wasn't so simple, though. Nothing ever was.

"What," she said, the smile widening, "they offered you two hundred and fifty grand and a BMW when you had your heart set on a Porsche? Are you kidding me? I'm barely holding on to a C average in sociology." She waved a hand around her. "This is probably the best job I'll ever get."

"Thanks for the sympathy, Cindy."

"No, seriously, Josh. I'm starting to tear up. I better go get a tissue."

She swayed back to the bar, and once again, he watched. She seemed to get more perfect every time he saw her. Not only the long legs disappearing into the ridiculous plaid miniskirt that the bar's waitresses were forced to wear but the fact that the sun always seemed to be shining around her.

Which, in a way, it did. Her parents were rich, her grades were irrelevant, and half the guys on campus would kill the other half to get a date with her.

He, on the other hand, was screwed.

He'd just left his last on-campus interview, and though the interviewer had been perfectly nice, it was clear that he—like all the rest—could spot a loser when he saw one. It was easy for Josh to hide his past from his friends but not so easy to keep it from a professional recruiter with half a brain and an Internet connection. Every corporate interaction he'd had followed the same pattern: the recruiter's initial excitement at seeing his résumé and setting up a meeting followed by a cool, disinterested interview, culminating in a polite letter saying that he wasn't what they were looking for.

The rest of the beer went down even more easily than normal, and a moment later Cindy returned with another one. When she tried to take his empty glass, he grabbed it and wouldn't let go. Her brow furrowed and her head tilted, but she finally retreated to the bar empty-handed.

Josh slid it to the edge of the table—the first of many. A monument to the weight of the responsibilities bearing down on him and the fact that he'd lived up to none of them. His medium? Pint glasses and dying brain cells.

His cell phone rang, and he looked down at the incoming number. Laura.

His sister had an uncanny ability to remember his interview schedule and religiously called after each one to see how things had gone. Amazingly, this wasn't new—she'd done the same thing when he'd been looking for engineering jobs after getting his undergrad degree. She'd been twelve at the time.

He turned the phone off and jammed it back into his pocket. What would he say to her? She was annoyingly difficult to lie to, so he'd have to spend some time devising and rehearsing something plausible—a creative recasting of the truth.

And what exactly was the truth? That strapping yourself with a mountain of debt to get an MBA because no one would touch you with a ten-foot pole after you graduated near the top of your class in engineering school wasn't a work of genius?

The worst part, though, was that deep down he'd known that the whole time. He'd run away from the world, retreating to the only place he could convincingly pretend not to be a loser. School.

He sat there for well over an hour, slumping farther and farther into his seat as the alcohol slackened his muscles but not his anger—at himself, at the companies that had no concept of the idea of second chances, at the world. He leaned forward and looked through the empty glasses lined up along the table's edge, trying to focus on the distorted image of the building beyond. A guy in a suit had just taken a stool at the bar and was trying to get a conversation going with Cindy. He clearly wasn't a student—suit, tie, and a midsection in irreversible-growth mode. Traveling salesman. Vacuum cleaners. Maybe encyclopedias.

Josh snorted at his own bad joke and pulled a pen from his pocket. Using a damp napkin and his six-figure education, he calculated how long it would take to pay off his student loans working at a Jiffy Lube. If he went back to his ramen-and-hot-dog diet, lived under a bridge, and managed to hold on for the average American life span, he'd make his last payment two years after he was dead.

"Cindy!" he yelled, noting that the telltale slurring had begun. "Tequila!"

He watched her approach through the lens of the glasses and immediately downed the shot she slid onto the table.

"Tequila and self-pity don't mix so well," Cindy said disapprovingly.

He squinted up at her. "Okay. Now I've hit rock bottom. I'm being lectured by a twenty-one-year-old waitress."

"I'm twenty-two, and you're being an asshole, Josh." She

slapped the side of his head and started back toward the bar. This time he just stared down at the grain in the tabletop.

She was right. And not just about her age. He pushed himself into a sitting position and took a deep breath to clear his head. Sure, he'd come up with a big goose egg from on-campus interviews. But the world didn't end at the well-manicured lawns of the university. What about the interview he had next week at a local company that was advertising in the paper? He was wildly overqualified, and the pay probably wouldn't be much more than he could make fixing cars, but at least it would be a foot in the door that led to the mysterious world of the white collar.

"Mind if I join you?"

He hadn't noticed the man who had been sitting at the bar approach and would have been startled if he hadn't been so drunk.

"Why?" was all he could get out.

The man laughed and slid into the opposite side of the booth. "You're Josh Hagarty, aren't you?"

"Do I know you?" The response was just a reflex. The man was probably in his midforties with an acne-scarred complexion and an oddly shaped bald spot that would be hard to forget.

"I'm John Balen." He reached across the table and shook Josh's hand before leaning back and loosening his tie. "I'm a recruiter for an organization called NewAfrica. We're based in New York."

That sobered Josh up a bit. "I didn't see you on the schedule."

"We weren't on it. We've never been all that impressed with the on-campus interview format, you know? Kind of a clusterfuck, and in our experience you don't end up getting the right people. Everyone's angling and got their game face on."

Josh's mind was still running at less than half speed, and he couldn't figure out where this conversation was going. Was the guy just bored and wanted someone to talk to?

"So, who are you interviewing?" Josh asked, more to be polite than anything. He could see Cindy coming their way. Maybe to save him.

"Just two people, actually. A guy from California and you."

And in the end, she did save him—arriving just before he could start to stammer.

"Can I get you guys anything?"

Josh looked at the line of glasses on the table and silently cursed himself. For very good reasons, he almost never drank. One Newcastle a week when he wasn't saving up for interview clothes. And now here he was looking like the poster child for Alcoholics Anonymous in front of a guy who had come from New York just to interview him.

"Uh, just the check, Cindy."

Balen held a hand out. "I got it."

She looked at him with an expression that suggested their conversation at the bar hadn't gone all that well. "They're on the house."

"No way," Josh said. "You don't have to do that."

She ignored him and began writing on a napkin she'd pulled from her apron. When she was finished, she slid it into the breast pocket of his jacket. "That's the address of my new apartment and my phone number. Why don't you come over tonight and I'll make you dinner."

If it had just been the five pints he'd consumed, he could have handled this many things coming at him at once. But the tequila had put him over the edge.

"Uh, I don't think I'd be very good company."

"Come anyway. You wouldn't believe the lengths I'll go to to cheer you up."

Josh stared blankly at her as she once again walked away. Finally he turned back to Balen. "I'm sorry. What were we talking about?"

"We were talking about our interview process."

"That'd be the process where you sneak up on people in bars."

Balen smiled. "We do our research from New York, narrow

down our prospects, and then do a few interviews. It's kind of un-usual, but it's been pretty effective, you know?"

"Why me?"

"Jesus, Josh. Have you looked at your résumé lately? Why not you?"

Josh chewed his lower lip for a moment, his badly impaired mind spinning things in ways he knew he'd regret. But he was fed up. It was time to get off this roller coaster and settle for something realistic. "You should just hire the guy from California, John. You're wasting both our time."

"Yeah, but it's my time. And if you don't mind me saying so, you don't look all that busy."

Out of the corner of his eye, he could see the line of glasses on the table and wondered why the hell Cindy hadn't taken them un-til he remembered wrestling with her to keep the first one.

"So. Any interest, Josh? Can I tell you a little about the com-pany?"

"I guess."

"We're a nonprofit focused on creating sustainable agricultural projects in Africa. The motto of the charity is 'Helping people who are willing to help themselves.' We've had a lot of success and done some good things for people who really needed it."

"Africa?"

"That's what I said. Africa."

Josh had never even been west of Missouri. Or was Africa east? He'd never thought about it.

"So, have you ever considered working for a charity, Josh?"

"Not really, no."

He regretted the words almost before they were out of his mouth. The conversation was starting to counteract the effects of the booze, and the memory of his desperation was getting the bet-ter of his cynicism.

"Why not?"

It was a good question that would have been complicated to

answer dead sober. The truth was that it just wasn't in his culture. His people were the *recipients* of charity, not the providers. That was a whole other world.

But that would be a little too much honesty. Balen had clearly done this on purpose. He could have called and set up a meeting. Hell, he could have come over before Josh had plowed through half a keg. He wanted Josh off guard. But he was going to be disappointed.

"Honestly, I think it would be incredibly fulfilling work, John. But I've never known anyone who's worked for a charity. And business school, doesn't really push you down that path. . . ."

"I'll bet. They tell you to graduate, make a bunch of money, buy a big house. It's the American way. But not the only way, you know?"

Josh nodded in a manner that was calculated to look deep as Balen pulled an envelope from his pocket and held it out across the table.

"First-class plane ticket. Flies out tomorrow morning."

"To where?"

The surprise must have been audible in his voice because Balen did a bad job of stifling a laugh. "Relax, kid. New York, not Congo. We'd like you to come out, meet some of our people, get the tour. You know, see what you think."

Josh opened the envelope and stared down at the ticket. He'd never been on a plane before. And he sure as hell had never been to New York City.

"Thanks, Mr. Balen. I don't know what to say. I really appreciate you giving me the opportunity."

"You know how you can thank me, Josh?"

"By doing a good job for your organization?"

"Well, that would be nice, but no. I was hoping you could tell me how you get free beer and a hell of a lot more than a dinner invitation from that waitress."

Josh hadn't been ready for the change in subject, and he blinked dumbly. "Uh, I had a little help on that one. We used to go out."

Balen leaned forward over the table. "Really? My old girl-friends all hate my guts. What's your secret?"

Josh thought about it for a moment and shrugged. "I like them."

2

It had been an unpleasant and undignified trip, but he'd finally made it.

Josh Hagarty stood on the corner with his back pressed against the building behind him, watching people flow by. Every few seconds there would be a break in the pedestrian traffic sufficient for him to see the brownstone he'd been given the address to. And every glimpse was followed by a wave of nausea.

He'd thrown up twice in the plane's minuscule bathroom—a combination of anxiety, his first time flying, and a moderately bad hangover. The taxi had been worse—the driver seemed to think that the only appropriate position for an accelerator pedal was completely released or pressed to the floor. But Josh had held it together. Barely.

Josh looked down at his watch and followed the second hand on its trip around the face. When it hit the 12, he started across the street, breathing into his hand to make sure the pack of Altoids he'd purchased was doing its job.

The door was mostly glass, with "NewAfrica" etched into a stylized representation of the continent. He looked into his reflection, smoothed a few waves from his hair, and searched briefly for anything that might be stuck in his teeth.

When he stepped through, he found an interior that was nice, but not the antique mahogany and Oriental rugs he'd daydreamed about during those endless tax-law classes. He wasn't exactly in a position to be critical, though. It was a hell of a lot more swanky than the Formica counter and cash register that might be his alternative. Besides, too much opulence would undoubtedly work against him—amplifying the city's uncanny ability to disorient and intimidate him. He'd seen hundreds of movies set in New York, but they'd done little to prepare him for the overwhelming reality of it.

A man wearing a vaguely threadbare blue blazer pulled open the door that led from the foyer to a small reception area and smiled widely. "Josh! How was the trip?"

"Good, thanks. No problem."

The man pumped Josh's hand and went into a cheerful diatribe about the incompetence of airlines. A small crowd gathered as he spoke, but none of the people were what Josh had expected. No Birkenstocks or tie-dyes, and not even a hint of patchouli oil. While his was the only tie, everyone was conservatively groomed, clear-eyed, and confident. It wouldn't be that much of a stretch to think he was in a successful boutique law office on casual Friday.

His research into NewAfrica hadn't been as fruitful as he'd hoped. Newspaper articles were surprisingly few, and the organization's website was longer on philosophy than on specifics. It was probably the worst-prepared he'd ever been for an interview, but so far it was going better than most. Why was a mystery.

"So are you finished with finals?" asked a woman with a foreign accent he couldn't place.

"I am. Day before yesterday."

"Can we assume you aced them all?"

"I think I did okay."

The group, which had swelled to seven people, laughed politely. It was clear that they knew his history and had little doubt about his performance.

"Did you just get in, or did you come last night?"

"I just landed an hour or so ago."

"First time in New York?" the man who had opened the door for him asked.

"It is. First time."

"Shame you couldn't have done the town a little bit. There are some amazing restaurants in this neighborhood. Don't leave without getting these cheapskates to take you to lunch."

"I heard that."

The group parted and let the man who'd spoken through. He was probably in his midforties, with a tan too dark to have been earned in New York and blond streaks in his hair that looked honestly sun-bleached. When they shook hands, his skin was smooth but didn't have the softness that Josh had come to associate with the city people who had interviewed him in the past.

"I'm Stephen Trent. I ride herd over this rabble."

"It's nice to meet you, Mr. Trent. I really appreciate you inviting me up here."

"Stephen. And I appreciate you taking the time to talk to a little charity like us. We know you must have big-money offers coming in from all over the country, but I think we might be able to offer you something unique."

The crowd quietly scattered before any further introductions could be made, and Trent led Josh through a narrow hallway toward the back of the building. The walls were lined with photographs of happy Africans in agricultural settings—sometimes working, sometimes posed with their arms around each other, sometimes in large groups with Trent's relatively pale face hovering near the center. The last picture before they entered the door at the back depicted Trent shaking hands with a sturdy African man in a military uniform. President Umboto Mtiti, Josh knew from last night's African charity cram session.

"Have a seat," Trent said, pointing to a comfortable-looking leather chair. Josh did as he was told, and Trent took the chair next to him instead of going behind the imposing desk that dominated the room. "I assume you've done some research on us?"

"I have, but there wasn't much time, so I wouldn't say I'm an expert."

Trent nodded. "We're a small, focused charity, and we like it that way. Our donors are sophisticated enough to understand that Africa is too complicated a place to fix with strategies that can be summed up in a sound bite. How much do you know about foreign aid, Josh?"

"Only what I've read. I don't have any direct experience."

Trent didn't seem concerned. "Foreign governments and aid agencies have been pouring money and people into Africa for decades. And if you criticize them, they'll hit you with a bunch of excuses: This or that project didn't work out because of this or that extenuating circumstance. It's ridiculous if you think about it. Do you know why?"

"I'm afraid I don't."

"Of course you don't. Why would you? It's because there's *always* an extenuating circumstance. And if there's always an extenuating circumstance . . ." He paused, obviously wanting Josh to finish the thought.

"Then it's not an extenuating circumstance?"

"Exactly!" Trent slapped the arm of his chair loudly. "Let me give you a piece of advice, Josh. If you ever become a millionaire and someone comes to you looking for aid money for Africa, ask them to take you on a tour of their projects."

Josh tried to appear thoughtful, but mostly he was thankful that Trent was content to do most of the talking.

"But when you get there," Trent continued, warming up to his subject, "tell them you only want to see projects that are at least ten years old. Then watch them scramble."

"But the newspaper articles I could find on NewAfrica have been pretty complimentary," Josh said. "They say you've been pretty effective."

"Yes! But it's because we're different. Some people think we're hard-asses, but if we think a project isn't going to be productive in the long term, we won't touch it."

"And other agencies will?"

"Hell, yes. Look, don't get me wrong. They all have good intentions. But after they've hired a bunch of people, put infrastructure in place, and started a donation campaign built around this project or that, it gets pretty hard to just pull the plug."

"Everyone would be out of a job," Josh said. "And they'd have to tell the donors that their money had been wasted."

"Precisely." Trent leaned back in his chair and examined Josh for a moment. "Have you ever been involved in charity work?"

It was a question that Trent almost certainly already knew the answer to. Josh had thought about it from every possible angle, but he had nothing to work with. He'd never even been in the Boy Scouts.

"I haven't, Stephen. But I've been around it. I grew up in a pretty poor area of the South."

Trent nodded but didn't immediately respond. "Okay, then. Let me ask you this: Have you ever been the recipient of charity?"

With his ritual of meticulous preparation, Josh had never been surprised by an interview question, and that left him with no canned reaction when it finally happened. He felt his mouth tighten, and he ran his tongue slowly over his teeth, trying to decide if he should be pissed off and what he should say.

"You don't have to answer that if you don't want, Josh."

"No, it's okay. The answer is yes. I have."

Trent jabbed a finger in his direction. "You see? That's a unique perspective that no one here—not me, not anyone—has. It's the kind of diversity that I believe can help make this organization even more effective. I mean, in a way, you're the model of what we want for the Africans. You started poor and disadvantaged, and you overcame that."

"I would hope that I could bring something useful to New-Africa, Stephen. But I'm not sure I have any secrets."

Trent grinned. "I'm having a hard time reading you, Josh. You seem a little reticent. Is it because of the way we snuck up on you or because you wouldn't take a job with a charity if someone put a gun to your head?"

Another surprise question, though it shouldn't have been. He'd been playing this interview like a politician, figuring that the less he said, the less could be held against him. But what else could he do? He sure as hell wasn't the rich goody-two-shoes that he imagined charities went for. He wasn't looking for adventure before returning to the country club and going to work for Daddy's company. He didn't need to find himself, and frankly, he'd always been so concerned with his own family that he'd never had time to worry about anyone else's.

"That brings up an interesting point, Stephen. How exactly *did* you find me?"

"To be perfectly honest, I don't really know. Something to do with Internet databases and search parameters. I tell a company that specializes in these kinds of things all the unusual qualities we're looking for, and on the rare occasion that we find someone who has those qualities, we pursue them."

"Unusual how?"

"Maybe 'unique' would have been a better word. Look, I won't lie to you. The realities of Africa can be a little harsh. We need people who are smart and driven, but also people who have some experience with the real world. People who are tougher than average. But most of all, we're looking for people who have common sense, because that can get lost pretty quickly in the foreign aid business." He paused for a moment, obviously considering something. "What I'm trying to say is that when you're faced with some of the things Africa can throw at you, it's easy to lose yourself in your ideology. We fight against that. You see, we look at this as a business, Josh. Our product is projects—agricultural, medical, economic—whatever. We want to manufacture a product for our customers that's effective, durable, and cheap."

"Your customers being poor Africans."

"Right. I know it's a strange philosophy, but we find that it works. You've got an MBA, so you understand how a business should run, you come from a poor, broken family, so you know what people need. You're an athlete and a hunter, so you're not soft. And you've achieved things on your own, so you understand what it takes to better yourself. That's what we need on the ground."

Josh felt his eyebrows rise, and it didn't go unnoticed.

"We know a few personal details about you, Josh. We're not trying to pry, but we also don't want to hire someone who is going to be over their head ten minutes after they land. We ask a lot, frankly."

Trent had misinterpreted Josh's surprise. It was less that he knew those few personal details than that he had missed a number of others. Or had he? Maybe he didn't care. Or was this a test of Josh's honesty?

"So this is a position outside the country?" Josh said, deciding to let it go. He could always lean on plausible deniability if the shit hit the fan later.

"Yup. You'd be knee-deep in the African mud." Trent's mouth widened into another prizewinning smile. "Well, it's really not that bad, but it's not the Upper East Side, either."

Josh nodded slowly. Africa. How many miles away was that? About the same distance as the moon, as far as he was concerned. For a million dollars, he doubted he could name five countries on the whole continent.

"Look, Josh, I know you're probably looking at a hedge-fund job or something, but I can tell you from personal experience that you should consider this. It's a different challenge every day, you have a lot of autonomy, you're not chained to a desk, and at the end of the day someone's life is better because of you."

3

Stephen Trent sat down behind his desk but immediately stood again. A quick glance at the clock confirmed that he had less than a minute. Aleksei Fedorov had told him nine P.M., and he was never late. Never.

Trent took a deep breath and brushed at the imaginary wrinkles in his shirt, a nervous tic that was impossible to resist but entirely pointless. Fedorov didn't care about anything that didn't involve making money, holding on to money, and keeping money—and the power it implied—from his enemies.

The lights in the hall were off, and Trent walked through the gloom taking deep, calming breaths, finally stopping in the lobby where he could watch the front door. The second hand on the receptionist's desk was almost thirty seconds past the hour when the sound of a key sliding into the lock became audible over the hum of traffic outside.

"Aleksei! It's good to see you!" Trent said, a little too loud to seem calm and a little too cheerful to sound spontaneous. If there was one positive thing about spending so much of his time in one of Africa's more godforsaken backwaters, it was that Fedorov almost never set foot on the continent.

Unfortunately, this was not true of NewAfrica's offices in New York. Despite endless hints designed to prevent these visits, Fedorov seemed to enjoy using them as proof that he was untouchable. And maybe he was. But why endanger everyone else?

Fedorov shook Trent's outstretched hand disinterestedly, his deep-set eyes taking in the surroundings more like a camera than the windows to the soul that poets imagined. They twitched back and forth over a long, straight nose that hinted at his foreign birth and an expression that suggested it hadn't been a pleasant one.

"We've had a thirteen percent drop in donations. Why?"

It seemed that his accent became more imperceptible every time they met, and that was worrying. Fedorov had relocated to the United States less than ten years ago and now, at age fifty, was close to perfecting his fifth language. Trent had been blessed with an impressive intellect that had proven indispensable over his lifetime, but it also tended to make him uncomfortable around those rare people who were clearly smarter than he was. It was an advantage he was loath to give up.

"Let's go back to my office, Aleksei. I'll make you a drink."

"First you'll answer my goddamn question."

"We've got a few things working against us," Trent said as he started back down the hall, anxious to get Fedorov away from the windows looking out onto the street. "And they're all hard to control. The U.S. economy's weakened pretty significantly, and that makes people feel less generous. Also, after getting a good run in the press for a while, the problems in Africa are taking a back burner. The Middle East, political scandals, even global warming are getting better ratings."

He stopped and let Fedorov go through the office door first. Trent couldn't read the man's expression in the dim light and had no idea how he was taking what he was hearing, making it impossible to properly adjust his tone and approach.

"We're doing what we can, Aleksei, but . . ." He let his voice trail off as he poured two whiskeys and Fedorov wandered around the office examining things he clearly had no interest in.

After a few seconds, the silence became uncomfortable and Trent found himself speaking again, purely out of nervousness. "We're working on a large partnership with USAID right now, and I'm optimistic about it. We'd be the primary administrators of a twenty-million-dollar project. Right now it's between us and CARE, but I think we'll get it. The danger is more that the U.S. will pull funding entirely. Conditions in the part of Africa where we operate are getting worse, and it's hard to convince people that the money invested there is going to make a difference."

Fedorov turned and accepted the whiskey Trent held out to him, looking down at it as though he thought it might be poisoned. "I saw your new campaign, Stephen. It's shit. Another bunch of happy niggers with shovels."

"Aleksei—"

"'Our work is done,'" Fedorov continued, cutting him off. "Is that what you're trying to say? Because that's what I'm hearing— 'Africans so happy and healthy that I think they should be giving *me* money.'"

"Like I was saying, Aleksei, we have to show a certain amount of progress and stability. Our focus groups—"

"Your focus groups?" Fedorov shouted. "Why don't you give me your focus groups' addresses? Then I can have a conversation with them about why I'm not making any money."

"I think—"

"Am I wrong, Stephen? Tell me I'm wrong. Tell me that I can't do simple math."

"That's not what I'm saying—"

"Don't we have photos of dead children? Why are you the only person on the fucking planet who can't find dead Africans to take pictures of? You can't walk ten feet in that country without tripping over one."

"It isn't—"

"Remember that picture of the starving kid with the vulture standing next to him? *That* made people want to give money."

Trent tried to remember how many times that particular image had come up and how many times he was going to have to defend his decision not to use something similar.

"Going with something like that is going to work against us in this situation, Aleksei. And we'd have to deal with a certain amount of backlash and scrutiny that I think we both agree we don't need. We have to be very careful about controlling our image."

"Charities can't run on good intentions, Stephen."

It was impossible to know if the statement's irony was intended or if an acknowledgment of the joke was expected. In the end, Trent decided to pretend he hadn't heard. "We're still refining the campaign, and I agree that it could be more hard-hitting. Give us another week, and we'll send you something more polished. I think you'll be happy with it."

Fedorov clearly wasn't convinced but was willing to move on. "Have you hired someone to take over the farming project?"

"I met with the last candidate yesterday."

"And?"

Trent sat down at his desk and slid a file across it. Fedorov made no move to pick it up, glancing blandly at it from his position in the center of the office.

"His name is Josh Hagarty," Trent said. "He graduated from high school with a very average GPA—essentially As in things he was interested in and Ds in things he wasn't. After that he went to work for an auto shop near his home and, well, wasn't exactly a model citizen."

Fedorov remained silent, but for the first time that night, his expression showed a hint of approval.

"He had a few minor arrests for things like disorderly conduct and marijuana possession, but nothing stuck. Then one night, he and a friend stopped at a liquor store. Josh stayed in the car while his friend went in and robbed the store at gunpoint."

"But Hagarty just sat in the car?"

Trent nodded. "When the police started chasing them, though, he tried to escape. And because he was drunk at the time, he hit a tree, and both he and his friend ended up pretty seriously injured."

"How much time did he do?"

"He cut a deal and only spent a year inside. His friend swore that Josh had no idea he was going to rob the store and that Josh screamed at him the entire time they were running from the police."

Fedorov seemed disappointed. "And what did he learn in prison?"

"Apparently that he didn't want to go back. When he was released, he enrolled in a community college, got straight As, transferred to a four-year college, and graduated near the top of his class in engineering."

"He didn't find Jesus, did he? I hate those fucking people."

"He doesn't attend church, and there's no mention of religiosity from our private investigators."

Fedorov nodded noncommittally.

"Because of his background, he didn't get any good job offers, and that prompted him to pursue an MBA. He's just now graduating, again near the top of his class, despite holding a full-time job the entire time."

"And?"

"And he's drowning in student loans and every other kind of debt. He has a sister he's extremely close to who'll be graduating from high school next year, and he doesn't have the money to send her to college."

"Are any other companies sniffing around him?"

"He's had a fair number of interviews, but even with his qualifications, his background has kept him from getting any offers. He does have a meeting next week with a small company near his

school called Alder Data Systems. They don't have a terribly sophisticated hiring process, and according to our people, they may
have overlooked his problems with the law."

"I take it we're going to fix that?"

"It's being taken care of as we speak."

"I'm not impressed, Stephen. After all the time and money
we've spent on this search, this is the best you can do?"

If there was one universal truth, it was that Fedorov was never
satisfied.

"There's no such thing as a perfect candidate, Aleksei, but he's
smart as hell, charismatic, good-looking, and well-educated. More
importantly, he's desperate—for money, to rise above his upbring-
ing, to prove he's changed. He's no angel, and he has a sister who's
important to him. I'm not sure it would be possible to find someone who fits the profile you created any better."

Fedorov's expression darkened subtly. "Because of a few minor
scrapes with the law and the fact that he was driving the wrong car
at the wrong time?"

"There's only so far we can go down that path, Aleksei. I can
sell Josh to the board as a redemption story. And if it ever comes
up, I can play the same card with the press. If we go with someone
whose background is any worse, it's going to generate questions
that aren't so easily answered."

"More attention than we got from that little saint you hired
before? I told you he would be a problem. But you didn't listen
to me."

"You have to understand that—"

"What I understand," he interrupted, "is that I'm not here to
fix your fucking mistakes. What you should understand is that I'm
holding you personally responsible this time. Do you understand
me? *Personally responsible.*"

4

"Thanks for the ride, man." Josh slapped the side of the old pickup, and the driver pulled away, leaving him on the side of the deserted road with nothing but the duffel slung over his shoulder.

The leaves were starting to change, and they crunched beneath his feet as he made his way down a wide dirt track that split off from the asphalt. The sun hadn't hit the mountains yet, but when it did, the still air would turn cold quickly. He increased his pace, intent on making it home before he had to dig around for a jacket.

He'd exchanged the plane ticket from New York back to school for one to Kentucky. His finals were done, and he'd decided that the tiny fall graduation ceremony would be more depressing than uplifting, so it was a good time to squeeze in a trip home. Whether it would be a quick visit before starting his life or a permanent return to his disastrous past was yet to be seen. No point in dwelling on that now, though. Plenty of time to wallow later.

His sister hadn't been at the airport to pick him up as agreed, and when he'd called, he'd found that the phone was out of service. Not that this was necessarily a cause for alarm. The old Ford he'd scammed from an auto shop he'd worked for had probably broken down again, and the phone service was always in the process of being cut off or reinstated. But there was no point in lamenting that, either. It was just the way things were. Positive thoughts, he told himself. Positive thoughts.

It was easy to forget how beautiful Kentucky was, but he was quickly reminded whenever he returned. The sugar maples were dense and vibrant on the sides of the road, marred only by the occasional poorly maintained trailer home. He waved to the few people who were outdoors, and they waved back unenthusiastically. Most he'd known since he was a kid, but he'd never really fit in. He still didn't.

His lunch with Stephen Trent had gone even better than the interview, and it was hard not to let his guard down, to fantasize about being offered the job at NewAfrica. Or maybe "romanticize" would be a better word. Josh Hagarty: World Traveler. International Sophisticate. Perhaps even Jet-Setter. The idea of actually going somewhere, seeing the world, had never occurred to him. But now that it did, he had to admit that it was just a little bit appealing.

Another fifteen minutes passed before he crested a hill and spotted a teenaged girl reading a book beneath a shedding tree. Laura.

Instead of immediately jumping up, she sat there contemplating his approach. It wasn't lack of excitement, he knew, but just the way his sister was.

"I'm sorry I wasn't there to pick you up, Josh."

She spoke with a slow, soft cadence made necessary by the fact that she considered every word—a trait she'd had since she'd first learned to talk.

Laura had been born more than a year after their mother's third divorce, at a time when she couldn't handle a new baby. Josh had only been seven, but he'd taken on virtually everything relating to the raising of his new half-sister. And despite the crappy job he'd done, she'd turned out to be the best person he knew.

"I'll eventually find it in my heart to forgive you. Now give me a hug."

When they embraced, she felt frailer than usual. But he always thought that. It was guilt more than anything—for being too young to be a real father. For not taking her away from all this long ago. And now for the likelihood that he would fail her again.

"You look good," she said, pulling away and looking up at him, her light-blue eyes, blond hair, and pale complexion washing out even more in the flattening sunlight. "Imagine. A Hagarty with a master's degree."

"Seems unlikely, doesn't it?"

"And how goes pimping yourself to the man?"

He laughed and took her hand as they started up the road. At seventeen, she was already a senior and seemed to have read every book ever written. He'd never figured out who her father was, and their mom wasn't talking. To this day, whenever he was in town, he was always on the lookout for blond men with the personality of a sarcastic Buddha. So far, zip.

"I've got some good offers, but I'm waiting for all of them to come in."

"Anything you'd love? Something that would make you happy?"

He hated lying to her and had to be careful not to exhibit the list of tells that she had learned years ago. "They're all pretty good, but there's a lot to think about. Money, location, opportunity for advancement."

"Fun?"

"As far as I'm concerned, anything that involves an obscene amount of money is fun."

She squeezed his hand, not looking completely convinced. "We're going to be okay, Josh. No matter what you decide."

"We don't deserve to be okay. We deserve to be great. And that's what's going to happen, right?"

She didn't respond.

"Right?" he repeated.

"Tell me about New York."

"It's really tall." He glanced over at her and once again regretted not being more insistent that she come live with him at school. She'd dug her heels in, and no amount of begging, yelling, or pictures of opulent local high schools had even made a dent.

"Tall? That's all you have to say? It was tall? What did you do? What did you see? Did you go to MoMA?"

"Who?"

She grimaced. "What about the Statue of Liberty? Did you know the French gave us that?"

"No and no."

"Did you see a play before you left?"

"Uh-uh."

"Geez, Josh. All that education and still a Philistine."

"Philistine? Jesus Christ, Laura, act your age. Use 'like' every other word. Talk about how lame your boyfriend is. You're creeping me out."

That actually made her laugh. It was a sound that hadn't really changed much since she was a baby, a rare and muffled gurgle that came mostly through her nose. It wasn't that she didn't have a cheerful soul. She was just discerning about what she thought was funny.

"What about you, kid? How are things going with you? I see the phone's out again."

"It'll be reconnected next week. We were just a little late. Things are okay. Nothing much changes, you know?"

He'd learned long ago that whenever she used the phrase "you know," she meant the opposite of whatever statement preceded it. Bad news would eventually follow.

"You're still doing okay in school?" he probed. "Valedictorian, right? Scholarship material?"

"What scholarship? You're going to be rich, right?"

"Don't evade the question."

"It's still between me and Erica Pratt."

He forced himself to shrug casually, though his stomach had cinched down a few notches. "Hey, no pressure. That girl's folks are richer than God, and she's two years older than you."

"It's not the two years, it's the rich part that's the problem. Her 'tutor,'" she said, making quotation marks with her fingers, "does all her homework and papers, and she cheats on the tests. Word is that her dad's car dealership isn't doing so hot, though. So I'm hoping he's gonna have to start hiring dumber tutors."

"Are you still working?"

"At the grocery store. They're nice."

The trailer that was his ancestral home became visible through the trees, and he slowed a bit, concerned that he still hadn't been able to ferret out what she wasn't telling him. Oh, God. She couldn't be pregnant, could she?

The tightness in his stomach suddenly started to feel like an ulcer in the making, and he silently repeated to himself that Laura was a smart girl with a historical distaste for the boys she went to high school with. How fast did things like that change? Hormones were powerful and unpredictable things.

He pointed numbly to the empty clearing where the car was usually parked. "Where's the Granada?" he said, trying to force out the doomsday scenarios bouncing around in his head with something more mundane.

She didn't answer immediately. "Now, don't get mad . . ."

He let out a long breath, feeling the tension leave his body. She wasn't pregnant. She'd just wrecked the car. "What happened, Laura?"

He'd barely spoken when the sound of an engine became audible behind them. He turned, seeing the worried expression on his sister's face and then the patchwork paint as the old Ford crested the hill fifty yards away.

"Fawn borrowed it," Laura said hesitantly.

He stared as the car approached too fast for the rusting suspension and then rocketed past them, its driver intent on whatever she was saying into her cell phone.

"You've got to be fucking kidding me. . . . "

"Josh—" Laura started but fell silent when he whipped back around to face her.

"I begged my boss on my hands and knees for that car and then didn't sleep for a week fixing it up. For what? So Fawn would have something to drive around in?"

"It sounds so bad when you say it like that."

"Don't sass me, Laura. This is why I had to hitchhike from the airport?"

"I said I was sorry."

"How much?"

"What?" she said gazing at the ground.

"You know damn well what. How much money has she gotten out of Mom?"

"Not that much."

"I want that thieving bitch out of here, Laura."

"I know, but Mom won't—"

She fell silent again when Josh turned and stalked off.

"Fawn! What the hell are you doing here?"

She stepped from the car, attempted a disinterested hair flip only to be thwarted by too much hairspray, and then ducked into the backseat to retrieve a box.

Fawn Mardsen was the daughter of their second stepfather. Not actually a blood relation but often mistaken for one because of her superficial resemblance to Laura. Though a few years older, she was the same height, had the same thin, slightly sickly physique, and wore her hair dyed to approximately Laura's natural shade. Her pale skin wasn't genetic like Laura's either, but a symptom of her aversion to the outdoors and anything resembling an honest day's work.

She hefted the box and turned confidently but hesitated when she was forced to look into Josh's face. "Hey, I didn't see you back there on the road. Congratulations on graduating—that must be a weight off, huh?"

He remained silent.

"Sorry about not coming and getting you at the airport, but you know, I've been super busy."

"Really?" he said. "Doing what exactly? Do you have a job?"

"Yes," she snapped back, "I have a good job."

"Fawn's starting a business," Laura said, subtly taking a position between them.

"Yeah, and it's going really well," Fawn said. "Actually, it might be an opportunity you'd be interested in. Your mom's getting in on the ground floor. It's a smart move."

"A smart move? What happened to the money Mom put into your last business, Fawn? What was that one again? Something about online pet grooming?"

When it became obvious that he wasn't going to step out of her way, Fawn set the box down and lit a cigarette. She took a long drag on it before she spoke again. "Yeah, and what are you doing? Other than sitting around in a classroom that costs a hundred grand a year—"

Josh's eyes widened, and Laura grabbed his hand. "Josh, she didn't mean—"

"Who provided the car you drive around in, Fawn? You? Or was it me?" He thumbed behind him at the broken-down trailer. "Who keeps the heat on in there? Oh, yeah. It's me. What exactly do you contribute?"

"Who the fuck do you think you are, Josh? Mr. I'm-better-than-everybody-else-because-I-went-to-college. You're never here. You haven't been for years."

"Get out, Fawn. I don't want to see you around here anymore."

She just laughed and threw her cigarette on the ground,

grinding it out with what looked like a fairly expensive shoe. "What are you going to do, Josh? You may pay the bills, but this is still your mom's place. And let me tell you something, *you're* out of here before I am. You just don't treat that woman right. And I do."

She picked up her box and brushed past him, pushing through the door and calling out for his mother. "Momma? How you doin' today? All right?"

Josh took a few deep breaths and tried not to grind his teeth. The one dentist he'd seen in the last six years had told him he wouldn't have any teeth left when he was forty if he kept it up.

"Josh," Laura started, "you've got to—"

He held a hand up, once again silencing her.

The thing that really pissed him off was that Fawn wasn't completely wrong. She gave his mother exactly what she needed— a loser to take care of. His mother wanted more than anything to feel needed, and her curse was that both he and Laura could make it better on their own.

"None of the money you're making at the store is going to her, right, Laura?"

"Come on. I'm not stupid."

The first time Fawn had shown up on their doorstep, Josh had been sympathetic. Her father was a world-class son of a bitch, and she'd obviously needed help. She stayed with them for a few months, contributing nothing, expecting him and Laura to wait on her hand and foot, and then one day disappeared at the same time as a piece of jewelry their grandmother had left them—probably the only valuable thing the family had ever owned. And now she returned at least once a year, broke and sniffing around for what she could get.

He climbed the cracked wooden stairs and yanked the screen door open, ignoring Fawn as he pushed past her and headed to the bedroom at the back.

He found his mother on her bed, wearing a robe that over the years had faded to the same color as the sheets. The ashtray next to her was full, and there were two empty beer cans on the floor.

"Mom?"

She just lay there, eyes closed and an arm hanging off the bed. Her nails were yellow and un-cared-for, some broken off close to the skin, others curling like claws.

Josh backed away and fell into a chair, watching her chest move subtly up and down. She looked like she had lost weight, and it caused the wrinkles in her face to deepen to the point that they were beginning to look like gouges.

They'd never had much, but you didn't really need all that much to be happy. To be a family. Poverty couldn't be blamed for what had happened to them. It was hundreds of little bad decisions that had added up to this disaster. And that was the problem. It made it too easy to dwell on "what if" scenarios. What if she hadn't been an alcoholic? What if his dad had hung around?

But he hadn't. And in his place, Josh had suffered through a procession of useless stepfathers. The last—number four—still stared at him from a crooked frame on the wall. He'd been a real prick—worse than numbers one and three but not quite as bad as Fawn's father. It looked like that was going to be the last picture, though. His mother, once a real natural beauty, was in no condition to attract another man. And since she didn't count her children, that left her pretty much alone.

His cell phone rang, and he picked up.

"Hello?"

"Josh Hagarty, please."

"Speaking."

"Hi, this is Bill at Alder Data Systems."

Josh sat a little straighter. "Bill! It's good to hear from you. I'm really looking forward to meeting with you and talking about joining your team."

"Yeah. About that. I'm afraid we're going to have to cancel."

"Can we reschedule for some time that would be more convenient?"

"I don't think so, Josh. Your résumé looks great, but we've decided to go with someone else."

Josh suddenly felt nauseated. "Bill, you're making a mistake. If you think I'm looking for some insane amount of money, you're wrong. I understand you're a small company, and that's what's exciting to me. I think I can really help you achieve the potential—"

"The decision's been made, Josh. I'm sorry it didn't work out."

Shock turned quickly to anger. "Jesus Christ, Bill. I'm scheduled to be back in town for that interview, and I've been stalling other companies until we talked. Now you're telling me you're just blowing me off?"

"You're just not what we're looking for, Josh. I'm sorry."

"But—"

The phone went dead, and he swallowed hard before looking back at the source of the rustling behind him. Fawn was standing in the doorway, looking down at him with a broad smile splitting her face.

5

The sense of déjà vu was somewhat diminished by the fact that this was Josh Hagarty's first experience with a second interview. Of course he'd listened hungrily to his friends' stories about them, but those narratives had always had the faded impact of someone describing color to a blind man. Now all that was going to change.

He glanced at his watch and jogged across the street, aware that he was doing everything exactly as he had before—a slip into superstition and compulsive behavior, for sure, but there was no point in taking chances.

The receptionist smiled and called him by name, telling him to "just go on back." The informality felt like a good sign, and his confidence rose as he navigated the hallway to the waves and greetings of the people behind open doors. It was like he'd worked there his whole life.

"Stephen?"

Trent rose from behind his desk and waved him in. "Josh! I really appreciate you coming on such short notice. I know how busy you must be."

"My pleasure. I appreciate you inviting me back." Josh sat and tried to relax as Trent dragged up a chair to face him.

"I don't see any reason to beat around the bush. We'd like to offer you the job."

Josh felt his breath catch in his chest but managed to get normal respiration going again before it became obvious. Or he turned blue.

"The salary we're offering is forty thousand a year." The moment he said it, Trent immediately raised a hand to head off the uncontrollable laughter he apparently expected. "You've got to understand that it's really difficult for us to compete on salary with the private sector guys who are courting you. Our donors would be understandably upset if they thought everything they were giving was going to American employees and not the Africans we're trying to help. It's hard to explain to them that getting good people saves us money in the long run."

Josh nodded sympathetically but was actually barely listening. Instead he was calculating the payments on his student loans and making assumptions about financial aid for Laura's college tuition. Forty thousand was incredibly low. It was a number that forced him to consider what he could make running the service center of a decent-sized car dealership.

"What we can do, though, is support you in less direct ways," Trent continued. "For instance, we'll make the payments on your student loans as long as you work for us. Our donors value education, so it's not such a hard sell."

That made Josh stop thinking about rebuilding transmissions and focus on the conversation again.

"We also provide full medical benefits for you and your family. If and when you might decide to start one."

"I have a sister," Josh said.

"Well, what we're talking about is more for wives and kids."

Josh didn't react, and Trent smiled. "Let me see what I can do.

In fact, let's just say we'll figure out a way to get your sister on the policy."

Josh nodded noncommittally.

"We also cover most tuition for your dependents. Normally that wouldn't include your sister, but for the sake of argument, let's say it does. Is she in school?"

"She graduates high school this year."

"Then we'd cover the costs of her college."

"When you say cover . . ."

"I mean cover. Tuition and living expenses as long as she lives on campus. Also, I want you to keep in mind that all your housing, food, and expenses are taken care of when you're in Africa. So while the salary doesn't sound that impressive, most of our people just have it deposited in a bank here in the States and never touch it. Compare that with how much you'd be able to save living in New York—even if you were making five times as much."

Josh leaned back in his chair and struggled to keep his expression hovering between skepticism and mild boredom. Trent was talking about Laura having medical coverage for the first time in her life and getting to go to an Ivy League school instead of shopping around for the cheapest in-state school they could find. If he worked at NewAfrica for five years, Laura would graduate from college free of debt, he'd have the better part of two hundred grand in the bank, and he could play his experience and philanthropy against his criminal record to prospective employers. And as an added bonus, he'd get to see the world and maybe help a few people out along the way.

Unless, of course, somebody hacked his head off with a machete.

"I've had some time to do a little more research on the part of Africa you operate in, Stephen. It seems really . . . fascinating."

In truth, he hadn't needed to do any research at all. Laura had gone nuts on the subject, following him around reading excerpts from the information she found surfing the Net and poring over books and magazines. But when balanced against the compensation package Trent had just rolled out, what did a little brutal violence, deadly disease, and crushing poverty matter?

"I won't lie to you, Josh. We're not talking about sending you to London, here. It's an area with a lot of problems. If it wasn't, they wouldn't need us."

"From what I read, a lot of charities have pulled out."

Trent nodded. "The country is basically split into three sections. In the North the Xhisa tribe has a strong majority. It's the seat of the government, and that's where some very profitable mining goes on. Overall, it's fairly stable. In the South, the Yvimbo have a weak majority, and there's a fair amount of tribal violence and rebel activity."

"And the middle section?"

"Is where you'd be working," Trent replied. "There have been a lot of refugees coming up from the South to escape the fighting—both Xhisa and Yvimbo. So we're working there to get the people out of the refugee camps and back to productive lives."

"The president of the country is Xhisa, right?"

Trent nodded. "Umboto Mtiti. He's a decent guy who's working hard to unite the country, but it's an almost insurmountable task. Tribal animosity runs deep in that part of the world."

It was an interesting take on the situation and more or less mirrored the sentiments of the American press. Laura had been more thorough than that, though, and she'd printed articles from all over the world. The European papers made no bones about Mtiti getting and holding his position through brutality and corruption but conceded that allowing a power vacuum to be created would be a dead end for his country. The South Africans were more pessimistic, with one editorial suggesting the country was completely hopeless and going the way of Somalia and Sudan.

"Sounds exciting."

"I guarantee it."

"So what would I be doing?"

Trent smiled. "You'd be managing a Yvimbo agricultural project not too far from one of the main refugee areas. The hope is that we can move a bunch of people out of the camps and into this self-sustaining farming community within a year or so."

"And when would I need to make a decision?"

"I'm sorry to say that we basically needed an answer yesterday. The project's adrift, and we're a little desperate."

6

"D on't touch that!"
Josh released the box in his hands and let it drop back onto the table. Fawn was standing in the middle of the trailer, hands planted firmly on her hips.

"That stuff's valuable and it's complicated and it has to stay in order."

"Order?" Josh said, looking around the tiny trailer at the boxes stacked on virtually every surface. There was no writing on the sides, so he peeked into an open one, ignoring Fawn's noisy protests. It was full of large plastic bottles. According to the labels, most contained diet pills, but some also made vague promises about liver function and increased muscularity.

"Stop it! Get away from those."

He dipped a hand into an open box nestled behind the kitchen table and came up with a container of pills that claimed to be the ancient secret to penis enhancement.

"So this is it? This is your new business?"

Fawn snatched the bottle from his hand. "While you're off in Africa, someone has to take care of this family."

He actually managed to laugh, and for a moment his fantasies about killing Fawn became less violent—tending toward strangulation as opposed to throwing her in a vat of battery acid. The power of gainful employment to bolster his mood was no less than amazing. And the two thousand dollars in cash Trent had given him to help with moving expenses was making him downright giddy.

"Well, I appreciate the contribution, Fawn. I really do. But I have a rental car full of my stuff from school, and there doesn't seem to be anywhere to put it."

Fawn smiled and retreated a bit until she was standing as close to his mother as her boxes of medical miracles would allow. Clearly not a good sign, but the roll of hundred-dollar bills straining the worn seams of his wallet would undoubtedly soften the blow. "Okay, Mom," he said. "Go ahead. Let's hear it."

She was sitting in a threadbare orange velour chair that he remembered being delivered when he was barely old enough to see over the arm. Her eyes were their typical red, and a cigarette hung loosely from her fingers. He'd been worried about her smoking for a long time, but honestly it seemed like every year she had less energy to actually take a drag. It was quickly becoming nothing more than a carcinogenic security blanket.

"Sweetie, you're not going to be around much. We were thinking you could put your things in the shed. It'll be okay there—she's not leakin' anymore since you fixed her."

Josh sighed quietly. "Look at all this, Momma. Is this the kind of thing you want Laura around?"

She put an elbow on the arm of the chair and propped the side of her head on her hand. Gravity had its way with her sagging skin, and for a moment she became almost unrecognizable. "Laura'll be okay. Laura's smart."

"Yeah, Laura's smart, Mom. But she's just a kid. She's . . ." He let his voice trail off. How many times had they had this conversation? What was the point?

He threw his duffel over his shoulder and started toward the door.

"Hey, Josh."

When he looked back, Fawn threw the bottle of penis-enhancing pills at him. It was only a lucky catch that kept them from hitting him in the face.

"On the house," she said. "You know what they say about those African guys. I'd hate for you not to measure up."

Josh pushed through the screen and out into the sun, taking a deep breath of air that didn't smell of old tobacco and even older mold. There had been happier times. Or maybe that was just his mind contorting the past into something better than it really was. It didn't really matter. What was the harm in slipping on a pair of rose-colored glasses when you looked backward?

═══

The trail that had been faint in his youth was nonexistent now. It didn't matter, though, he could have found the way blindfolded.

Josh navigated through the loose rocks and tangled under-brush, reveling in the peaceful silence like he always had. To his left, the slope dropped off steeply, leading down to a small ridge obscuring the trailers that made up his neighborhood and giving him the impression that he was the last person on earth. Sometimes not such an unpleasant fantasy.

Laura had been gone when he'd come out of the trailer, but it wasn't hard to figure out where. He plunged into a tangle of dense bushes, holding his hands out in front of him to protect his face.

When he emerged, it was into a clearing dominated by an ancient oak tree with an elaborate tree house in its branches. Working seven days a week with lumber stolen from a nearby construction site, he and Laura had taken an entire summer to build it.

Laura had been eight years old at the time, and their mother had been dating one of the more abusive assholes she'd ever gotten involved with. The construction project had been a great excuse to get him and Laura out of the house until that prick had finally moved on.

He walked to within a few yards of the trunk and looked up at the bottom of the deck fifteen feet above and the tennis-shoe-clad feet hanging over its edge.

"Laura! Come down from there. It's not safe anymore."

She leaned forward and peered down at him. For the first time, he could see a very different future for her: a nice house, a good job, and a husband who loved her. Maybe a few kids and an SUV with a bumper sticker bragging about their grade school academic victories.

"So did they tell you?" she called down.

"About being moved into the shed? Yeah."

He climbed up and entered through the trap door leading into the enclosed section of the house. It was more or less empty now, but still dry and surprisingly solid. A testament to his adolescent engineering skills.

"I don't want you to go," she said as he took a seat beside her. "Forget about this and stay here with us. You could get a job in town."

"Doing what?"

"Who cares?"

"I care, Laura. This is an opportunity for both of us to get out of here. To do something better."

"The place they're sending you is horrible and dangerous. A lot of times there's no electricity, and there are all these diseases, and people get killed every day." She turned to look directly at him. "Do you know how? They don't just use guns, sometimes they—"

"Enough, okay? I've heard the gory details. That's why I'm going, right? To try to change all that."

"Because you're such an expert on Africa?"

"Jesus, Laura. You act like I'm an idiot or something."

She pulled a piece of paper from her pocket and held it up. There was a map of Africa with no country names printed on it. "Point to where you're going."

He squinted at all the little colored blocks, but the truth was they all looked about the same.

"You've been waiting all day to do that, haven't you?"

"I'm not stupid either, Josh. This is it, isn't it? This is the only job you could get."

There was no point in lying—she'd see through it.

"This is a good gig for us, Laura. I—"

"Because it'll pay for my school? I can take care of myself."

"That's what I hear."

She lay back on the rough wood and stared up at the sky through the leaves spread out above them. "There are so many evil, stupid people in the world, and *you're* the one who can't get a job. It's not fair."

"You know what they say about life being fair."

"Don't do this for me, Josh. If something happened to you, I wouldn't know what to do." Her eyes began to fill with tears, and it brought back memories of the last time he'd seen her cry. His sentencing.

"It's going to be okay," he said, lying back beside her. "I don't think I'd have liked sitting behind a desk all day anyway."

7

Josh shaded his eyes and watched two shirtless men tossing the luggage out of the plane. None of the other passengers seemed alarmed when their suitcases crashed onto the pavement, and he mimicked their disinterested calm as one of his duffels made the eight-foot drop.

When he started toward it, he discovered that the bottoms of his sneakers had actually begun to melt and now made a perceptible sucking sound as he walked.

Kentucky had been hot in the summer—sometimes brutally so—but this was different. It was like God was following him around with a magnifying glass, punishing him for all those ants he'd burned when he was a kid. He'd never given a lot of thought to why some people were black and others white, but suddenly he was envious of the Africans' excess melanin. If his last bag didn't hit the tarmac soon, he was going to end up the color of an over-ripe tomato.

When it finally did appear, he retrieved it and teetered toward the only building in sight—a small, single-story construction covered in a patchwork of faded paint and leaning noticeably to the east.

By the time he arrived, other passengers had formed into lines, waiting their turn to throw their belongings on tables manned by pissed-off-looking soldiers. Josh dropped his bags and shoved them along with his foot as the line slowly progressed, the heat and stink of sweat becoming stronger and the soldiers' moods deteriorating visibly. Above, a larger-than-life-sized mural of Umboto Mtiti kept an eye on things.

By the time he made it to the front of the line and hefted his bags onto a table, he was feeling a little light-headed—a combination of the heat, jet lag, and the disorientation of being so far from home. He hadn't been prepared for how different it would be. The sound of the local languages' bizarre clicks and grunts, the haze of oddly scented smoke that mixed with the air, the fact that his was the only white face in the crowd.

Josh handed over his passport, and the soldier flipped through it, taking in the blank pages with eyes that were an alarming shade of yellow rimmed with red. Finally he looked up but didn't hand it back.

"Liquor?" His accent was almost too thick to decipher.

"No. No liquor."

His mouth turned down in irritation.

"Books? Magazines?"

"Yes."

"What magazines and books?" Now he looked vaguely hopeful.

"Uh, I've got a *National Geographic* and a copy of *Lord of the Flies*."

His brow furrowed in a way that suggested he'd had a mental list of acceptable responses that hadn't been matched. He pointed to Josh's luggage, turned, and motioned for him to follow.

He did, but hesitated in the doorway when he saw the small, empty room the soldier was standing in the middle of.

"Come!"

"Is there a problem?" Josh asked, starting to feel disorientation turn to nervousness. "I work for a charity. NewAfrica. Someone is supposed to be meeting me here. Do you—"

"Come!" the soldier barked.

Josh did as he was told, clutching his bags to him like a shield as the soldier slammed the door closed. A few moments later, he was rifling through the duffels, tossing whatever didn't interest him on the cracked tile floor.

"Hey, come on," Josh protested. "There's nothing in there."

It didn't take the soldier long to come to a similar conclusion, and he stood, slapping the clothes Josh had picked up from his hand and pushing him against the wall. The frisking was the fastest and most efficient Josh had ever been subject to, and before he knew what was happening, the soldier had pocketed his MP3 player and all but twenty of the five hundred dollars that had been in Josh's wallet.

This was starting to get serious. He was about to find himself standing in the middle-of-nowhere Africa with no money, no possessions, and a NewAfrica guide who had decided not to show up.

"This is bullshit! You can't do that. I came here to—"

The rest of his protest was lost in the sound of the door behind him being thrown open and slamming against the wall. The man who stalked in was probably four inches taller than his own six feet, with a shaved head and a muscular chest that glistened beneath a partially unbuttoned shirt. His skin was noticeably lighter than the soldier's, but his expression was a hell of a lot darker—even with eyes hidden behind a pair of mirrored sunglasses.

Josh took a couple steps back, starting to wonder if he would ever leave this airport. What would Laura say at his funeral? "I told him this would happen."

But the man didn't seem to even notice him, instead shouting something in his native language at the soldier, who quickly started repacking and zipping up the bags on the floor.

"Does he have anything of yours?" the man said in easily understood English.

"What?"

His jaw tightened, and he enunciated slowly, clipping off each word. "Did he take anything?"

"Uh, yeah. My MP3 player and a bunch of money. Are you the person who was supposed to meet me from NewAfrica?"

He ignored Josh's question and shouted something else at the soldier, who shook his head in what was obviously a rigorous denial.

The man's expression turned to fury, and he slapped the soldier's hat off, grabbing his hair and nearly lifting him off the ground. He clamped his free hand around the man's throat and drove him back, slamming him into the wall with enough force that puffs of dust were ejected from the cracks in the wood.

"Hey, it's not that big a deal," Josh said, suddenly afraid that it would be the soldier who never left this room. Four hundred and eighty dollars was a lot of money, and he liked the MP3 player, but it wasn't worth somebody getting killed.

The man had released the soldier's hair and began a search of his pockets, almost immediately finding what he was looking for. He let go of the soldier's throat and turned, holding Josh's possessions out to him and leaving the man behind him to slide down the wall, gasping for air.

"I'm Gideon," he said, impatiently shaking the money and MP3 player to entice a hesitant Josh Hagarty to reach for them. "I'm here to collect you."

═══

"I must apologize for my countryman."

With the luggage safely stacked in the Land Cruiser's cargo area, Gideon jumped in and accelerated onto the dirt road running along the front of the airport.

"No problem," Josh mumbled.

"You're wrong. It is a problem. You don't understand the situation here. President Mtiti is a great man, and he tries to include everyone in his government, but some aren't well-suited. Some are stupid and corrupt."

Josh wondered if that was a swipe at the Yvimbo tribe and a suggestion that Mtiti's Xhisa followers were pure as the driven snow.

"It seems like you've figured out how to handle it," Josh said, remembering the terror on the young soldier's face. He'd been pissed about getting ripped off, but Gideon's reaction had been something he hadn't experienced before. Sure, there had been some guards in prison who had been complete sons of bitches, but there was always a sense that things were under control. That they would only go so far. He hadn't felt that way back at the airport.

"These behaviors cannot be tolerated," Gideon said. "If you do—even just once—there will be no future here."

From what Josh had seen, the future seemed a long way off no matter what Gideon did. So far, Africa was poorly maintained planes, crooked soldiers, unbearable heat, and air that swallowed everything less than a few miles away in a yellowish haze.

As they entered the city, Josh's list got longer. The transition from desolate countryside to a claustrophobic crush of humanity seemed to happen in an instant. Suddenly there were people everywhere—milling around in the street, crammed into outdoor markets erected in front of brightly colored colonial-era buildings, hanging out of windows, and filling open doors. Gideon didn't slow, piloting the vehicle through the crowd as though the people rushing to get out of their path didn't exist.

Josh looked out the window at countless shacks, wired together out of what looked like garbage, clinging to steep hills west of town. It seemed that the slightest rain or breath of wind would send them and their inhabitants crashing back to earth.

Gideon skidded the truck down a side street, and Josh fixated on a giant wall mural, visible only because the building next door had collapsed. It depicted President Mtiti patting a child on the head while doves flew around them. Inexplicably, a large, neatly printed caption read, "Lo Be Thy Name."

When he sat back, he saw that Gideon wasn't watching the road so much as watching him. His face was a blank, and his eyes were invisible behind his glasses, so it was impossible to know exactly what he was seeing.

"Why do you come to my country?"

"What?"

"Why do you come here?"

It was an interesting question. He'd been asking himself the same thing since his plane's wheels had touched ground. "To help people."

The answer didn't register on Gideon's face, but it was enough to get him to start looking at the road again. Josh did the same, taking in the unidentifiable food cooking on oil-barrel grills, the tiny trucks and vans packed to triple capacity speeding along the dirt road. And the continued lack of white faces.

He'd never considered himself in the least bit racist, but it was impossible to not feel his uniqueness and wonder if this was how the few blacks in his classes had felt every day.

They broke out of the city, and he felt a wave of relief at the empty road climbing steeply ahead of them and the clearing air that had the distant mountains gaining sharpness and turning green.

Josh pulled a bottle of pills from his pocket and shook one into his mouth.

"What are those?" Gideon shouted.

It was hard to hear. The radio was blasting African music, which was actually kind of appealing, but even that was barely audible over the tires and suspension being brutalized by the road.

"Malaria pills."

Gideon smirked.

"I once read that half the people who ever lived probably died of malaria," Josh yelled. "Fascinating, don't you think?"

It was clear that he didn't—or at least it wasn't as compelling as what was in his rearview mirror. Josh twisted around and saw another vehicle coming up fast from behind. It was identical to the one he was in, except most of the roof had been cut away to make room for a mounted machine gun. The man standing behind it eyed them from behind glasses similar to Gideon's as they passed. On the vehicle's door, the Save the Children logo was still visible beneath a thin coat of white paint.

"How much farther?" Josh said, facing forward in his seat again and watching the makeshift military vehicle recede in front of them.

"Not far. The roads are paved."

It was hard to know exactly what he meant by that. They were driving in the dirt, ten feet to the left of pavement so potholed that it was virtually undrivable even in a four-by-four.

"Are you from around here, Gideon?"

"Not far."

"Not far" was starting to look like the universal measure of distance in Africa.

"Family?"

"Yes. Why wouldn't I have a family?"

The conversation went on like that for another few minutes until Josh got the hint and shut up. The humid air poured through his open window, not having much of a cooling effect but keeping things bearable as long as their speed stayed over fifty kilometers an hour.

The villages they passed were nothing more than collections of small, round buildings spaced out over green hills and surrounded by farmland. Kids chased their vehicle, shouting, laughing, and holding out their hands for a gift they seemed to know they wouldn't get. Josh wondered if they did that to everyone who drove by or if it was his pale skin that attracted them.

The only buildings with any permanence seemed to be the bunker-like funeral homes. It had been one thing to read about the thirty percent AIDS rate but another to see the cinder-block monuments to the virus dotting the otherwise beautiful countryside.

Gideon slowed as they came to a village of concrete-and-thatch houses. Two were on fire, sending black smoke rising into the still air. The former Save the Children vehicle that had passed them earlier was parked at the edge of the road, with the man in back covering twenty or so soldiers as they dragged people screaming from their homes. Josh turned around in the seat, but in a few moments, the village was lost in the distance and smoke. Like it had never existed.

"What the hell was that all about?"

"Rebels."

"They looked like farmers."

"And what would you know of this?"

Josh fell silent again, staring out at the increasingly remote countryside, thinking about what he had just seen and, for the second time in his twenty-six years, pondering death. It was a subject that had been so efficiently swept under the rug in America—as though it were a rare disease that would someday be conquered.

After only a few hours in Africa, hints of death's presence seemed to be everywhere. In fact, it was hard to see anything else.

8

Over the course of the punishing seven-hour drive, the landscape had transformed. The dry, open plains had been taken over by jagged, grass-covered hills that rose hundreds of feet into a sky that had turned nearly black with clouds. What sunlight remained was slipping in sideways from the distant horizon, causing the endless carpet of vegetation to glow an otherworldly shade of green.

Josh stepped from the Land Cruiser, taking a deep breath of the humid air and trying to drive away the nausea that had replaced exhaustion over the last hour. A quick glance at his watch suggested it was early morning in Kentucky, and he guessed that his disoriented body clock was still working on the assumption that he wasn't a million miles from home.

"Who's in charge?" he asked as Gideon walked to the front of the vehicle. This stop hadn't been the African's idea, and he clearly wasn't happy about it.

"You are."

Josh let out a frustrated laugh. Getting a straight answer out of his new assistant might turn out to be the biggest challenge of his new job. Josh had been expecting a smart, enthusiastic guide who could teach him to maneuver effortlessly through the complicated politics, culture, and languages in the country. Someone who had dedicated his life to helping his people. Someone Josh would form an immediate and lasting friendship with.

Of those qualities, Gideon seemed to have one: He was clearly no idiot. What his motivations or interests were, though, was a mystery. And the chance that Josh would feel anything but wariness toward him seemed remote at this point. On the other hand, he'd only been in the country for a few hours. No point in setting any of his impressions in concrete yet.

"I know I'm in charge, Gideon. What I meant was, where's the foreman? Where are the agricultural experts?"

The African shrugged thick shoulders, his face unmoving except for the reflection of the boiling clouds in his glasses. It was a surprisingly expressive gesture that even Josh's jet-lagged mind could decipher. He wasn't saying he didn't know where they were—he was saying they didn't exist.

The steep slope in front of them was being systematically hacked into sections by what Josh calculated to be about a hundred workers using hand tools of varying effectiveness—nothing more sophisticated than a rusted shovel and nothing less sophisticated than a pointy rock.

The plan was for the entire butte to be terraced, creating fertile agricultural land that would not only support a village built on the narrow swath of flat land surrounding it but also produce excess food that could be sold on the open market. Trent had given him only a short briefing on the project, responding to nearly every question Josh asked with "Why don't you go down there and get the lay of the land, then we'll talk."

Trent's attitude had seemed reasonable at the time, but now Josh wondered if his new boss hadn't been intentionally vague in an effort not to scare him off.

Not that Josh knew the first thing about this type of agriculture, but even to his eye, something had gone seriously wrong here. The individual terraces sloped every which way, there was no uniformity to the depth of them, and there was nothing supporting the vertical slab of earth the digging had created—a dangerous situation highlighted by what looked like a large mudslide on the eastern edge of the project.

"The rain is coming," Gideon said. "We'll go to the compound now."

It was tempting, but Josh knew he wouldn't be able to sleep with this many unanswered questions spinning around in his head.

"Let me just look around for a minute."

"The rain," Gideon warned as Josh moved away from the Land Cruiser. "There's nothing to be done here tonight."

"I can take a look. It'll give me time to think."

"Think tomorrow. We're going."

There was a finality to his tone that sounded like an order and made Josh pick up his pace. Who was working for who here? And what exactly were they trying to accomplish? To stay dry or to help these people feed themselves?

He aimed himself at the project's most interesting feature—a small but prominent field at the base of a hill that had been terraced with incongruous precision and was planted with corn that had grown to a height of about five feet.

The first raindrop hit him on the back of the neck with impressive force and an audible splat. He wiped at the warm water as he waded into the rows of corn. "What's up with this?"

"I don't know what you're asking," Gideon said, obviously angry, but not so much that he was willing to wait in the car. "It's almost ready for harvest."

"What I'm asking is why one little section is done and perfect, while the rest . . ." He wasn't quite sure how to describe the rest of the project, so he just waved his hand in its general direction.

This time Gideon's shrug was more disinterested. "I'm not in charge of this project. You are."

"That's what I keep hearing."

"We have to go now."

The rain was coming harder, the drops shaking the leaves and exploding in the dust around their feet. Above them, the people had stopped working but didn't seem in a hurry to leave. Instead they formed groups, talking animatedly and looking in Josh's direction.

"Okay, fine. Let's go," Josh said, deciding it was a little early to make an enemy of the man who was supposed to be his lifeline here. When they turned to go back to the Land Cruiser, though, he was distracted by a flash of yellow through the corn, and he set off toward it instead.

"Where are you going?" Gideon shouted. "This way!"

"Head back to the car," Josh yelled back, trying to be heard over the rain that had now completely soaked through his clothes. "I'll be there in a sec."

For some reason, Gideon didn't take the suggestion and appeared from the corn just as Josh started to circle the small earthmover he'd found next to a dilapidated shed.

Trent had mentioned the tractor but had neglected to say that basically every part on it that could be easily unbolted had been stolen. The fact that it had treads instead of tires was the only thing saving it from the indignity of being up on blocks.

"What the hell happened here?"

Gideon's jaw stiffened just as it had right before he'd gone crazy on the soldier at the airport, and Josh felt his resolve wavering. But he refused to let his uneasiness show and just stood there waiting for an answer.

"It's a tractor that NewAfrica provided. It no longer works."

"I'd say that's an understatement. Where's the rest of it?"

Another shrug. Josh could already tell that those were going to get really irritating.

"Can we get new parts?"

"It's difficult."

"Maybe we should find the people who stole them and buy 'em back?" Josh forced a smile, though he hadn't actually been joking. Gideon just stared at him, the water running in sheets down his glasses.

There was movement to Josh's left, and he turned to watch a long line of workers coming up a path toward them. They examined him carefully as they passed and put their tools inside the shed. Some scattered, but others hung around and listened to a man who had begun to speak. On the surface, he didn't look much different than his audience—same strong but slightly malnourished build, same dirty jeans and ratty T-shirt. But his voice was clear and strong, and everyone seemed to be paying attention. Overall, he seemed to be a person Josh should get to know.

He strode up to the man and interrupted him by sticking a hand out. "Hi, I'm Josh Hagarty. I'm from NewAfrica."

His new status seemed to hover between celebrity and roadside oddity, and all eyes were on him. The man fell silent, not moving at first but finally taking Josh's hand. He looked directly at Josh with an intensity that was impossible to match, so he let his eyes wander. The man's skin seemed impossibly black and camouflaged the creases around his eyes and along his cheeks.

Whatever he saw obviously didn't impress him all that much, and he said something that was meant for the men he'd been speaking to. Josh expected them to laugh, but instead they just nodded gravely.

"This is Tfmena," Gideon said with obvious reluctance. "He's what you would call a village elder. He says that he is pleased that you're here and grateful for your and your organization's commitment to his people's welfare."

That might be who he was, but Josh was fairly certain that wasn't what he'd said. If he had to guess, it would have translated more as, "Look at this arrogant asshole straight out of school who's here to tell us how to live. He was born a white American male, and he managed to screw even that up."

Despite that, this was a man who had the respect of his people, and that didn't seem like something easy to win in this part of the world. Undoubtedly a step in the right direction from the two Africans Josh had interacted with so far—the soldier at the airport and Gideon.

"Tfmena," Josh mangled, trying to keep the rain from flowing into his mouth as he spoke. What did these people have against vowels? "It's good to meet you, sir. I want you to know that I'm going to do my best to make all this work."

9

The rain ended as suddenly as it had begun, though the sound of dripping was still audible as Josh's and Gideon's clothes drained onto the Land Cruiser's seats.

The metal gate they were stopped in front of was covered in rust but still looked much more formidable than the guard standing next to it. He was at least seventy, armed only with a tiny bow and dart-like arrows that were in danger of falling from their quiver as he threw his weight behind the gate.

The compound that was to become Josh's home for the foreseeable future was perched on the summit of a low hill and glowed unnaturally in a landscape that was descending into inky darkness. The concrete walls that surrounded it were more than ten feet high and topped with jagged chunks of glass to discourage anyone considering climbing over.

Gideon revved the engine and gunned the vehicle forward, nearly brushing the old man as they passed. The unease that Josh felt at the similarity to the prison he'd been so anxious to leave faded as they skidded to a stop in a gravel courtyard overflowing with bougainvillea, fruit trees, and white Land Cruisers.

He barely had a foot out the door when a thin African man

with cheeks that hovered somewhere between extraordinarily chubby and dangerously swollen rushed toward him. His grin was full of teeth almost white enough to outshine his garish Hawaiian shirt, but they disappeared when Gideon began barking unintelligible orders. A moment later, he had pulled Josh's bags from the back of the vehicle and was teetering away with them.

"Hold on!" Josh called. "Let me help you with those."

He turned to thank Gideon for the ride, but the African was already reversing the Land Cruiser toward the gate. Josh swore quietly to himself. Making friends left and right.

"Hey, you! New guy!"

He spotted a white face emerging from a path that had nearly been reclaimed by the banana trees lining it.

"Come on over here and introduce yourself, son."

Josh pointed in the direction he'd last seen his luggage heading. "There's this really skinny guy trying to carry about two hundred pounds of my stuff, and—"

"Luganda?" the man said in an accent that suggested northeastern United States. "Jesus Christ, kid. He doesn't need your help. He could twist your head off like a bottle cap. Now, who the hell are you?"

After one last glance back, Josh walked over to shake the man's hand. He was probably in his late forties, though his shaved head and sun-damaged skin made that more of a guess than an estimate. His clothes were standard mail-order safari, though their style and threadbare condition suggested that the catalog dated back to somewhere in the early '90s.

"I'm Josh Hagarty."

"NewAfrica," he said, contemplating Josh with the same skepticism everyone else on this continent did.

"That's right. Who are you?"

He didn't answer immediately, instead taking a pull from a sweaty glass topped with a paper umbrella. "JB Flannary. Maybe you've heard of me."

"No."

"America's youth has become virtually illiterate, hasn't it? I blame those Ataris."

"I have no idea what you're talking about."

Flannary paused to take another drink, an act that went on long enough to turn the scene slightly awkward.

"Well," he said finally, "you bothered to come all this way, so I guess I should show you where you're staying. Where are you from, anyway?"

"Kentucky."

"How'd a good ol' boy like you get hooked up with New-Africa?"

"It's kind of a strange story," Josh said, nearly tripping over a coconut as he followed the man on a detour through the landscaping.

"Yeah? How so?"

He was about to answer when Flannary came to a sudden halt, their path blocked by a white woman in her midtwenties. She wore her mouse-brown hair in a short, square cut that seemed to have been designed to fit around her sturdy-looking glasses. Blue fatigue pants and a similarly colored top gave her a vaguely SWAT feel.

"Hey, Josh, let me introduce you to Katie—one of our quickly dwindling crew. She's with the African Women's Initiative."

"Nice to meet you. I don't think I'm familiar with your charity."

"They do firewood," Flannary said before Katie could respond.

"What?"

"Firewood," he repeated.

"So people can cook," Katie cut in. "Most of the area has been clear-cut, so the women have to go farther and farther to get wood. And with the lawlessness, they're getting raped and mutilated by rebels."

Josh squinted his tired eyes, trying to process that. "Why don't men get the wood?"

"Because they'd be executed if the rebels caught them."

"You're telling me that African men are such cowards that they stay home while their daughters and wives get raped and mutilated?"

She froze, staring at him with an expression of shock, colored with just a hint of disgust.

"Well," Flannary said, throwing an arm around Josh's shoulders, "on that note, I think we'll just head on over to your bungalow."

"It was good to meet you," Josh said lamely, allowing Flannary to drag him away. The feeling was clearly not mutual.

"Christ, that came out sounding racist, didn't it?" Josh said when they were alone again. "That's not the way I meant it. I'm just really tired. Or maybe it's the malaria pills . . ."

Instead of letting him have it, which would have been completely justified, Flannary started to laugh. And once he got started, he couldn't stop. He bent forward at the waist, convulsing wildly but somehow not spilling any of his drink.

When he started coughing and choking, Josh slapped him a few times on the back. "JB? Are you okay?"

When Flannary finally managed to catch his breath, he started leading Josh down the path again as though nothing had happened.

"I hate to say it, kid, but I think I'm warming up to you."

"What do you mean?"

"You want to know why she was so upset?"

"Because it was a really asshole thing for me to say?"

"Guess again."

"Because I just got here and have no idea what I'm talking about?"

"An enlightened attitude, but that's not it either."

"Then why?"

"Because you're right. The simple truth—and it's one of the

few here—is that men don't gather firewood. Period. It's women's work, and there's no amount of rapes and mutilations that's ever going to change it."

———

The bungalows were simple concrete affairs, similar to the wall that surrounded the compound but with a few incongruous architectural details that showed some effort. Flannary led Josh through the open door of one of them and waved his drink around in place of a tour.

It wasn't bad—a combination of his family's trailer and a dorm room, but with the strong scent of mold being circulated by a rickety window AC unit.

"It's got a bathroom in the back," Flannary said. "Nothing fancy, but it's a flush toilet, and on sunny days the water's . . ."

He lost his train of thought when a young girl entered carrying a beer and another umbrella-topped gin and tonic.

"Falati," Flannary said, "you're like the daughter I never had." There was no comprehension in her expression, but that didn't seem to bother him. He handed the beer to Josh and took the gin for himself.

"Nice to meet you, Falati."

She nodded politely and disappeared back through the door.

"So what do you think?"

"I was expecting a mud hut, so I think it's great."

"Mud huts don't happen around here. Hard to get top dollar."

"What?"

"This place is owned by President Mtiti's cousin, and let me tell you, they're charging rent that would get you a Central Park view back in the States. Plus, having us all corralled like this makes us easy to keep track of."

Josh took a pull on his beer and then held up the bottle. "How much is the president's cousin going to charge me for this?"

"You don't want to know. But don't worry, the tabs all say stuff like 'children's antibiotics' and 'children's mosquito nets,' so it'll sail right through your people."

"What's the difference between antibiotics and mosquito nets for kids and ones for adults?"

"There is none. But the word 'child' tends to grease the skids in the industry."

"Maybe I should have ordered a Shirley Temple."

"Funny! You're a funny guy."

The man who had carted off Josh's luggage came through the open door, emptied one of the suitcases onto the floor, and started carefully going through the contents—folding, organizing, and finally selecting an appropriate drawer or shelf.

"Hey, don't worry about that. I can do it."

"Don't sweat it," Flannary said. "This is his job. He's paid to do this. Right, Luganda?"

The man looked up from his position on the floor and displayed those amazing teeth again. "I'm at your service, JB. Like always, yes?"

"Luganda is a national treasure," Flannary said to Josh. "He knows everybody, can get anything, and has all the choice gossip. If you need something, you go straight to him and he'll take care of you."

"I appreciate that, but he doesn't really need to . . ."

Flannary's frown silenced him.

"Look, sport. You're not at home anymore. Here, you're rich. And as a rich person, you have an obligation to hire people less fortunate than you to do your work. There's nothing an African hates more than some rich, fat white guy who comes here and decides he's going to do his own laundry and gardening and whatnot."

"I'm actually not rich, JB."

He laughed but this time managed to not almost die. "As far as the Africans are concerned, all white people are rich. And you know what? They're right."

"I don't think that's—"

"Let me tell you something about the Africans that's going to serve you well. Are you listening?"

Josh glanced uncomfortably at Luganda pawing through his boxer shorts and then back at Flannary, who seemed completely comfortable talking like the man wasn't there.

"Yeah. Sure, I guess."

"Africans are the world's greatest pigeonholers."

"Huh?"

"When an African meets someone, they immediately put that person into a category, and that category completely controls how they treat you. You're a European. Period. Whether you're Charles Manson or Mother Teresa makes absolutely no difference."

"I find that hard to believe."

Flannary rolled his icy glass across his forehead. "We had a black kid from Chicago come work here about a year ago. He lasted less than two months before he damn near went nuts."

He paused, and it was obvious that he meant for Josh to inquire as to the cause of the mental breakdown.

"Okay. Why?"

"Because he didn't look European but also didn't have a tribe, so the Africans didn't know how to deal with him. The only thing they could figure out to do was completely ignore him. Strangest thing you ever saw. It was like he was a ghost only white people could see."

Flannary started for the door, pausing at the threshold. "I'll let you settle in for a bit. Drinks are served by the pool starting in about an hour."

"There's a pool?"

"Sure. Why wouldn't there be?"

Music began to play outside, and Josh pressed the phone tighter to his ear. Luganda, apparently finished unpacking for him, now sat behind the counter of the compound's office watching a speech by Umboto Mtiti on a black-and-white TV.

Stephen Trent had provided a state-of-the-art GPS-enabled satellite phone but made it clear that Josh was to use it only for official business and emergencies. That left him at the mercy of the local phone system.

"Hello?" he shouted into the handset. "Laura? Are you there?"

"Josh! I can barely hear you. Are you in Africa? Did you make it okay?"

JB Flannary wandered in and leaned on the counter, looking at the television and halfheartedly pretending not to listen in on Josh's conversation.

"Yeah, I made it. But it took forever. It's nighttime here."

"I've been waiting for you to call. I was starting to get—"

Her voice was drowned out by hysterical shouting on her end.

"Hang on a sec, Josh. . . . Calm down, Fawn! I don't know what's wrong with it."

"Bullshit!" Fawn's muffled but still unmistakable screech. "You did something, you little bitch! I know you did. You're standing between me and enough money to get out of this shithole."

"I don't know anything about cars, okay, Fawn? Call a mechanic."

"Your mother—"

The crash of the screen door sounded as Laura retreated outside.

"Sorry about that, Josh. How are you? Is Africa amazing?"

"What the hell was that all about?"

He wasn't sure if it was a sigh or just static, but either way his sister sounded tired. "Fawn convinced Mom to let her sell the car to raise money for the Internet pill business she's doing."

"I bought that goddamn car! You—"

"Calm down! Geez, everybody's yelling at me." She lowered

her voice. "I rearranged the wires on the distributor like you showed me, and for good measure, I hid the title."

"Jesus Christ! Laura, you need to—"

"Did you see any lions yet?"

"They all got killed in cross fires."

"What? I couldn't hear."

"Nothing."

"What's it like there, Josh? Are you in a hut by the edge of the jungle? I saw a movie once where lions hunted and killed people. No. Wait. Maybe that was India. . . ."

He looked down at his sweating beer bottle and then through the open door at a tiki bar wound with Christmas lights. "I don't think I have to worry too much about that."

10

Where are we going?"

The turn leading to Umboto Mtiti's compound slipped by, and the driver shrugged, continuing to follow the armored vehicle in front of them. Stephen Trent twisted around in the backseat of the heavily armored limousine and looked at the machine gun mounted to the chase vehicle tailgating them. A bored-looking youth was holding on to it, more to keep himself from being thrown from the truck than out of interest in defending them against attack. More often than not, Trent noticed that the barrel was aimed directly at him.

"We're supposed to be meeting the president," he said, trying to prompt one of the men in the front seat to speak, though it was unlikely either spoke English. He moved to the center of the seat, staying as far from the tinted windows as he could and taking measured breaths. He'd hated everything about Africa since the first time his feet had touched the hot, blood-soaked, poverty-stricken ground there. But mostly he hated Umboto Mtiti—a wildly unpredictable and paranoid man who considered any discussion that didn't take place at gunpoint to be a waste of time.

Trent wondered again how he had ended up trapped halfway

between the psychotic Umboto Mtiti and the icily sociopathic Aleksei Fedorov. Too many wrong turns and impossible choices. Too much fear.

And now that fear was growing with every mile the motorcade traveled away from Mtiti's compound. In the distance, he could see the new prison looming, though in truth it was neither new nor a prison. Europeans had originally built it as a factory during their brief attempt to "civilize" the country. It had long since been shut down until Mtiti had decided its stone-and-steel construction would be an ideal place to contain anyone he saw as a threat to his power. It had become a potent symbol inside the country, the way he imagined the Bastille had been in France. The mere mention of it made grown men go weak.

And he was no exception. Despite the limo's air conditioning, the sweat was running freely down his back as they passed through the gate. Above, unused and slightly leaning smokestacks rose into the glare of the sky.

Trent stepped from the limo and into the cloud of dust its abrupt stop had created. Hundreds of dull, hungry faces watched him, though none of the stooped, skeletal men packing the courtyard dared approach. A small contingent of soldiers surrounded him and ushered him forward, shouting and occasionally using a rifle butt against any prisoner who didn't have the strength to move out of the way fast enough.

They passed through a metal door and immediately started down a set of stairs illuminated by a single bare bulb. The heat was stifling, and the smell of excrement and rot made Trent put a hand over his face.

"I think there's been a mistake," he said trying to keep his voice from shaking. "I was supposed to meet the president."

They kept moving downward, the men behind him not quite pushing but unafraid to make contact when they thought his pace was slowing.

He managed to keep from panicking, but only barely. There had been no mistake. Within the narrow context of his backwater country, Umboto Mtiti never made mistakes. He understood the subtle relationship between every faction of every tribe, knew exactly where to draw the line between terrorizing the people and inciting them, and had an uncanny nose for men with charisma and brains. Few survived much past early adulthood.

The steel door they arrived at had the look of one that you entered but never came back out of. Why did Mtiti have him brought here? Did he think he'd been betrayed? Had he decided that NewAfrica had outlived its usefulness? Was he looking to send Fedorov a message?

The lead soldier pulled the door open, but Trent put a hand on the jamb and wouldn't go through. "No. This is a mistake. I—"

"Stephen!"

Inside, Umboto Mtiti moved from the shadows and left Trent with little choice. He stepped hesitantly over the threshold as the enormous African strode toward him and embraced him tightly. The claustrophobia of being wrapped in his thick arms was magnified by the clang of the door shutting behind him.

"I'm sorry for our surroundings, Stephen, but I find myself with little time and much to do. Your trip was a pleasant one, I trust?"

"It was fine, Mr. President, thank you for asking." Trent wiped the sour-smelling sweat from his face and tried to ignore the two men kneeling by the back wall. They were the only other things in the room, naked, bound, and bleeding from various wounds.

"And Aleksei?"

"He sends his regards, Excellency."

Mtiti smiled widely and tugged at the army uniform he'd favored when he'd seized power but had forsaken in recent years in an effort to soften his image with the international community.

His rise to power had begun twelve years ago, at a time when violence was rare and his people's only concerns were feeding themselves and raising their families. The country was being run by a man with strong tribal credentials but not much interest in doing anything other than living a life of relative opulence in the capital.

When the foreign mining companies began to take an increased interest in the region's natural resources, the former president was slow to recognize the shifting paradigm. He had everything he wanted, his people weren't starving or restless, and he'd always distrusted the whites. Unfortunately, that distrust hadn't extended to Mtiti, whom he'd thought of as a son.

Almost overnight, there was money and power to be had that was actually worth something. The coup was comically simple. Mtiti simply walked into the then-presidential palace with a few trusted men and beat his mentor to death with a shovel taken from one of the gardeners. To this day, no one was sure why he'd chosen that method. He'd had a sidearm.

"I wonder, Stephen. What are you doing for me?" His tone was still cordial, but the dull eyes began to sharpen—a warning sign Trent was all too familiar with.

"I'm sorry, Excellency, I don't think I understand."

"The rebels in the south are getting stronger, and your government is talking about cutting back its military aid to me. I wonder how this could be happening."

"I'm sure you know, Excellency, that our economy has taken a turn for the worse and a lot of our resources are going to the war on terror—"

"What about my war on terror?" Mtiti said, his deep voice reverberating in the small room. Out of the corner of his eye, Trent could see the two prisoners stiffen at the sound. Mtiti's smile was still broad but now seemed empty.

"Sir, we—"

"Is that what America wants, Stephen? For this country to fall into a civil war? Maybe I should get rid of the American companies and replace them with Europeans and Asians. You know I'm courted by them every day."

"Excellency, we don't really have control over—"

"Excuses! When we began our relationship, I expected more than this. Now I wonder why I continue it."

It was becoming harder and harder for Trent to remain calm, and he wiped at his forehead again. Business relationships didn't just end in this part of the world. One of the parties ended up begging uselessly for their lives.

"Sir, we're working hard to maintain your image. Our charity sends consistently favorable reports to both USAID and the UN, and we do everything we can to highlight what you're up against. And on the ground we've helped you take care of problems in ways that otherwise would have attracted the attention of the foreign press—"

"So I rule because of your help?" Mtiti shouted, the spit spraying from his mouth visible in the glare of the bulb overhead. "Is that what you're saying to me? That I'm powerless in my own country without you?"

"Of course not, Excellency. We're here to make your life easier. That's all."

"Well, you're not doing a very good job, are you? Because my life isn't easy. And it gets worse every day."

Trent pulled an eight-by-ten picture from the portfolio in his hand and held it out in an attempt to divert Mtiti from a subject that could only end badly. "This is the location of the photo shoot we've set up for you."

Mtiti's face darkened. "With the Yvimbo."

"Yes, sir."

"I've decided not to do it."

Trent didn't let anything show in his expression. "Excellency, we've talked about this. It's critical to your image abroad. We have to show you reaching out to the other tribe—to prove that you're trying to create an inclusive, peaceful government."

"And what about *my* people? How does this look to them? Me

posing with these pigs? Me allowing your agency to feed them when my own family goes without?"

"Excellency, you know that we've already made provisions for controlling the distribution of the photos and for the project's long-term prospects. The photographs will only be available where they can benefit you."

"You tell me that and ask me to trust your words?" He pulled his pistol from the holster at his side, gesturing with it but not actually pointing it in Trent's direction. Yet.

"Sir, I—" He fell silent when Mtiti stopped gesturing and he found himself looking down the dark barrel of the gun.

"Shut up! Shut your mouth! Your stupidity put me and my country at risk."

"I don't understand," Trent said, careful to remain completely motionless. He saw the men at the back of the room straighten to the degree their bonds and wounds would allow. Their heads moved in bird-like jerks, first toward Mtiti, then to Trent, and back again.

"I spoke with Gideon," Mtiti said. "He tells me that your new man is no different. No different at all."

Trent nodded slowly, unsure how best to answer.

When he had discovered that Dan Ordman was beginning to ask questions that were better left unanswered, he'd immediately called Aleksei with the recommendation that they shut down the terracing project and use the excuse of a lack of funding to lay Dan off.

How Mtiti had come to know of the situation, he still wasn't sure. Maybe it was the spies that he had on every street corner. Maybe Aleksei had told him. The bottom line, though, was that Dan was dead. And not only dead but dismembered as a pointless attempt to warn anyone who might be thinking of following in his footsteps.

"On the surface, I agree, Mr. President. Josh Hagarty doesn't seem much different. But that was our goal—to find someone who would seem credible. I promise you, we won't have the same kinds of problems again."

Mtiti was clearly unconvinced. "I've told Gideon that at the first sign of a problem, he's to deal with your new man just like he did the old one. If that becomes necessary, and I'm the first one to find out that it's necessary, it will make me wonder if you're more of a danger to me than a help."

"Yes, sir," Trent said contritely. "I understand."

Mtiti turned toward his two prisoners and gestured with the gun. "These men worked for me. They were honest men—they didn't steal or sympathize with the Yvimbo. But after a time, they came to believe that their own interests were more important than mine. They became lazy and . . ." He scratched his cheek with the barrel of his pistol, searching his moderate English vocabulary for the proper word. "They became . . . entitled."

The first bullet caught the man on the left in the forehead and exploded through the back of his skull, ricocheting off the concrete wall and causing Trent to dive to the floor. Mtiti didn't seem aware of the danger and fired at the second man, who had fallen to the floor and was wrenching futilely at his bonds. The side of his neck was torn away, but this time it was accompanied by a wet gurgling instead of the deafening ring of a ricochet.

Trent pushed himself to his knees, but the room had lost focus. He clenched his teeth together in an effort to stop what was coming, but a moment later the contents of his stomach were on the floor in front of him.

The killing of two helpless men who had never really sinned against him seemed to raise Mtiti's spirits, as did the fact that his point had obviously been made. He holstered his weapon and crouched next to Trent, helping him to his feet. "I'm sorry, Stephen. I wasn't aware you were ill. I'll take you to my personal doctor immediately."

11

Josh Hagarty pushed his way through the people moving urgently along the dirt street and tried to imagine what their lives were like. He'd hoped his visit to town would teach him something, but now he wondered if he wouldn't have been better off just downing a few of Luganda's brutal margaritas in the compound's pool. Everything here was so different that he was having a hard time even finding a context to place it in.

The buildings on either side of him were colonial in design—still imposing, but peeling paint and the occasional collapsed balcony hinted at inevitable disintegration. As did almost everything else.

He winced when one of the children swarming him grabbed his hand and squeezed the blisters raised by moving too quickly from pushing paper to swinging a pick.

"You give me money," the boy said cheerfully.

It seemed to be his only English, but if you only knew four words, Josh had to admit, those were good ones.

"I'm flat broke, kid. You're looking at a true American loser."

None of them understood, but all ten or so laughed, displaying spirits unbroken by their surroundings and dim prospects. He actually did have some change in his pocket but had been warned against passing it out. Something about turning African children into beggars and destroying their future. He understood the concept, but standing there staring at the reality was an entirely different thing. He thought he'd had a pretty good handle on poverty but was quickly realizing that he didn't know the first thing about it.

The kids lost interest when it became apparent he wasn't going to cave, leaving him to the mildly curious stares of the adults around him. The crowd became more dense as he approached an outdoor market operating under the watchful eye of Umboto Mtiti, staring down from a large wall mural. This depiction was a bit more modern than the ones he'd seen in the capital, and the caption was scrawled in the style of graffiti: "Gates are doors to the future."

He had no idea what that meant, but it seemed to capture the competing waves of possibility and hopelessness that had been buffeting him since he'd arrived.

Gideon hadn't shown up that morning, so Josh had spent a frustrating day using his charades skills to try to get the people on his project digging in straight lines. Not that he was sure the terraces necessarily needed to be straight, but he didn't have anything else to do.

The main obstacle they were facing was drainage, and he'd waded back into the cornfield to see how its designers had dealt with the problem. He didn't find the elegant, ancient solution he'd expected, instead uncovering a sophisticated system of pipes and gas-powered pumps. Where they'd come from and where he could get more was a mystery.

Josh wandered past stalls selling the gravy-soaked dough that seemed to be the country's national dish, past fabric vendors hawking material polka-dotted with Umboto Mtiti's image, finally entering the sector dominated by meat vendors. He stopped short in front of a table containing what looked like a charred child, its swollen tongue still pink where it protruded from a lipless mouth. Josh held off his revulsion and inched closer as the woman behind the table waved away the flies. He let out the breath he'd been holding when he realized it was a monkey.

She chattered at him unintelligibly, but he held out his hands and backed away. "Looks tasty, ma'am, but no thanks."

The heat, smoke, and sweat-soaked people sliding past started to close in on him, and he ducked down an alley, happy for a little shade and urine-scented solitude. The thick, colonial-era walls deadened the sound of the plaza, and the increasing quiet created an illusion of serenity as he penetrated deeper. He was going to be all right. He'd just gotten there. Had he thought it was going to be easy? That he was going to roll in there and turn an entire continent around overnight?

He was too lost in thought to hear the footsteps coming up behind him until someone grabbed his shoulder and spun him around. He managed to get an arm up and deflect the club before it connected with his head, but the force of the blow still knocked him back against the wall of the narrow alley.

There were two of them, both probably in their early twenties, and both shouting with the same unbridled fury that he'd seen in Gideon at the airport. Adrenaline quickly cleared his head, and the instincts he'd developed in jail turned out to still be with him.

"Take it easy," he said, trying to buy some time in a situation that he already knew wasn't going to end peacefully. A quick glance in either direction confirmed that his attackers knew exactly what they were doing. There were no windows looking down on them and no doors to run for. The alley dead-ended in about thirty feet, and they had blocked off any hope of an escape back in the direction of the plaza.

"You want my money? I don't have much, but you're welcome to it." He began to reach for his pocket, but when he did, they charged. Josh focused on the one with the club, ducking just in time for it to pass over his head and strike the wall behind him with the sound of splintering wood. As it did, though, the other man landed a kick to his chest. The bottom of his foot was hard from a life spent shoeless, but nowhere near as damaging as the boots favored by the people Josh had tangled with in his youth. He managed to catch hold of the man's leg and flip him onto his back in the dirt, opening a path out of the alley.

He was just a little too slow, giving the man on the ground time to slap his ankle and cause him to stumble as he tried to escape. He regained his balance quickly, but the split-second delay gave his other attacker time to slam what was left of his club into the small of Josh's back.

This time he wasn't able to maintain his footing, and he landed hard on his stomach, skidding across the dirt and colliding with the wall to his right. The sensation of a hand snatching the wallet from his back pocket prompted him to flip instinctively onto his back and grab at the man's wrist. The loss of a few dollars and his IDs shrank to insignificance when he saw the club, almost entirely intact as it turned out, arcing toward his skull.

Josh abandoned his efforts to retrieve his wallet and tried to pull his hand back to ward off the blow, but the man anticipated the move and grabbed him in a sweaty but unbreakable grip.

The combination of being out in the sun all day, jet lag, and the disorientation of being so far from home made it hard to fully accept what was happening. It was simple, though. In less than a second, the club was going to land and he was going to die lying in an alley thousands of miles from home. For nothing. For a wallet containing barely enough money to buy a Big Mac and fries.

Josh closed his eyes and waited for the impact, but nothing happened. No pain, which he supposed was understandable, but also no disorientation or loss of consciousness. No blinding light surrounded by angels or fiery pits guarded with pitchforks.

The pressure around his forearm disappeared, and he opened his eyes to discover that there were now two more men in the alley, and everyone was trying to kill each other. The one with the club was on the ground and absorbed a kick to the head so vicious that Josh's stomach rolled at the sound of it. The man he'd knocked to the ground tried to run but quickly discovered his own plan working against him. There was nowhere to go. A moment later he was on all fours trying desperately to dislodge the man snaking an arm around his throat.

There was something about the man on top that was familiar—the way he moved, the wiry power of his arms. Josh's mind was still coming to terms with the fact that he was alive, and it took a few seconds for him to realize that he actually knew one of his saviors.

The man beneath Tfmena Llengambi was much larger and younger, but so far he hadn't been able to use that advantage to escape. One of his hands came off the ground and dipped into his waistband, reappearing a moment later with something that gleamed in the sunlight angling into the alley.

Adrenaline hit Josh full force again, and he jumped to his feet, sprinting the few yards to the struggling men and sliding across the dirt just in time to stop the knife from lodging in Tfmena's ribs.

It was the opening the older man had been looking for, and he picked up a broken piece of concrete, bringing it down on the back of the man's head with a sickening crunch. Josh released the now limp arm, pedaling his feet in front of him as he scooted away. Tfmena brought the block down again and again until the blood flowing onto the ground mingled with what Josh assumed were pieces of the man's brain.

And then it was silent again. Josh glanced behind him and saw that his other attacker was in a similar condition, having become the victim of his own club in the hands of a young man wearing a Britney Spears T-shirt over a heaving chest.

Tfmena stood and held out a steady hand to help Josh to his feet, then brushed the dust off him. His expression was strangely calm and seemed to contain a bit less disdain than it had before.

Tfmena picked up Josh's wallet and held it out to him, saying something in Yvimbo that was easy to decipher from the tone: "Get out of here. This is none of your business anymore."

Josh mumbled his thanks, shaking the man's hand and trying not to look at the two corpses as he backed away. Finally he turned and ran. When he burst into the blinding sun of the plaza, he was at a full sprint. He ran past bemused Africans rushing to get out of his way, past the charred monkey that still hadn't been sold, past tables of knockoff watches and boom boxes, not stopping until exhaustion and heat overcame him.

He bent at the waist, breathing hard and trying to think about what had just happened. When he finally managed to straighten up again, he discovered that he was standing in front of a clothing store with a well-appointed sign reading "Dead White Man Shoppe."

"Forget your undies?"

He spun, fists raised, to find JB Flannary standing behind him.

"Whoa, tiger. Peace, okay?"

Josh just stood there, his breathing still not controlled enough to answer.

Flannary pointed to his chest. "You got red on you."

Josh looked down and saw the blood splattered across his white T-shirt. Was it his? Or did it belong to the man he'd just helped kill?

"They were slaughtering chickens in the market," he heard himself say.

Flannary nodded knowingly. "You should be more careful. Sometimes bloodstains don't come out so easy."

12

The front of the bar was completely open, but it seemed to
have been less an architectural decision than a violent history.
Whether the makeshift terrace was the work of a bomb or an out-
of-control vehicle was hard to say.

"Hey, look who I found wandering the streets," Flannary said
as he ducked into the relative darkness of the bar's interior and approached a table where Katie was nursing a beer alone, despite the
fact that the bar was dominated by the white faces of aid workers.
Josh recognized a few of them from the compound, and he returned their waves reflexively as Flannary pushed him into a chair
across from Katie.

She frowned and mumbled a stiff greeting, obviously still
working out whether she should forgive him for his insult the
night he'd arrived.

"What can I get you?" Flannary asked.

Josh adjusted himself in the chair, still too full of nervous energy to sit comfortably. "I could really use a beer."

"I think that can be arranged," he said, walking to the back of
the building and initiating negotiations with a man guarding a bar
built into a street vendor's cart. Josh just stared down at the table.

"Are you all right?" Katie said after a minute or so.

He barely heard her, his mind still replaying what had happened. How could he have been stupid enough to go into that alley alone? Now two men were dead. Should he tell someone? Stephen Trent? The police?

Flannary returned and slapped a beer down on the Formica-topped table before falling into a chair. Josh reached for it and took a sip. It tasted like water, but it seemed to have a hint of the alcohol bite he desperately needed.

"What the fuck am I doing here?"

Josh wasn't fully aware that he'd spoken aloud until he noticed that the conversations at a number of the tables closest to him had gone silent.

"Wasting your time?" Flannary said and then jerked when Katie kicked him under the table.

"Everyone eventually asks themselves that question," Katie said.

Josh looked up from the table and met her gaze. "Have you? What was your answer?"

She took a long pull from her beer and then set it back on the table. "I learned to focus on winning small, everyday battles. If you let yourself think about the big picture . . ." Her voice faded.

A pudgy man sitting at an adjoining table finished her thought. "You'd go crazy."

He was from CARE, Josh remembered, and wondered if it was his Land Cruiser that was driving around the countryside with a machine gun mounted in the back.

"I feel like I'm on another planet," Josh said.

"How so?" Katie asked.

He considered telling her and Flannary about the alley but decided to keep his mouth shut. If he didn't talk about it, maybe someday he'd be able to tell himself that it hadn't happened.

"I've been working my ass off since I got here, and you know what *I've* learned? Nothing. I went through all the project's books, and I still have no idea where all our money's gone. I don't know how much we pay people or even who works for us. There's actually an entry in the ledger for 'diarrhea mountainscape.' What the hell does that mean? All I can tell you is that it cost two hundred and seventy bucks."

"Why don't you ask Gideon?" Flannary suggested.

"I would, but whenever I ask him something I get an answer that doesn't mean anything. And that's only when he actually shows up . . ."

That elicited a bitter laugh from Katie, but it was Flannary who spoke. "Things are different here, kid. You'll get used to it."

Josh wasn't so sure, but didn't say so. "What charity do you work for, JB? I don't think you've ever said."

This time Katie's laugh had some humor in it. "He doesn't work for an NGO. He'll tell you he's a reporter and that his brother's a big deal with the *New York Times*, but the truth is that he's just a crazy expat. He likes slinking around Africa and every once in a while writes an article to keep him in liquor money."

"You know, I *am* sitting right next to you," Flannary said, though he didn't seem particularly upset.

"Yeah? Tell me I'm wrong."

"I'm too busy trying to remember how many little kids like you have come and gone over the last twenty years and what exactly it is you've accomplished."

"Touché," she said, and she clinked her beer bottle against Flannary's glass.

"You see," Flannary started loudly, "the charities didn't start showing up in this country until the mining took off. . . ."

The conversations at the tables around them suddenly erupted in a chorus of groans. A number of wadded-up napkins were thrown in Flannary's direction, one hitting him in the ear and clinging to the sweat for a moment before fluttering to the ground.

"JB thinks we're to blame for everything that's wrong with Africa," Katie explained.

"Josh, do you know what the largest industry in this country is?" Flannary asked.

"Wikipedia says mining."

"Wrong. It's foreign aid. Every year international charities pump tens of millions of dollars into an economy that shouldn't be worth a bucket of spit. And with all that money flying around, feeding yourself from a farm doesn't seem all that attractive anymore. Better to get a gun and see if you can't carve off a few bucks for yourself." He lowered his voice. "If you can find any that haven't ended up in Mtiti's pocket . . ."

"You may get your wish," Katie said. "We may all be gone soon. Things are getting too unstable for most of the NGOs. They're pulling out, and they're taking their money with them."

"Even I can't blame them after what happened to Dan," Flannary said.

"Who?" Josh said.

Flannary's head tilted slightly. "Dan. The guy you replaced."

"Oh, right. Dan Ordman. Do either of you know how I can contact him? I've been thinking maybe he can help me figure out where the project money's gone."

Katie was staring at him with her mouth partially open, and Flannary seemed to be at an uncharacteristic loss for words.

"I said something stupid again, didn't I? What is it this time?"

"He's gonna be a hard guy to get in touch with," Flannary said. "They found him dead in the jungle a little over a month ago."

Josh froze with the beer halfway to his mouth. "Natural causes?" he said hopefully.

"By African standards, I suppose. He was hacked to pieces with a machete."

━━━━

Josh shaded the screen of the satellite phone against the glare of the sun as he walked away from the bar where he'd left JB Flannary. It began to ring, and he pressed it hard against his ear, finding trying to hear over the noise of the crowd preferable to going somewhere quieter.

"Hello? This is Stephen Trent."

"Stephen, it's Josh."

"Josh? What's up? Is everything okay?"

"Actually, I'm having a pretty bad day."

"I'm sorry to hear that. Is there anything I can do?"

"Yeah. You can tell me why you never mentioned that the guy I'm replacing didn't quit. That he was dismembered."

"I never said he quit, Josh."

"No, but you seemed to have skipped the dismembered part, too."

"Honestly, I didn't think it was relevant."

"Not relevant? He was cut into little pieces, Stephen!"

"I think we've established that. Thank you. Look, he'd driven out of the compound alone and gone more than a hundred miles into politically unstable territory. We've stepped up security for our people everywhere, but honestly, it really isn't necessary unless you decide to go driving off into the countryside in the middle of the night. And you're not going to, right?"

Josh didn't respond. The idea that Trent hadn't thought this was pertinent was bullshit. And so was his story about picking only the best people. He picked the most desperate people because no one else would touch this job with a ten-foot pole.

"Josh? Are you still there?"

"Yeah," he said, trying to calm down. As bad as this gig was shaping up to be, he couldn't afford to lose it. Not yet, anyway.

"Look, I'm sorry. I should have mentioned it. But I promise you this isn't because somebody has something against us."

"Then what?"

"Look, I don't want to speak ill of the dead, but we have reason to believe that Dan had gotten involved in some things that he shouldn't have. That's one of the reasons we were so careful with our hiring process this time. We needed someone we could fully trust."

"Yeah . . ."

"Josh, if you ever feel you're not safe or there's something else we should be doing to make sure you don't have any problems, pick up the phone and tell me. That's all you ever have to do."

A group of children spotted him and began running toward him with their hands out. He turned and started walking in the other direction.

What choice did he have? He was banking over thirty grand a year while NewAfrica covered basically every expense he and Laura had.

"Fine."

"Great," Trent said, the relief audible in his voice. "How's it going otherwise? Is there anything we can do to help you?"

"Get me someone who knows something about farming. And you might as well burn the books they've been keeping."

"It's not that complicated, Josh. They're digging. You just need to keep it on track. You're a smart, resourceful guy. Those are the qualities that got you the job."

The group of children had almost overtaken him, so he dropped a handful of change on the ground and increased his speed as they wrestled over it.

"Send me some books on agriculture and terracing."

"Absolutely," Trent said. "I'll do it today."

"Fine."

"And Josh, keep in mind that you just got there. You'll get it."

"Like Dan did?"

Trent either didn't hear or chose to ignore the comment. "Look, I don't want to pile things on you, but in a few days we've got some photographers coming in to take shots of the finished parts of that project."

"They look great," Josh said. "And that's something else I'd like to talk to you about."

"And we will—I'm coming for the shoot. . . ." The way his voice trailed off suggested there was more. "And so is President Mtiti."

"Please tell me that's a joke."

"Take it easy, Josh. There's nothing you need to do. Like you said, that part of the project looks great. Just try to keep the rest of it moving forward, okay?"

13

It was after nine A.M. before Josh finally walked out of his cabin. He'd been awake for hours, tossing and turning in a futile attempt to retreat back into unconsciousness. A hangover, combined with the memories of the two dead men in the alley, made sleep come hard.

He shaded his eyes against the glare of the morning sun as he made his way to breakfast but stopped when he noticed that the door to the Land Cruiser NewAfrica had provided him was open. Through the windows, he could make out the shape of a man digging around in the driver's seat.

Out of instinct, Josh began to run toward the vehicle, but a moment later he had slowed to a jog, and shortly after that he was walking toward breakfast again. Screw it. If the guy wanted it, he could have it. Josh would call Stephen Trent after he finished his oatmeal and get a new one.

"Josh! Where the hell are you going?"

He turned and saw Flannary waving to him over the roof of the Land Cruiser. "We're all packed up and ready to go!"

"Cut me some slack, JB. I'm hungover, I'm hungry, and I'm not in a very good mood, you know?"

"Did someone wake up on the wrong side of the bed this morning?"

Josh waved a hand dismissively and was about to leave when Flannary held up something wrapped in foil. "You know what this is? A breakfast burrito made with my personal stash of authentic tortillas and salsa. We'll throw it on the engine and in about fifteen minutes, the genuine imported cheddar cheese will be all melty. . . ."

"No, JB. I've got about a thousand years of work to do—"

"But only about another fifty before you're dead. So since you're clearly doomed to failure, why not come out with me and learn something?" He dropped the burrito and held up a cocktail shaker. "I've got Bloody Marys."

Josh took one last look at the path to the breakfast area and then walked over to the Land Cruiser and climbed in. What the hell. Africa would still be here tomorrow, and it would still be a disaster.

Flannary gave him an approving slap on the leg and began backing up, almost clipping Luganda, who had burst from the trees behind them.

"Where you going?" he said, poking his impossibly round face in Josh's window and gripping the sill as he jogged alongside the vehicle.

"Just a little field trip," Flannary said, slowing but not stopping. "Nothing to be concerned about."

"Where? Let me send people with you. It's not safe."

"We'll be fine—back in time for happy hour."

He accelerated again, and Luganda was forced to release the sill. He stared at them through the billowing dust as Flannary sped toward the gate.

"Maybe we should take him up on his offer, JB. You never know what we could run into. On the way here I saw—"

"Quit being such an old lady and fix me a drink."

"Pothole!"

Josh held his cup out the window, letting the tomato juice and vodka slosh over his hand and drip into the road.

"Sorry," Flannary shouted over the sound of the wind and the clanking of the empty beer bottles rolling around on the floorboard.

The countryside they were bouncing across seemed lost in time. The dirt road clung to precipices that descended into distant emerald valleys, and villages were few and far between, consisting of small, round houses with conical roofs perched neatly on what little flat terrain could be found. Cattle wandered about looking for choice grass, and women in colorful garb sauntered along the sides of the road carrying impossibly large loads on their heads. In some ways it could almost be mistaken for idyllic.

"Watch the kid!" Josh yelled, grabbing the dashboard as Flannary eased to within inches of the cliff they were skirting to avoid a small boy holding up a dead rat that must have weighed almost as much as he did.

"*Cricetomys gambianus,*" Flannary said. "The giant pouch rat."

"Jesus, JB," Josh said, his heart still pounding desperately in his chest. "You shouldn't be driving."

"Why?"

It was obviously meant as an honest question. Driving drunk, one of America's great sins and an act that had contributed in no small way to the destruction of Josh's life, was such a trivial infraction here that it was beneath notice. Like worrying about a hall pass during a school shooting.

"Never mind."

"He'll still be there on the way back," Flannary said, pulling a long black cigarette holder from a duffel stuffed between the seats. "We'll see if we can get a deal. Those things are pretty good with the right marinade. More tender than you'd think."

"What are you doing?"

Flannary put a cigarette in the holder and struggled to light it in the damp wind coming through his open window. "I'm considering going through a Hunter S. Thompson phase." Smoke billowed from his mouth as he spoke. "It was between that and a Jim Morrison phase."

"The leather pants would be hot."

He slammed his hand emphatically against the steering wheel. "My thought exactly."

———

Flannary swung the wheel hard to the left, and they climbed a hill steep enough that Josh had to put a hand over his drink to keep it from spilling down the front of his shirt. The engine protested loudly, but they finally crested a low plateau and entered a village similar to all the others except for a whitewashed church that looked as if it had been stolen from the set of *Little House on the Prairie*.

Flannary skidded to a stop and jumped out, stumbling and nearly falling as his alcohol-soaked brain relearned standing after three hours in the car. "We're here."

Josh was more cautious, holding on to the door for support as he exited. The foliage had turned dense over the past hour and seemed to be looking for spots where the village's defenses were weak enough for it to take over. The one exception was to the east where meticulously cleared farmland was filled with women fawning over a crop he couldn't identify. Children in different states of nakedness played with whatever was at hand but, unlike the city kids, didn't seem all that interested in their arrival.

"Where are we?" Josh said, unaware that their trip had a destination. He'd assumed it was more of a moving bar.

Flannary didn't respond but motioned for him to follow. When they cleared the line of huts to their right, Flannary stopped and pointed with a dramatic flourish to a tall, blond woman working a hand-operated water pump.

"Who the hell is that?" Josh said, immediately struck by the way she threw her entire body into working the rusted handle.

"Annika Gritdal. Kind of a hard-ass, and I think she may hear voices, but a fairly good egg."

She was too intent on her battle with the pump to notice them, which gave Josh an opportunity to stare. She was thin in a way that suggested endless physical labor, with deeply tanned skin that set off the gleaming hair stuck to her sweat-soaked shoulders.

"She's done amazing things here," Flannary said. "Two years ago this piece of land couldn't have supported a cockroach."

"You sound almost like you admire her. I thought you said all this was bullshit."

"Oh, don't get me wrong. I think she's wasting time, but at least she's doing it with style and a refreshing lack of hypocrisy."

She glanced up and spotted them, abandoning the pump to wave.

"Annika! Good to see you, my sweet," Flannary said, staggering slightly as he approached and gave her a hug that left the front of his shirt even wetter than it had been before. "Let me introduce Josh Hagarty. He's Dan's replacement."

She gave him a sad smile and shook his hand, saying something about how sorry she was about the fate of his predecessor, but he wasn't really paying attention. He'd met a few Scandinavian girls in school, but they hadn't been all that remarkable. Annika looked like a descendant of the Vikings should—a powerful figure, standing unfazed by her hostile surroundings. Was he romanticizing? Sure. But it was hard not to.

She pointed to the pump and yelled something at a group of men drinking on the porch of a particularly dilapidated hut. One of them gave a brief response and then went back to his jug. An argument ensued that was fascinating to watch. The native language, which sounded surreal in any setting, was almost otherworldly when flowing from a European mouth. No one he'd met yet could do much more than approximate "Another beer, please."

She finally got frustrated and said something that clearly meant "Just fucking forget it" and turned back to them.

"That was amazing," Josh said.

"Being ignored?"

"Not so much that as the fact that they seem to understand you."

She shrugged. "It's the curse of being from Norway. No one's going to speak your language, so you have to get used to speaking theirs."

"What's with the pump?" Flannary said. "New fitness craze?"

She let out a frustrated breath and pointed to a mechanical pump sitting idle in the dirt. "That one cracked about a month ago, but I haven't had any luck getting it fixed."

Josh looked at the damage. "Doesn't look all that serious."

"Are you a water-pump expert?"

"Not specifically, but I do have a degree in mechanical engineering."

She rolled her eyes. "You all have such impressive-sounding degrees, but I've never seen any of you do anything useful with all that expensive education."

There was a playfulness to her tone, but Josh still felt like he'd been chopped down to about half his normal size.

Flannary laughed. "I told you she's kind of a hard-ass. All nuns are that way as near as I can tell."

"You're a nun?" Josh said, immediately regretting the wide-eyed shock and disappointment in his delivery.

"In fact, I am *not* a nun. I was a novice for two years but never took my vows."

"The Catholics are scumbags," Flannary pointed out.

"The Catholics aren't scumbags, JB. You just—"

"Oh, come on. You ran out of that convent like your ass was on fire."

"I'll admit that they're a bit misguided on how to prevent the spread of AIDS here and gave too many orders for me. And then there's the sex . . ."

"Excuse me?" Josh said, again regretting opening his mouth.

"Sex. The idea of never marrying, never having children." Her expression turned thoughtful. "I felt as though I was closing doors at a time in my life when I should have been opening them." A beautiful smile preceded a sudden change of subject.

"Come with me, Josh. As an engineer you'll appreciate this. My church took up a collection and sent me a brand-new, very good welder." She paused for a moment. "Do you go to church?"

"Not really."

"Why not?"

"I guess I haven't quite reconciled the whole God thing in my mind yet."

"That's okay because He—"

"Believes in me," Josh said, finishing her sentence. "I know."

"Actually, I was going to say that He can get back at you by sending you to the fiery depths of hell for all eternity." Another one of those camera-flash smiles. "Anyway, like an idiot I asked for the welder instead of a new pump. I said, 'Annika, you should learn to fix things.' You want to see it?"

"The welder? Uh, sure."

He was having a hard time concentrating and sounded increasingly stupid, even to himself. Flannary had obviously noticed and was enjoying himself immensely.

She pointed to a tarp lying next to a pile of junk, and Josh pulled it off to examine what looked like a car alternator with cables sticking out of it.

Flannary shook his head in disgust.

"Sometime after it entered the country, someone stole the one my church sent and replaced it with whatever that thing is," Annika said. "But do you know what really makes me mad? I know in my heart that right now my welder is being used to fix one of Mtiti's Rolls Royces."

Josh grinned and poked at one of the cables with his foot.

"What? You think this is funny?"

"Kind of."

"I wonder how you'd feel if you had to stand there by that pump all day in the sun?"

"Tell you what," Josh said. "Why don't you and JB go have a drink? In about an hour, come back and just try to resist asking me to marry you."

———

Josh finally understood the phrase "Africa hot." He was sitting in the full sun wearing one of Annika's old sweatshirts, gloves, and a welding helmet, basking in the glow of the molten metal in front of him. And to make matters worse, the Land Cruiser was idling only inches behind him.

"I feel so stupid!" Annika said as Josh continued to fuse the cracked pump.

The thing under the tarp actually had been a welder—but one designed to be powered by a car motor as opposed to being plugged into an outlet.

"How would you know?" Josh yelled through his helmet. "Sometimes you just need a redneck. Nothing else will do."

"'Redneck'?" she said.

He laughed. "JB, maybe you could come up with a good definition."

"I don't think she'd have a context. Most of the American NGO people she's met are more Ivy League types. Like Dan."

"Were you friends?" Josh heard her say.

"Never met him."

"I liked him," Annika offered.

"Does anyone know what happened?" Josh said.

There was no immediate response, but finally Flannary spoke. "He got killed. It's Africa, kid. No reason to look deeper."

Even over the crackle of the welder, his tone suggested there was every reason to look deeper. Josh flipped up his helmet and looked back at Flannary, who was sipping from an expensive-looking martini glass.

"Africa can be a dangerous place," Annika said. "A beautiful place filled with wonderful people, but still . . ."

"I'm hoping to avoid getting killed," Josh said. "That's definitely not what I came here for."

"That brings up an interesting question," Flannary said. "Why *did* you come here?"

Annika sat down on the Land Cruiser's bumper and searched his face in a way that suggested she thought something was hidden there.

He flipped the helmet down and went back to work. "To help out my fellow man?"

"Really?" Flannary said.

"Why not?"

"Come on, Josh. I'm the world expert on those fresh little faces. You don't have one."

"Okay, how about this: It's the best job I could find, and I've got a lot of debt."

"Better, but I still don't love it."

"Why not?"

"Didn't you say earlier that you have an engineering degree?" Annika said. "And don't you have an MBA, too?"

He stopped what he was doing. "How would you know that? Is someone passing out my résumé in backwater African villages without telling me?"

"You've got to admit, though, it's a pretty impressive résumé. One that would get you a job just about anywhere, I would think."

Josh didn't answer.

"Did you rob a bank or something?" Flannary prodded.

"What's it to you?" Josh shot back.

"In this part of the world, it makes sense to know who you're dealing with."

"I didn't rob a bank."

Annika had wisely decided to sit this one out, but Flannary wasn't so easily deterred. "Drugs? Stuffed a little too much up your nose? That can—"

"What the fuck's your problem?" Josh said, wrenching off his helmet and jumping to his feet to face Flannary. Annika pushed herself off the Land Cruiser, but instead of preventing a fight between them, she had to grab Josh around the waist as the sudden movement and heat caused the blood to rush from his head.

"So what, then?" Flannary said as Josh's knees collapsed and Annika lowered him to the ground. "You got caught cheating on your finals?"

"JB! That's enough!" Annika scolded. "Josh, are you all right?"

She pulled his sweatshirt off and then snatched Flannary's drink, dabbing the cool gin on his forehead. "Josh? Are you with me?"

By way of an answer, he held out a hand in Flannary's direction and lifted his middle finger.

14

Josh Hagarty found himself in an increasingly familiar position: lying awake in bed, watching the sun spike around the curtains.

It was hard not to turn the previous day over and over in his mind. Annika Gritdal may well have been the most amazing woman he'd ever met. Of course he'd known women in school who were forces of nature in their own right—ones who would end up earning millions of dollars, dining with senators, and putting the fear of God into the financial markets. But they would also be in actual danger of perishing if the local Starbucks ran out of soy milk.

He closed his eyes and breathed the increasingly thick scent of smoke wafting in from hundreds of cooking fires burning in the refugee camps over the hill. Annika's image hovered in the darkness.

Not that he had a chance in hell with her. He had a not-so-vague feeling that Flannary's interrogation had been planned and that she'd been complicit. Why they would be interested enough to bother escaped him, but how he'd come off didn't: a violent jerk with something to hide. Or more accurately, a violent jerk prone to fainting spells with something to hide. Quite the chick magnet.

Josh coughed and opened his eyes. The smoke had become thick enough to put the other side of his room slightly out of focus. That had never happened before.

He slipped out of bed and was pulling on a pair of jeans when someone started pounding on his door. The muffled shouting was completely unintelligible, but the tone and volume made his breath catch in his chest.

His first reaction was that they were under attack, though he wasn't sure why or by whom. He managed to get his pants buttoned and ran to the door, finding Luganda on the other side, speaking in a jumble of his native language and English.

The column of smoke bisecting the horizon behind him bore no resemblance to the yellow haze that hung over the town. It took a moment for Josh's mind to process its distance and location, but when he did, he took off shirtless and barefoot toward his truck.

By the time Josh skidded the vehicle to a stop, the flames were rising more than twenty feet into the air, moving quickly across the field of corn toward the shed that housed the irrigation controls and tools. He jumped out and ran toward the shed, ignoring the rocks cutting the bottoms of his feet and holding a hand in front of his eyes to protect them from heat. Smoke billowed over him as he tried to work his way closer, but there was no way. The hair on his arms and bare chest was beginning to singe, and the derelict tractor next to the shed was already being engulfed. He was finally forced to retreat, backing away until the air cleared enough for him to see a few workers who had arrived early watching the inferno.

They weren't moving or shouting or even talking among themselves. Instead they just stood there watching the flames with blank expressions. One of the men was standing with his son in front of him, hands reassuringly on his shoulders as everything they had lived and worked for was consumed. The boy was too young to have learned the resignation displayed by his elders, though, and despair was clearly etched in his face.

Josh ducked involuntarily when the gas that hadn't been siphoned from the tractor exploded, causing the flames to waver for a moment before gaining even more strength. He ran behind his Land Cruiser and fell to the ground, pressing his back against the closed door and putting his face in his hands. These people had been out there every day for God knew how long, breaking their backs to try to turn their lives into something. To create something they could give their children. And now it was gone. Now they had nothing.

When he remembered that President Mtiti was scheduled to be there in a week for a photo op, he slammed an elbow into the side of the car in frustration. How the hell had his life turned out this way? Despite what the paperwork might say, he wasn't a bad person. He'd worked hard to make something of himself. And he'd been ready to work hard to help the people here do the same. But he couldn't. Everything he touched turned to shit. God hated him for some reason. And He hated him so much that He was willing to destroy everything and everyone around him.

Josh looked up when he heard the crunch of approaching footsteps and discovered Tfmena looking down at him with what he interpreted as a mix of disappointment and inevitability. The African was probably regretting saving his ass in that alley.

"I don't know what happened," Josh said, though he knew Tfmena wouldn't understand.

The African grabbed him by the arm and stood him up, taking hold of both his shoulders and looking him in the eye. "And what would you do if you did know?"

Josh blinked a few time trying to process what he'd just heard. "You . . . you speak English?"

"Enough," Tfmena said.

"Why didn't you tell me before?"

"I had nothing to say to you."

"But now you do?"

"I begin to think you are someone worth saying things to."

Josh let out a bitter laugh. "You're wrong. A few weeks ago, I couldn't find your country on a map. And you know what my experience with farming is? When I was sixteen, I tried to grow pot behind my family's trailer and it died."

Tfmena's expression turned exasperated. "But now isn't a few weeks ago. You are here. And you know where you are now. Yes?"

Josh nodded numbly, but it was just a reflex. Africa was breaking him. Turning him into someone who just sat around and whined about injustice instead of doing something about it. Even prison hadn't been enough to do that.

Tfmena opened his mouth to say something but fell silent when he spotted Gideon running in their direction.

"What has happened?" Gideon shouted. "What have you done?"

"I didn't do anything," Josh said as Tfmena took a step backward. "It was already on fire when I woke up this morning."

Tfmena shook his head in disgust and picked something up off the ground. It looked like a cat, but there was no way to be sure. It was completely blackened, the body twisted unnaturally, like the monkey Josh had seen in town. A thick wire, maybe a coat hanger, was wound around what was left of its tail, and it was by that that Tfmena held it out to him.

Josh screwed up his face in disgust and was about to take a step backward when Gideon made a grab for the burned animal. The urgency of his movement suggested that it wasn't just some witch-doctor talisman or African delicacy, and Josh lunged forward, cutting him off and snatching the wire from Tfmena's hand.

"Give me the animal," Gideon said as Tfmena walked back to

the people silently watching what was left of their hope being carried off by the wind. "I will dispose of it."

"Thanks," Josh said, jerking it away when Gideon reached for it. "But I'll deal with it."

"Give it to me," Gideon repeated, the smoke moving across his mirrored sunglasses. "It isn't for you."

When Josh spoke again, he surprised even himself with the force of his voice. "*I said* I'd deal with it."

15

The pool area was empty, but Josh just sat there staring into it as though something profound was about to be revealed. Something that would put his life on track. Some hint that the universe wasn't laughing at his futile efforts to redeem himself.

He didn't notice JB Flannary's approach until the reporter leaned over to sniff at the charred carcass of the cat lying on the table. "We could probably still get it stuffed. A little souvenir of your trip to the dark continent."

"Screw you."

"Too soon?" Flannary said, falling uninvited into a chair and waving at Luganda for drinks.

"Not now, JB. Okay?"

"Why not?"

"Because I'm about to get fired, and all those people who were counting on me are going to starve."

Flannary snorted. "Yeah, all that genetically engineered corn, gone. What a shame."

Josh watched as Luganda started toward them with their drinks. "You got something to say, JB? Go ahead. Just come out and say it."

"I don't know what you're talking about," Flannary responded innocently.

"You're so full of shit."

Flannary examined him, drumming his hands thoughtfully on the table. Finally he seemed to come to a decision. "The way agriculture has always worked here is that when farmers grow a crop, they eat part of it and save part of it as seed for next year's planting. Your engineered corn is tough as nails, but it's sterile. So now these people are dependent on you to provide seed. What happens when your donors get bored or you decide it's getting a little too dangerous to stick around?"

Luganda arrived with their drinks, saving Josh from having to come up with an answer. What was it that Stephen Trent had said about providing sustainable solutions for Africa? But then, it was starting to seem like that was all Stephen was good for. Pretty speeches.

"Did you have a good trip?" Luganda asked.

"What?"

"Your field trip. Where did you go? North? You know I grew up there."

Josh accepted the beer the African was holding out to him but didn't answer. There was no reason for him not to like Luganda. He had been nothing but gracious and helpful, but there was also something not right about the guy. The overly wide grins, the endless procession of new-looking Hawaiian shirts, the downcast gaze. It all seemed a bit strained. And the fact that he hadn't so much as mentioned the fact that Josh's entire project and the food source for over a hundred of his countrymen had just burned to a crisp was downright bizarre.

"It wasn't that interesting," Flannary answered. "Drove around, looked at a few animals. You know how it is."

Luganda bobbed his head and just stood there. When the phone in the office started ringing, he was forced to retreat.

Josh pointed to the cat. "Gideon says the fire was an accident."

"Shit happens. Right, kid?"

The silence between them stretched to thirty seconds before Josh spoke again. "Go ahead."

"What?"

"You know you pretty much live to show all of us how stupid we are. I'm saying go ahead."

For once Flannary didn't seem particularly inclined and instead pointed to Luganda, who was striding toward them with a phone in his hand.

"Shit," Josh said quietly as the African held it out to him. This was it. He was about to go from being an overeducated felon with a job that no sane person would want to being an overeducated felon who couldn't hold a job that no sane person would want.

"Hello?"

"Josh?"

His brow furrowed at the unexpected voice. "Laura? Why are you calling me? Are you okay? Is everything all right?"

"I just wanted to hear your voice. You haven't called in a long time."

She didn't sound like herself. Her normally deadpan delivery had an audible hopelessness to it that he'd never heard before.

"We talked a few days ago, Laura. What's going on?"

"Nothing."

He stood and walked out of earshot of Flannary and Luganda, stopping beneath a banana tree. "Is Mom okay?"

"Sure. I—"

"What's going on with Fawn?"

Silence.

"Laura? Are you still there?"

"She's okay. She has a new boyfriend. I think you knew him in school."

"Who? What's his name?"

"Ernie Bruce."

Josh swallowed hard and tried to stay calm. Bruce had been

the quarterback of his high school football team, and despite play-ing together for three years, Josh had always steered well clear of him. Not that Josh and his friends had exactly been angels, but Ernie Bruce was different.

"I want you to listen to me, Laura. You're too young to remem-ber this, but when Ernie and I were seniors, he was accused of rap-ing a cheerleader. It was his word against hers, and he was a hell of a good football player, so it kind of went away. But he did it."

"I wasn't too young. I remember."

Despite the deep shade provided by the tree spreading out above him, the sweat began dripping from Josh's chin.

"Is he living there?"

She didn't answer.

"Laura?"

"Yeah. Most of the time."

He gnawed on a fingernail, trying to think and barely noticing the taste of blood as he tore it. His little sister—the only worth-while thing in his life—was living a half mile from their nearest neighbor with a rapist, a thieving bitch, and a mother who split her time between dead drunk and passed out.

"Can you stay away from him?"

"Yeah. When Fawn's around, he's okay. She's really jealous, you know? But when she's not, I go to the tree house. I've taken some stuff up there. It's real nice now."

He continued to chew on the bleeding nail. It was bad enough that he'd left her there in that broken-down trailer, but now she was holing up by herself in an old shack in the woods.

"You're going to have to get Mom to call the cops. Sit her down and—"

"They're buying her vodka, Josh. And I heard Fawn talking to her about making a will."

He'd obviously been in Africa too long because all his fantasies about killing Fawn now involved a machete.

"Josh? Did you hear—"

"I heard!" he snapped back, stalking deeper into the trees to get farther from Flannary, who he knew would be straining to make out his conversation.

The only way they kept their mother from drinking herself to death was to make sure she drank only beer. Josh had known the owner of the liquor store almost since he was born and had arranged it so he would overlook Laura's age and supply her with just enough Bud Light to keep their mother from striking out on her own.

The trailer and the land it sat on were owned free and clear—his father had paid off the mortgage before he died. It was hard to say what it was worth, but it was probably nudging into the six figures. He'd always considered Fawn a complete scumbag, but he'd never thought of her as a murderer. It made perfect sense, though. She and Bruce would get his mother to make them the beneficiaries of her will and then provide her with case after case of hard liquor. When she finally drank herself to death, they'd own the property and no one would be the wiser.

"I don't want you to worry about this," Josh said finally. "I'm going to deal with it. I'm going to figure something out, okay?"

She didn't answer.

"Laura? Answer me. Okay?"

But she wasn't there anymore. The connection had gone dead.

16

The crumbling colonial building and rutted dirt road were luxuries completely lacking in the refugee camp. Flannary slowed the vehicle and proceeded tentatively into an oily puddle that came nearly to the bottoms of the doors before he gunned it out the other side. Homes were built of whatever was available—plastic sheeting, old signs, baling wire—and crammed together so tightly that it seemed to have been a conscious decision. As though the only thing keeping the makeshift buildings from collapsing was the fact that they were leaning against each other.

"Still sulking about the fire, kid?"

Josh continued to gaze out the window as they passed an aid agency building enshrouded in the smoke of the cooking fires of the people waiting to get inside. He scanned the faces but didn't recognize any as people he'd been working with. It could only be a matter of time, though.

He'd gone to the project that morning to organize a cleanup and get things moving again but had quickly come to the realization that there was nothing left to fix. Everything of use or value had been incinerated, and none of the workers had even bothered to show up.

Flannary had found him a few hours later, sitting alone in the dirt, trying futilely to get through to Laura on his sat phone. At that point, the offer of a tour of the refugee camp had been a welcome one—an excuse to delay telling Stephen Trent what had happened and a way to divert his mind from the subject of Laura and Ernie Bruce.

Now the trip was starting to look like a mistake.

"I'm not sulking," Josh said. "And you're one callous son of a bitch."

"You think? When you were crapping in your diapers, I was here. And after you and all the others run back home with your tails between your legs, I'll still be here."

"You won't have to wait long."

"What?"

"I'm quitting."

Flannary took his eyes off the muddy track, and Josh could feel him staring. "Because of the fire?"

"Because of a lot of things."

"And how do you feel about that?"

"How do I feel about turning my back on these people after completely fucking up what little hope they had? I feel great, JB. Just great."

"It wasn't your fault, Josh. That project was doomed a thousand years before you got here."

"Because they're African?"

Flannary grinned. "I've lived here too long to be prone to political correctness, Josh, but I'm not the racist kook you think I am."

"Then why?"

"It's disputed land, son."

"What do you mean."

"The people you have working for you are from two different factions of the Yvimbo tribe who have always lived here. They're not refugees from the south. That hill you're digging up has been disputed territory as long as anyone can remember."

Josh turned away from the window to look at him. "If that's true, why would NewAfrica have started a project there?"

"It's a good question," Flannary said, reaching into the back-seat and retrieving the charred cat he'd insisted Josh bring along. "Notice anything strange?"

"Are you kidding?"

"The wire on the cat's tail. You know what it's for?"

"I thought it was to make it easier to carry around."

"Nice that you haven't lost your sense of humor. Actually, they tie a gas-soaked rag to it, light the rag, and then set the cat loose in the field. Simple, cheap, effective, and not exactly a new trick, if you know what I mean."

Josh didn't respond, not wanting to believe what he was hearing but also having a hard time ignoring the loud ring of truth.

"Honestly, it's a miracle this didn't happen earlier," Flannary continued. "If anyone is responsible for that, it's Tfmena. He actually has support on both sides—something that's virtually unheard-of here. Gideon's a Xhisa. And the brother of one of Mtiti's wives to boot."

"Are you saying he had something to do with this?"

"What I'm saying is that your project was never meant to succeed. Mtiti, for all his talk, isn't going to let a bunch of Yvimbo start feeding themselves in his backyard. How would that look to his people? I'm trying to think of an analogy here, and this is the best thing I can come up with: It would be like the American president closing down a U.S. orphanage and using the money to build free housing for al-Qaeda."

"But he's been trying to reach out to the other tribes," Josh said. "Chaos isn't good for him, either."

Flannary let out a condescending snort. "What if you succeeded, Josh? Hell, what if all the aid agencies succeeded and made this country some kind of middle-class utopia? That would be the end of Mtiti. A lot of his power comes from controlling who gets aid and who doesn't, and a lot of his money comes from siphoning off that aid money into Swiss bank accounts. And it would be the end of the aid agencies because you would have worked yourselves out of a job."

"I don't believe people like Katie are that divisive."

"No, I'd agree with that. But I think it's possible that people like Katie are blinded by their own idealism and seduced by their ability to help."

The makeshift road continued to narrow, and the smell of the sewage flowing across it grew stronger. Faces they passed seemed less and less welcoming the farther they penetrated into the camp.

"Where are we going?"

"There's something I want to show you."

Flannary steered around a group of soldiers unloading food from an armored vehicle. They stopped and stared at the Land Cruiser as it eased by.

"You know, I read some of your articles. My sister printed them out for me before I left. They seem a little unrealistic."

Flannary shrugged. "I did some negative pieces back in the day, but according to my editor, it was a little more truth than his readers wanted to deal with. No one likes complicated, Josh. People want to hear that if you give Africans food, they don't starve. So now I write happy stuff, and the charities love me."

"And that allows you to stay."

"It allows me not to have to go home."

"Have you ever written something about my charity?"

"No, you guys are different. You're a small, results-oriented organization, creating sustainable projects for the long-term benefit of the African people through a culturally sensitive partnership with the government."

Josh recognized the quote from NewAfrica's most recent brochure. "Don't be patronizing."

"Never!"

"So have you written about us or not?"

Flannary stopped the vehicle and pointed through the windshield at an open-air general store with shelves full of every imaginable product. Bags of food with "Donated by the People of the United States—Not for Sale" written on the sides, tools, clothing, and, piled haphazardly in the dirt, the missing parts for the project's earthmover.

"Gideon's little side business," Flannary explained.

Josh threw open the door and jumped out of the vehicle, dodging when Flannary tried to grab the back of his shirt.

"Don't get out of the car, Josh!"

A woman appeared from around a pyramid of disposable diapers and chattered nervously at him. She made shooing motions with her hands.

"One of Gideon's wives," Flannary said, coming up beside Josh but keeping most of his attention focused on what was going on behind them. "We should go. This isn't a part of town that a couple of crackers should be walking around in, you know?"

Josh ignored him, wandering through the myriad products as the woman followed along, her voice getting louder. He stopped when he came to a table stacked with individual cans of hairspray. Nothing here made any sense. His impression at the airport had been right: He'd landed on another planet.

"Josh, we should really get out of here. We're starting to attract attention?"

Flannary's nervousness was starting to turn to fear, but all Josh could feel was anger. At Gideon, at Stephen Trent, at Fawn Mardsen. And at himself for being so stupid for so long.

He reached out for a can, but Flannary snatched it from his hand and slammed it back on the table. "The American company that makes that stuff gets a huge tax break for donating their surplus, which goes on American freight ships that get paid four times the going rate to bring it here. Okay? Are you satisfied?"

"And the Africans get hairspray."

"Don't be so cynical, Josh. The kids love it," Flannary said, grabbing his arm and dragging him back toward the Land Cruiser. Up the road, a group of raggedly dressed men were approaching, talking among themselves but keeping their eyes locked on the two white men who had penetrated their territory. "They have this game where they throw it in a fire and see which one of them runs away last. Of course sometimes they stay too long and the thing blows up in their faces. But that's the way it goes, right?"

———

Flannary was concentrating more on his driving than usual, obviously not anxious to let the sun set on them so deep into the refugee camp. When they turned onto what passed for a main road, he seemed to relax a bit.

"Think, Josh. Why is it that your dinky little charity can accomplish more at the snap of a finger than huge organizations like CARE and UNICEF can in a month of red tape?"

"How the hell should I know?" Josh said, still fuming about Gideon's store. If he had the tractor parts, what else did he have? How many of those mysterious payments in their books had gone straight into his pocket while the people on the project dug in the dirt with sticks?

"Have you ever seen any of NewAfrica's other projects?"

"No."

"Do you know anything about them?"

"Why ask me? It's a matter of public record, right? The U.S. government puts money into them, so they must have to file some kind of report."

"Charities have two sets of documents: the ones they send home and the ones that never leave Africa. Care to guess which ones actually reflect reality?"

Josh watched a young boy with a missing leg lurching out of their way. He wondered if he'd lost the limb throwing hairspray into fires.

"Why doesn't NewAfrica operate in any other countries, Josh?"

"What are—"

Machine-gun fire sounded, and they both ducked involuntarily. Flannary's foot went a little deeper into the accelerator as he peered through the steering wheel at the darkening street. "Rebels," he said. "They're coming farther north every day. I've seen it before in other countries. The government's losing control."

17

The cornfield was still smoldering, making it impossible for Josh to enter. Not that there was any reason to. Nothing had changed. And nothing would.

"It's all gone," Josh said into the satellite phone. "Everything."

"I don't understand what you're telling me," Stephen Trent responded. He didn't seem as controlled as usual, and the fact that his buttery-smooth exterior had cracked so easily made Josh wonder if it was fake.

"Then you're not listening. The corn's all burned. The shed and the tools, too. And the irrigation system is a twisted pile of junk. Oh, and the tractor with all the missing parts? No need to worry about that anymore."

"Jesus Christ, Josh. We're flying in photographers from the States right now. And do you have any idea how hard it was to convince President Mtiti to come there?"

"I can't say that I do, Stephen."

"Does Gideon know about this?"

Gideon. That was a whole subject in and of itself. He considered telling Trent about Gideon's store but decided against it. After his conversation with an unusually circumspect JB Flannary the night before, he was even less comfortable with who everybody was and where they stood.

"He said it was an accident, Stephen. But I wouldn't trust that guy as far as I could throw him."

"You wouldn't trust him? You've barely been in Africa long enough to unpack, and you're already making pronouncements about the trustworthiness of people we've worked with for years? I don't seem to remember anything like this happening before you got there. When Gideon was running things."

"Then maybe you should put *him* in charge."

"Fuck!" Trent shouted into the phone and then fell silent.

Josh had no idea what to say that wouldn't just be throwing gas on the fire, so he turned and took in the scene behind him. Many of the workers had shown up that morning, but with no tools there was nothing to do. They had formed small groups, and most seemed to be arguing, occasionally pausing to glare at another group but maintaining their distance. It seemed so obvious now. The pure, harmonious tribal ideal he'd seen when he'd gotten there had been a fantasy. He'd seen exactly what he wanted to. Or maybe what he was supposed to.

Josh walked toward a group of nine men squeezed into the shade of a small tree, talking heatedly. They watched him as he approached but clearly saw him as completely irrelevant now. If anything, their conversation grew in intensity, as did the urgency with which they passed around a jug of homemade liquor.

"When you say it's all gone," Trent said finally, "are you certain *all* of it's gone? There isn't an angle we could shoot from that would disguise the damage?"

Josh wasn't really paying attention, instead concentrating on the unintelligible words of the men in front of him. What he wouldn't give to know what they were saying.

He dug out his MP3 player and flipped on the record function.

"Josh?"

"I already told you," Josh said, putting the player in his back pocket and turning away from the group of men. "It's all gone. If you want a good angle, you might want to think about flying Mtiti to Florida."

"You're making jokes now?" Trent said, the volume of his voice rising. "I'm glad you're so damn broken up about this."

"Jesus Christ, Stephen. Do I want to help these people? Hell, yes. But I have no idea what I'm doing. And what's worse is that I have no idea what *other* people are doing. I mean, I expected to have to deal with some corruption and inefficiency, but . . ." He let his voice trail off for a moment. "The bottom line is that you hired the wrong guy."

When Trent spoke again, he had managed to reconstruct some of the calm that Josh was so familiar with. "Look, I'm not going to lie to you, Josh. This is a disaster. But I'm not trying to dump a bunch of blame on you. You're right. This is an incredibly hard job, and sometimes things happen that are beyond anyone's control."

"I appreciate the vote of confidence, Stephen, but it's misplaced. As much as I wanted it to, this isn't going to work out."

"I don't understand. You're quitting?"

"The truth is, I've got some family problems that can't be dealt with from here."

There was a long pause.

"I'm sorry to hear that. Is it anything we can help you with?"

"No."

"We need to talk face to face, Josh. We put a lot of effort into finding you, and I'm still convinced we made the right choice."

"I'm not sure what you base that on, Stephen."

"Look, there aren't many planes going in and out of the country anymore. I'm going to reserve the soonest available seat for you. But I won't put the money down until we get together and talk. Fair?"

Josh had no interest in meeting or talking with anyone. He just wanted to go home, rescue his sister, and get on with his life. Whatever that life might be.

Tfmena Llengambi had taken a position at the base of the hill, and he motioned to the groups milling around to come to him. Some did, but the men behind Josh just talked louder, their speech slurred from the liquor and their laughter turning malevolent.

"I don't want to waste your time, Stephen. I need to—"

A hand suddenly gripped his shoulder and spun him around. Out of reflex, he dropped the phone and threw a hand out, landing a fist firmly in Gideon's chest. The African staggered backward a step, though it was more from surprise than the force of the blow. A moment later, Josh found himself pinned to a tree with Gideon's thick forearm jammed against his throat.

Everyone had gone silent, but no one seemed inclined to interfere. The men he had been recording gathered around expectantly, and in the distance, Tfmena just watched.

"I hear you've been traveling to places you shouldn't," Gideon said, bringing his face close enough that Josh could smell the stolen food on his breath. Of course he'd expected Gideon's wife to mention the two white men poking around her merchandise, but he hadn't been prepared for a reaction this violent.

The pressure on his neck increased to the point that it was hard to breathe, but if Gideon was trying to scare him, his actions were having the opposite effect. Just who the fuck did this guy think he was?

He rammed his palms into Gideon's chest and shoved as hard as he could. The tree provided enough leverage that, despite his superior size, Gideon was driven backward hard enough to almost land him on his ass. A muffled gasp went up from the ever-expanding peanut gallery.

"Yeah, why didn't you tell me you were in the tractor-parts business? I was in the market, you know?"

Gideon took a menacing step forward but recognized his delicate position when Josh balled his fists. While Gideon would almost certainly win a fight between them, it might not be easy.

There was a lot of face to be lost in a narrow victory over a pampered white boy from America.

"This is not your country," Gideon said, holding his ground. "You come here and you judge us and you tell us how we should live. But my people have been here for thousands of years. We don't need you. And if you stay too long, things can happen. Like they did to your friend Dan."

18

When Josh got out of the Land Cruiser, the women Annika Gritdal was talking to began to giggle and whisper to each other. One gave Annika a nudge in his direction.

"It's still working," she said as she approached.

He'd spent the long drive preparing himself to see her again. This time, instead of acting like a smitten fifteen-year-old, he was going to be a suave, James Bond–like figure.

"What?" he said.

Not bad. He'd managed to maintain just the right amount of disinterest despite the subtle flow of her T-shirt and the tan legs extending from grimy work shorts.

"The pump you fixed! It's working great."

"I guess you're going to have to take back all the horrible things you've said about me."

"We'll see."

She squinted through the windshield of his vehicle, probably looking for Flannary. "So why do I have the pleasure of your visit, Josh?"

It was a good question. He should have been hiding out in the compound's pool, drinking heavily and figuring out what he was going to do with his life.

"I needed to talk to you. And to ask a little favor."

"It seems that I owe you. What do you want to talk about?"

"Is it true that the ownership of the land my project is on is disputed by the people working there?"

"Did JB tell you that?"

"Does it matter?"

She thought for a moment before speaking. "It's true."

"So the project was never going to work?"

She started toward the church, waving for him to follow. "Let's go sit down."

They didn't actually enter the building but instead went around back, passing through a rickety gate into an oasis carved from trees hung with fruit he couldn't identify. Large, carefully placed rocks gave it a Japanese feel, though the metal table in the middle was more Italian. She gestured for him to wait and disappeared through the back door of the church. He sat gingerly in one of the chairs, noticing that, despite the meticulous paint job, it was about ready to collapse.

"It doesn't make it easier, though," Annika said when she reemerged.

"Doesn't make what easier?"

"Watching something that was so hard to build, so important, be destroyed. It's always in the back of your mind here—that something it took hundreds of people years to build can be destroyed by a few people in minutes. And often for no reason at all."

"Do you think that's going to happen to you?" he said.

She didn't answer, instead ceremoniously unwrapping a small piece of chocolate, breaking it in half, and holding one of the pieces out to him. "Here. This will make you feel better."

The way she was handling it made it obvious how rare and precious it was to her. "No, I can't accept that."

"Of course you can. It's just a little piece. I'm afraid that's all you get for your project burning."

He accepted the candy reluctantly, popping it into his mouth and licking the residue off his sweating palm. "What would have to happen for me to get a big piece?"

"Oh, you should hope you never deserve a big piece. Sometimes you don't survive big-piece days."

She chewed slowly, savoring the chocolate for the treasure it was.

"So you never answered my question," Josh said.

"Do I think the same thing could happen to me?" She frowned subtly. "It's becoming more dangerous for us. Our crops have done well, and we've been able to sell some on the open market. That's drawing the attention of the government."

"Why would the government have a problem with you selling your crops? Isn't that what you're supposed to do with them?"

She swallowed and ran a tongue across her teeth, making sure she didn't miss anything. "In one way or another, the government—and by that I mean Mtiti—controls all the food the aid agencies bring into the country. In fact, the main job of his agriculture minister is to get his hands on it and sell it or give it to Mtiti's supporters. Successful local agriculture throws a, uh, hammer into their machine."

"Wrench."

She screwed up her face in an expression that was impossibly endearing. "Yes, of course. A wrench. You can imagine how this could lower the prices they can get from their stolen food and how it could feed people they want to stay hungry."

He shook his head miserably.

"What?"

"Why do you do it, Annika? How do you keep going?"

"I believe that things can be better. I believe that God wants us to help people who haven't been as lucky."

"I guess. But it seems like Jesus had the good sense to split two thousand years ago."

"You sound just like JB. Africa is a very hard place. Everything can disappear in a moment. Violence is always just under the surface. And no matter how long you're here, you'll always be an outsider. But still you came. You're trying to help. So you must understand."

"Not for much longer."

"What do you mean?"

"I quit yesterday. I'm just waiting for a flight out."

There was a flash of something in her expression that looked like sadness, but he decided that he was just projecting.

"I'm sorry about that, Josh. I think you could have helped a lot of people here."

"That's what I thought, too. But now I know I was just fooling myself."

She nodded sympathetically. "You mentioned a favor before. What is it?"

He reached into his pocket and pulled out his MP3 player. "I recorded some people talking yesterday. I was wondering if you could tell me what they're saying."

She accepted the player and turned it over in her hands, staring down at it. "If you're leaving, why all the questions? Why this?"

"I have some problems with my family at home," he said. "It's not something I can deal with from here. But before I leave, maybe there are some things I can set straight. I'd like to leave something more positive than a bunch of burned corn and melted irrigation equipment."

19

Josh glanced over his shoulder as the sun made its way to the horizon. The confused faces staring at him from the edges of the dirt track were receding more and more into shadow, giving his surroundings an increasingly menacing feel. Ahead, the refugee camp's roads narrowed further, forcing him to stop.

A boy of about twelve watched fascinated from the doorway of a house constructed primarily of mud, and Josh motioned him over. "Tfmena? Do you know him? I'm looking for Tfmena Llengambi."

The boy just shook his head, so Josh pointed to his Land Cruiser and pressed a five-dollar bill into the kid's hand. "Can you watch that for me?"

The boy nodded excitedly and climbed up onto the hood, making a show of scanning for ne'er-do-wells. Josh started up the road on foot, certain he'd never see the vehicle again.

The narrow street turned to a path, and now the ramshackle houses and tiny stores all selling the same things were only a few feet to either side of him. People and cows pushed past, always staring but not otherwise acknowledging his presence. When a plump older woman in traditional dress smiled at him, he seized the opportunity.

"Tfmena?"

She stopped and tilted her head slightly. "Tfmena Llengambi?"

"Yes! That's right. Tfmena Llengambi."

At best he had hoped that she would point him in the right direction, but instead she motioned for him to follow and led him deeper into the chaotic maze of the refugee camp. After five minutes of walking silently behind her, the initial relief he'd felt started to wane. His sense of direction had completely abandoned him, and it was now fully night. This woman could have been taking him anywhere.

He was about to turn around and take his chances finding his way out when she suddenly stopped and pointed to a small dwelling with a door fashioned from a faded Pepsi sign. She gave a short bow before waddling back the way they had come.

"Thank you!" Josh called after her, but she didn't acknowledge it. He knocked hesitantly on the door and waited. An eye appeared in a crack about waist high, and Josh crouched. "Hey, there. Is Tfmena here?"

The eye widened in fear and disappeared. He heard the panicked shouts of a young girl followed by the soft padding of feet on dirt.

The woman who answered had a similar style of dress as the one who had led him there, but she was quite a bit younger and rail thin.

"Tfmena Llengambi?"

She leaned through the door to see who was watching and then pulled him inside.

The interior was probably ten degrees hotter than it was outside, lit by a single kerosene lamp and smelling of damp earth. He was starting to wonder where the hell he was when Tfmena entered through a door at the back.

"Why are you here?"

His expression conveyed the same calm dignity it always did but couldn't hide his surprise at finding Josh on his doorstep.

"You and your family have to get out of here. Right now."

"What? I don't understand what you're saying to me."

"I want you to listen to this," Josh said, handing his MP3 player to Tfmena and helping him with the earphones.

Annika had struggled to translate the voices on the poor recording, but after four listenings she'd gotten the general gist: Now that the project was destroyed, there was no reason Tfmena and his family couldn't be murdered and the payment for performing that assassination couldn't be collected.

Judging by Tfmena's expression, her translation was dead-on. The African finally pushed the stop button and handed the recorder back to Josh before taking a seat on a low bench that was the only furniture in the room.

"You must think we are a very strange people."

It was peculiar how out of place the man seemed there, on the dirt floor with old magazine clippings serving as artwork on the walls. It was hard not to wonder what someone like him could have become if he'd been born under different circumstances.

"I don't suppose it matters what I think."

"When you came to us, I would have agreed. But now I think you may be a man with . . ." Tfmena's voice trailed off while he tried to retrieve the correct word. "Weight."

"I appreciate that. Coming from you, it really means something. But shouldn't you be getting—"

Tfmena waved a hand dismissively. Whether he knew something Josh didn't or it was just that irritating African fatalism was impossible to discern.

"We've lived this way for a long time. And for a long time it was good. The tribes, the big families. These protected us against Africa. Because this is a place that always wants to kill you. It does this with droughts, with floods, and with sickness. But the whites came, and the world changed. Now the things that once protected us kill us."

"The world changes faster and faster," Josh said. "Sometimes it's hard to keep up."

"This thing is much more difficult than you can understand, Josh. There are many people who want many different things."

"Like who?"

Tfmena smiled. "I wonder if this is something you want to be a part of. No one will win. Not in my lifetime. Not even in yours."

Josh glanced back at the dark cracks around the door, trying to discern movement—evidence that the men he'd recorded were outside sharpening their machetes. There was nothing, though. He pulled what little money he had from his pocket and held it out to the man. "I want you to have this. To help you get your family away."

Tfmena shook his head. "I saved you. And now you've saved me. You owe me nothing."

Josh set the cash on the shelf holding the lamp. "Then pay me back someday."

20

The main road was blocked by an armored vehicle, forcing Josh to turn onto a side street and once again recalculate his path.

He barely recognized the capital city he'd driven through when he'd first arrived. Illumination was provided by fires built in rusting oil drums, occasional bare bulbs hanging from wires, and a few brightly lit and heavily barricaded storefronts. The women and children darting about were gone, too, replaced by young men talking and drinking on street corners. When he passed, they always fell silent.

Unwilling to stop at a crossroad, he gunned the vehicle through it and aimed at a dull glow hanging over the east side of town. The powerful security lights made the capital's high-rent district look a little like Oz. Now if he could just find the yellow-brick road.

After fifteen more stifling minutes in the closed-up Land Cruiser, the dirt road turned to pavement, and idle men were replaced by neatly kept trees. Razor wire gleamed atop fences that allowed only brief glimpses of the colonial mansions behind them.

Josh pulled up to a small guardhouse and rolled down the window, happy to feel the damp breeze again.

"I'm here to see Stephen Trent," he said, squinting as a uniformed man approached him and shined a flashlight in his face.

"There are no visitors tonight. Come back tomorrow."

"Could you tell him Josh Hagarty is here? It's important."

The man scowled before walking back into the guardhouse. A few moments later, the gate began to swing open.

Josh eased the vehicle across the cobbled courtyard and parked in front of a house that was impressive by any standard—probably five thousand square feet of white stucco, Roman-style columns, and cathedral-like windows.

"Josh, what the hell are you doing here?" Stephen Trent said, coming out onto the wraparound porch wearing wrinkled slacks and an untucked linen shirt that suggested Josh had gotten him out of bed.

"I needed to talk to you."

"I know I said we'd get together, but I didn't mean tonight. Did you drive here alone?"

"Yeah."

"Jesus Christ," Trent said, ushering him inside. "Next time you want to come here in the middle of the night, at least call me so I can send some people to escort you in. It's insane to drive around the city after dark."

The interior was even more impressive than the facade. True to the period in which the house had been built, it was filled with exotic woods and well-polished European antiques. A far cry from Annika's tiny church or Tfmena's ramshackle hut.

Trent led him into an office much more expansive than the one he kept in New York and took a seat behind his desk. Josh remained standing, glancing at a wall lined with filing cabinets. Most were normal, but the one on the far right was forged of thick metal with locks that looked like they could stop a tank. It was hard not to wonder if those were the files Flannary had talked about—the ones that never made it back to the States.

"Look, Josh, I know I said we'd talk about us helping you with your family problems and getting you home, but you haven't exactly given me much time. With the fire and Mtiti's photo shoot, my plate's a little full."

Josh pulled his MP3 player from his pocket and set it down on the desk.

"What's that?"

"I recorded some men at the project talking."

Trent's expression was almost too placid, showing no anticipation at all. "So?"

"They say they're being paid to kill Tfmena Llengambi and his family."

"Who's Tfmena Llengambi?"

"The most respected tribal leader out there. He's probably the main reason the project got as far as it did."

Trent put one of the earphones in and played a few seconds of the recording. "Who translated this?"

Josh opened his mouth to tell him but for some reason checked himself. "It was a guy who was just passing through. He told me his name, but you know how it is. I couldn't pronounce it, let alone remember it."

"Where was he going? I'd like to find him. We're always looking for people with language skills."

Josh just shrugged.

"Did you tell Tfmena about this?"

"Hell, yes. With a little luck, he's long gone already."

Another nod, but that was it.

"This project has a hell of a lot more problems than you told me about, Stephen. Did you know that the ownership of that land is disputed? Or that Gideon has a store in the refugee camp where he sells stuff he's stolen from us?"

Trent held up a hand. "Okay, Josh, let's talk reality for a

minute. Did I know this was disputed land? Yes. There isn't a goddamn piece of dirt an inch wide in this country that isn't disputed. This tribe hates that tribe, this faction hates that faction, this village hates that village. If that wasn't the case, we wouldn't need to be here. And I'll be honest. Dan never had any trouble with this. He had them all getting along fine."

"This would be the Dan who's lying in pieces out in the jungle?"

Trent ignored the comment. "And as far as Gideon goes, he's got three wives and fourteen kids to support. He's going to wet his beak just like everyone in this part of the world. I don't think you should ignore the fact that he's well-educated and speaks almost perfect English—"

"But he's kind of self-serving in the way he uses that English. I don't believe he's translating what people say accurately. And as far as him wetting his beak, I understand that kind of thing happens, and I wouldn't care if we were talking about a shovel here and a bag of food there. But disassembling our tractor and selling off the parts is a little over the top. I don't have to tell you how far the loss of a piece of equipment like that has set the project back."

"I don't need a lecture from you, Josh. Let me put it in starker terms: Gideon is President Mtiti's brother-in-law."

Josh crossed his arms in front of his chest, still unwilling to sit in one of the empty chairs in front of the desk. "Kind of makes you wonder how committed to this project Mtiti is, doesn't it? In fact, it makes you wonder if Gideon is involved with the men who want to kill Tfmena. He told me the fire was an accident when he knew it wasn't."

Trent sighed quietly. "He's just telling you what he thinks you want to hear, Josh. The Africans have a certain stoicism that, to us, comes out as lying. It's not intended that way. And as far as Mtiti goes, I can personally guarantee you that he's committed to this project. If for no other reason, he needs it to maintain his image abroad."

"Does it ever seem to you that everyone here is working against everything—even their own self-interest? I understand it's complicated, and I haven't been here very long, but it's hard not to wonder if there's really anything we can do. If there's anything we can build that will last."

"Things are different here, Josh. Think about how African Americans were treated before the civil rights movement. Why? What had they done other than work themselves to death in cotton fields so that the whites could get rich? Well, here some of the grievances are a hell of a lot more serious than that. And a hell of a lot older."

"I'm not saying—"

"And what about the nepotism? In the U.S. people admire you for putting your ideals above family and friends. Why? Because we can afford to. For someone like Gideon, getting one of the few decent jobs available can be the difference between his family having nothing or having enough to eat and access to medical care. As far as the Africans are concerned, you'd have to be one crazy ingrate to screw over someone from your village or a relative because someone you've never met had better grades in school, or a better work history, or whatever. You owe a very real debt to your family and your tribe, and you spend your life repaying it."

"I never thought about it that way," Josh confessed. "But you have to admit, it's not working out so well for them."

"In the end, it's a losing strategy," Trent agreed. "But you're not going to come in here and change things overnight. You're a smart kid, and frankly, we both know you're no Boy Scout. That's why we hired you. Is the system a disaster? Yes. The question is, can you work with it?"

Josh didn't answer immediately, and Trent just sat there and watched him.

"If this project is going to have a chance, Stephen, you're going to have to make some hard decisions."

"Such as?"

"Get rid of Gideon. If what you say is true and Mtiti needs this project, then he isn't going to care about you canning some distant relative who's making trouble."

"Okay. What else?"

"We need to figure out a way to bring back Tfmena and protect him. He's got the respect of a lot of people, even some on the other side."

"So if I can get all that done, you'll stay?"

"No. That's the last thing. Get someone in here who actually has practical knowledge about agriculture. No Ivy League degrees, no twenty-five-year-olds. Find yourself some retired farmer who never graduated from high school but who actually knows how to get shit done."

Trent rose and walked over to a small refrigerator, retrieving two beers and holding one out to Josh. "I don't want to pry, but if you tell me what your family problems are, we might be able to help."

"Thanks, but I don't think you can."

"Don't underestimate me. You might be surprised."

Josh took a sip of the beer and then held the cold bottle to his forehead. The anger he'd felt on the drive there had faded a bit. As much as he hated to admit it, some of Trent's explanations rang at least partially true. To a point, you had to go along to get along. And now he sounded sincere in his offer of help.

"It's my sister. The environment she's living in has gotten bad enough that I think she could actually get hurt."

"You sound like you two are close."

"Very."

"What about your mother?"

"We don't have much of a relationship."

"But your sister . . . Laura, isn't it? She'll be going off to college soon."

"I'm starting to worry about that. I think she might not leave. Because of my mother's situation."

"Which is?"

"Drunk. And at the mercy of a relative who is looking to take advantage of her."

Trent nodded slowly. "I see. Look, I don't want to make you uncomfortable, but we *are* an aid agency. We have contacts in social work, not to mention lawyers who see these kinds of situations every day."

"I appreciate the offer, but—"

"Your ideas are good, Josh. There are going to have to be some compromises in implementing them, but it's this kind of smart, decisive action we're looking for. We don't want to lose you."

"My mind's pretty much made up, Stephen."

"But if I could help you deal with your family problems? Then you'd stay, right?"

The truth was, as frustrating as this job was, it also had its positives. And not only the compensation package and the fact that he had no other prospects. If Trent gave in to his demands, he might actually have a shot. He might actually be able to do something worthwhile.

"I don't know, Stephen. Maybe."

"Okay, then. I'm still trying to get you on a flight out of here, but in the meantime, I'll make some calls and see what we can do for your sister. I'll be down for Mtiti's photo op in a few days, and we'll talk again then."

Josh's beer stopped halfway to his mouth. "You're still coming?"

"Of course."

"Stephen, there's nothing left. I'm serious. Nothing."

"I don't have much of a choice, Josh. I promised the president, and we designed all our fund-drive materials for the season around this. I'll just have to figure something out."

21

Stephen Trent watched Gideon's jaw clench tighter and tighter, the muscles quivering as he listened to the recording on Josh Hagarty's MP3 player. His nose flared one last time, and he yanked the earphones out.

"Who translated this for him?"

"I don't know."

"Did you ask him?"

"Of course I asked him! He didn't know the man's name."

"He's lying," Gideon said.

"Then who? I thought you had people watching him twenty-four hours a day? Why don't you know?"

"I can make him tell us."

"I think you've already done plenty. You let the project burn before the president's visit, and you let Tfmena Llengambi get away."

"My people had nothing to do with burning the project," Gideon said indignantly. "It was some Yvimbo dog. They—"

"You want me to trust your people?" Trent shouted. "The same people who were standing out in the open talking about getting paid to kill Tfmena?"

"They had no way of knowing that they were being recorded. They—"

"Shut up!" Trent said. "Just shut up and let me think!"

Josh Hagarty had been exactly right: It was Tfmena Llengambi's unique ability to bridge the divisions in his tribe that had kept the project from descending into chaos long ago. But that status worked both ways. With him gone, there would no longer be anything keeping the two groups from each other's throats.

It had been a simple, virtually foolproof plan. Following Mtiti's visit, Tfmena would be brutally murdered, tribal violence would flare, and Gideon's people would make certain that what little had been accomplished on the project was completely destroyed.

Mtiti would have photos to demonstrate to the international community his fabricated commitment to crossing tribal boundaries, the project would be wiped out to demonstrate to his Xhisa supporters that he was dealing with the Yvimbo, and NewAfrica would have a heart-wrenching disaster to further loosen the purse strings of its donors.

But now that perfect plan had gone to shit. Like everything else on this godforsaken continent.

"Where is Hagarty?" Gideon said, ignoring Trent's outburst.

"Asleep in the guesthouse."

"When he leaves in the morning, I'll have my people follow him. He'll tell us what we want to know, and no one will ever see him again."

"You're not going to touch him, Gideon. Do you have any idea how many questions we had to answer after Dan's death?"

Gideon let out a disgusted, noncommittal breath.

"I mean it, Gideon. I'm going to talk to Aleksei, and I'll tell you what we decide. In the meantime, you're going to get rid of your store in the refugee camp."

"What?"

"You heard me."

"I will not! I have a right—"

"You have a right?" Trent yelled, jumping out of his chair and hammering a hand onto his desk. "I'm going to see the president in a few days, maybe I should tell him about your rights. Maybe I should tell him that you're willing to put him in danger so you can keep your fucking little store open."

Gideon looked as though he wanted to reach across the desk and snap Trent's neck, but at the mention of Mtiti his indignation began to falter.

"I didn't mean to say—"

"I don't give a shit what you meant to say. Do you think being related to Mtiti is going to help you? He'll send his people down here, and they'll kill you and your whole family. He's done it before to people he was a hell of a lot closer to than you."

The African didn't respond, and Trent reached for the MP3 player, slamming it repeatedly down on his desk until the pieces were scattered across its wood top.

"Now, listen to me very carefully, Gideon. You're going to find the person who translated this, you're going to find out if they've talked to anyone about it, and then you're going to kill them. Do you think you can handle that?"

———

Stephen Trent made himself a drink and held it to his lips with a shaking hand. How the hell had he ended up like this? A few years ago he'd been a reasonably successful con man, swindling people out of their life savings without harming so much as a hair on their heads. Now he was threatening to have the entire family of one of his employees butchered.

When Aleksei Fedorov had found him, Trent had been facing multiple counts of stock fraud and racketeering. Fedorov had provided enough money, lawyers, and God knew what else to get all the charges dropped. And in return, Trent had taken over Fedorov's latest criminal venture—NewAfrica.

At the time it had seemed like an incredible stroke of luck—a clean record and a mid-six-figure salary in place of prison. But every day he became less certain.

Wasn't that how deals with the devil always went? He'd bargained for his freedom and in the process had permanently lost it.

Trent picked up the phone and dialed, swilling the rest of his drink as he listened to it ring.

"Yes."

"Hello, Aleksei."

"What the fuck took so long? Mtiti's been calling every hour, and I can't keep ducking him."

"I'm sorry for the delay. I wanted to make sure I had all the facts."

"And what are they?"

"I'm taking care of the situation with Mtiti's photo op, but Josh Hagarty isn't as easy. I don't think he's going to work out."

"What do you mean he isn't going to work out? This was your plan—you found him, you trained him, and you told me he was perfect for this job."

Of course that was a wild distortion of the truth, but arguing with Aleksei Fedorov was always dangerous and most often pointless.

"He has suspicions—"

"Suspicions? What in the hell are you doing over there, Stephen? He just landed on a continent he's never been to before, he doesn't speak the language, and we have him isolated in a compound in the middle of nowhere. Are you advertising what we're doing on television there?"

"He has some family problems to deal with and wants to go home, Aleksei. No harm done—"

"No harm done? How much does he know?"

"Not enough that it's going to cause us a problem. We'll give him a good severance, and he'll never think about us or this country again."

"What guarantee do I have of that? How do I know he's not

going to come home and start talking to people? How do I know he isn't going to start a goddamn blog called 'My Time with NewAfrica'?"

"I'll talk to him. I'll—"

"Get rid of him."

"Aleksei, it's too soon after Dan. Our donors are going to start getting uncomfortable, and it's going to make it impossible for us to replace him."

"Replace him? With who? You searched the whole country, and he's the only thing you came up with."

"There was the candidate from Cali—"

"No. You told me Hagarty was the best man for the job. He's either going to stay on, or he's going to disappear."

Trent looked longingly at his empty glass and fell into the chair behind his desk. The idea had been that Josh was someone who could be slowly brought along and eventually told the truth about NewAfrica. That he, unlike a typical aid agency do-gooder, could be made to understand the situation for what it was and appreciate the financial opportunities it could provide. After their last meeting, though, Trent was beginning to realize that he'd misjudged his new employee—that Josh Hagarty would never be able to accept what they were doing here.

"I'm not sure either one of those options is the best course, Aleksei."

"What about his sister?"

Trent rested his head in his hand. It always came down to the children. The ones least able to defend themselves.

"Her name is Laura," Trent said quietly. "She's seventeen years old, living in a rural part of Kentucky with their mother."

"And they're close?"

"Yes."

"Then maybe we need to show him just how easy it is for us to get to her."

22

H ey!" Josh Hagarty shouted, running toward a soldier who had just sent a young boy sprawling to the ground.

Josh managed to grab the kid and pull him away before the soldier could deliver the kick he was clearly lining up for. A moment later he found himself staring down the barrel of a machine gun. Terrifying, but not exactly unexpected.

The malaise that had engulfed his project after the fire was gone. No fewer than forty of Mtiti's soldiers had come roaring up the road that morning in a convoy of flatbed trucks loaded with mature cornstalks.

Josh raised his hands and began to slowly back away as the soldier barked unintelligibly at him. On the hill, maybe three hundred yards away, he could see Gideon watching. Apparently, instead of firing him, Trent had put him in charge of whatever the hell it was that was happening.

Josh had to admit, though, that he'd never seen his workers move with the kind of urgency he was seeing now. There was obviously something extremely motivating about being chased around by fatigue-clad thugs wielding assault rifles and machetes. Despite a complete lack of organization, the burned tractor was already gone—dragged out with a team of cows and some rope. The remains of the storage building were in the process of being dismantled by a group of children, and the black ash was being swept away by an army of women armed with brooms improvised from handfuls of straw.

Most impressive, though, was the fact that almost half the field was already replanted, and the corn necessary to finish the job was on its way—passed hand to hand by a line of straining workers.

The soldier motioned with his gun for him to get out of there, but Josh remained frozen, uncertain what to do.

This was slavery, plain and simple. The men, women, and children he had been working with were being driven past the point of exhaustion by terror and violence. But what could he do? Tfmena was gone, he didn't speak the language, and he was seen as just another ineffectual white alien in this world. One last glance at a smug Gideon and Josh retreated back through the chaos.

———

"Busy little beaver today, aren't you?"

JB Flannary had set up two lawn chairs on a small rise that afforded a sweeping view of the mayhem below. He patted the empty seat next to him, and Josh dropped into it, too worn out and frustrated to do anything else.

"I'm done."

"Done with what?" Flannary said, fishing a beer from the cooler next to him and holding it out.

"Everything. You, this continent, Stephen Trent. By this time next week, I'm gonna be sitting in front of my mom's trailer wondering what the hell just happened."

"And that's a good thing?"

Josh accepted the beer and stared down at it. Of course it wasn't a good thing. All the problems he'd run from were still waiting for him. But at least in Kentucky there was someone he could actually help. Here he was useless. Or worse.

They sat in silence for a while, drinking and watching the field being planted. When all the corn was in, the trucks pulled back and the women went to work erasing their tracks from the dirt.

"Looks even better without the shed and the tractor," Flannary observed. "More authentic."

His voice carried more than a hint of sarcasm, but there was no denying that he was right. Tightly framed and from just the right angle, the newly planted field looked almost idyllic. Sun-dappled corn swayed in the breeze, endless green hills retreated into the horizon. If it hadn't been for the soldiers frisking various men and women before dragging them into an inexplicable line, it would have seemed almost peaceful.

A small dot appeared on the horizon, and a few moments later the drone of a helicopter became audible. The workers who hadn't passed muster were chased into the trees by screaming men with guns.

The afternoon rains hadn't come that day, and the dust turned into a choking cloud as the helicopter landed on the far edge of the project. When the air cleared, the door slid open and a few well-armed men jumped out, surveying the area before motioning behind them.

The workers began to cheer as Umboto Mtiti emerged, but it was less a sign of political solidarity than a reaction to the not-so-gentle urging of the men guarding them.

"His Excellency, the president," one of Mtiti's entourage called out in an impressive baritone. "Ruler of the country, commander of the armed forces, and savior of his people."

"Don't forget 'world-class scumbag,'" Flannary added, raising his beer in a drunken salute.

Josh had seen a few poor-quality photos of Mtiti, but beyond the roundness of his face and the uniform heavy with medals he'd awarded himself, they hadn't captured the man. First, they always

depicted him smiling—an emotion that seemed completely foreign to the face that Josh saw now. And second, they couldn't
replicate the sheer size of the man. He had to be at least six-four,
with the formless bulk of a retired power lifter.

Mtiti didn't acknowledge his fans, instead marching directly
toward the cornfield as a group of photographers hurried to keep
up. One skittered over to the recently formed line of workers,
finding an angle from which he could capture their cheers without
including the soldiers extracting them.

"Vultures," Flannary said.

"Who?"

"Photographers. I hate those sons of bitches. The root of all
evil, if you ask me."

"I thought money was the root of all evil."

"A distant second, son. Ever wonder how they get all those pictures of starving kids in a country like this—one that's drowning
in donated food?"

"I never really thought about it."

Flannary frowned deeply as he followed Mtiti's progress. "I
was at a hospital down south a few years back. A bunch of photographers from some NGO or another found a kid with dysentery,
took him out of his bed and laid him on a patch of floor where the
tiles were broken, and started taking pictures. But the kid was on
the mend, and he didn't look sick enough, so they asked the doctor
if he'd take out the kid's IV for a while."

"Bullshit."

"I swear on my mother's grave."

"Did the doctor do it?"

"I don't know. I went outside, slashed their tires, and got
drunk. Been that way ever since."

Josh wanted to believe that the story was an exaggeration, or
maybe even the fabrication of a booze-soaked brain, but like most
of what the reporter said, it had the depressing ring of truth.

Josh drained the rest of his beer as Stephen Trent appeared in the door of the helicopter wearing a pair of khaki cargo pants and a NewAfrica T-shirt. He looked a bit reluctant to get out but managed to overcome his hesitation and jog to Mtiti's side. He nodded respectfully as the president talked, but there was no indication that they were actually discussing the project. Neither man showed any interest at all.

"Aren't you gonna go down and press the flesh a little?" Flannary asked. "Mtiti is one of the greatest men in history. If you don't believe me, just ask him."

The truth was that Josh just wanted to sit there, get drunk, and wait for it to be morning in the United States so he could check up on Laura. Even with everything that had happened, though, it seemed a little disrespectful to sit there under an umbrella watching his boss and the president of the country like they were a sideshow in some grotesque circus. His chances for getting a letter of recommendation were looking pretty slim as it was.

Josh pushed himself out of his chair and walked down the hill, joining the carefully selected group of workers being marched toward the president. They seemed nervous, unsure what was going to happen to them, and some looked at him for reassurance. He considered giving them a composed smile, but it seemed too dishonest.

A shout and wave from Stephen Trent got Josh ushered through the makeshift barricades. He concentrated on looking nonthreatening as he approached, aware of the armed men watching him.

"Mr. President," Trent said, "I'd like to introduce you to Josh Hagarty. He's our man on the ground here."

Mtiti appraised him emotionlessly and ignored Josh's outstretched hand. Not that he could blame the man. It wasn't like the work that had been done here demanded a hell of a lot of respect.

"Who's that you're sitting with over there?" Trent said as Mtiti turned his back on them and started toward the photographers setting up equipment.

"Nobody. He's a reporter who lives in the compound."

"JB Flannary," Trent said. "Are you two friends?"

Josh shrugged. "There aren't that many people to hang around with, you know?"

"I understand, but I wonder if you could have chosen more wisely than a burned-out reporter who sits around all day and criticizes everyone who tries to do something positive with their lives. He's done real hatchet jobs on charities in the past."

The workers were being arranged in a way that would obscure the cornfield's lack of depth, and the photographers had descended into an argument about where to best put Mtiti.

"That was a long time ago. These days he just writes positive stuff." Josh paused for a moment. "If he didn't, I'm guessing he'd have been run out on a rail by now."

The photographers made their decision, and the president was positioned amid a group of children, who began cheering and waving their hands in the air on cue. With a little Photoshop, it would be quite the inspiring image.

"Any word on my plane ticket?"

"I think I've managed to get you a seat on the nineteenth."

"The nineteenth? That's almost three weeks from now."

"You're lucky it's not three months the way the flights are these days," Trent said, wiping the sweat off the back of his neck in a way that seemed to be a nervous tic. "Before you leave, though, we need to talk about your sister."

"I've been thinking more about that, Stephen. I appreciate your offer and all, but I don't think you can help. Actually, I know you can't. This is something I have to take care of myself."

"Shit," Trent muttered, but Josh realized it wasn't directed at him. After less than two minutes of having his picture taken, Mtiti waved a hand in frustration and started back toward his helicopter.

"Look, I've got to go," Trent said, joining the bodyguards and protesting photographers following along in the president's wake. "But we have to talk. I'll give you a call and we'll set it up."

——

"Looks like you and Mtiti hit it off right away," Flannary said, still lounging in his shaded beach chair.

"Fuck off."

"Would you like me to get you a drink while I'm fucking off?"

"Goes without saying."

The helicopter was already in the air, and the people beneath it scrambled to escape the stinging dust, temporarily deaf to the soldiers' orders. Flannary held out a beer, but Josh shook his head. "Got anything stronger?"

"Why?"

Josh sank into the empty chair and watched the helicopter gain altitude as the soldiers tried to regain control. "Because they didn't fix the irrigation system."

Flannary nodded thoughtfully. "I missed that. You've probably got enough people to hand-water them for a couple of weeks until you can rig something up."

"I don't think it'll be necessary."

Flannary's brow furrowed, and he handed Josh a half-full bottle of vodka. The air cleared, and the empty flatbeds pulled back up to the cornfield. Within a few minutes, the first stalks had been dug up and were being passed hand to hand back to the trucks.

"You knew that was going to happen," Flannary said, admiration clearly audible in his voice.

"I suspected."

Flannary reached over and clinked his glass against the bottle of vodka in Josh's hand. "You're one cynical son of a bitch, kid. I think I'm actually starting to like you."

23

They were going to assassinate Tfmena?" Flannary said. "Who was paying?"

They'd sat in those lawn chairs for almost six hours the day before, drinking and watching Gideon oversee the dismantling of the project. There had been nothing left when they finally got up and stumbled back to the compound. No corn, no tools, no people. Nothing.

Josh had been depressed and drunk enough to agree to get up before dawn to drive Flannary to the airport. At the time it had seemed like a good idea. Now, not so much.

Josh opened the door of the Land Cruiser and vomited onto the dirt rushing below, barely managing to pull himself upright in time to miss an animal-drawn cart meandering up the side of the road.

"Annika listened to the recording at least ten times, and she says she got pretty much all of it," he said, grabbing a warm Coke and swishing his mouth out with it. "No mention of who the moneyman was."

"Please tell me you still have it."

"The MP3 player?" Josh shook his head. "Stephen wanted it, so I gave it to him."

"Jesus Christ!" Flannary shouted. "How could you do something that stupid?"

"Don't bust my balls, JB. I knew it was a mistake, but he's my boss, and he said he needed it to justify getting rid of Gideon. What was I gonna do? Call him a liar and make a run for it?"

"Why the hell not?"

Flannary seemed impervious to lack of sleep, hangovers, and pretty much everything else. He was well-scrubbed, what remained of his hair had been trimmed, and his badly dated clothes were wrinkle free. According to him, this rare trip to the United States was for his brother's wedding, but he didn't seem particularly interested in the prospect of being reunited with his family.

"You know, when you first got here, I figured you were just some stooge NewAfrica had hired. But now I think you're too dumb to be a stooge."

Josh grimaced, though he was fairly certain the statement was meant as a compliment. "You know, JB, every time we talk, I get the feeling you're dancing around something. It's starting to make me want to punch your face in."

The reporter grabbed his travel mug and took a thoughtful swig of the Bloody Mary it contained. "Have you ever asked Trent what happened to Dan?"

Josh wasn't sure how he'd expected Flannary to respond, but that wasn't it. "Yeah. We've talked about it."

"What did he say?"

"Not much. He implied that Dan had gotten involved in something illegal."

"That's bullshit."

"How do you know?"

"Because Dan Ordman was an insufferable Boy Scout from a stinking-rich family of East Coast liberals. Now, if someone told me *you* were into something shady, I'd be open to the idea. But Dan? No fucking way."

"I'm driving you six hours to the airport, you know. A little respect would be in order."

"No offense intended," Flannary said. "But you're not exactly the prototype for this kind of work. As near as I can tell, you're nothing but a desperate guy with an armed-robbery conviction."

Josh slammed on the brakes, skidding to a stop and sitting there with the dust rolling over them.

"Are you throwing me out?" Flannary asked.

It was a good idea. Just shove him out the door and watch him recede until he was nothing but a little fleck in the rearview mirror. Some lucky hyena's evening snack.

Instead Josh stomped on the accelerator, and they fishtailed back out into the road. "What do *you* think happened to Dan?"

Flannary didn't answer immediately, a pause that Josh had come to suspect was him calculating how much to say.

"JB?"

"I think Dan was looking for NewAfrica's other projects."

"What do you mean, 'looking for' them?"

"A few days ago, when I asked you about your other projects, you told me you didn't know anything about them."

"So? Why would I?"

Flannary shrugged. "Maybe you wouldn't. The problem is that no one else does, either. NewAfrica has all these brochures with pictures of fancy agricultural projects and grinning refugees, but when I ask for specifics from the locals, all I get is 'Oh, it's west of here a ways.' Or 'I met a guy once who knew someone who worked on that project.'"

"I'm not following you."

"Yes, you are."

"Are you trying to tell me that NewAfrica's projects are fake and they killed Dan because he found out? I think you've been hitting the gin a little too hard, JB."

"Maybe."

"What about my project? That exists."

"Really? It looks like a burned-out hill to me."

"You know what I mean."

"Yours is different. Pathetic as it sounds, it's NewAfrica's flagship. The others are always in much more remote areas, always completely self-contained, and always manned with imported workers—not people indigenous to the area." Flannary reached into the backseat and pulled a manila envelope from his duffel.

"What's that?"

"Everything I've been able to find on NewAfrica's projects since they first started in business. I compiled it from brochures, notes of conversations I've had, and Freedom of Information Act stuff on projects the government was involved in." He dropped the envelope in Josh's lap.

"Why are you giving it to me?"

"I'm going to do a little digging while I'm in the States, and I thought maybe you could do the same here."

"I told you I'm not staying. I'm out of here in a couple weeks."

"Then you've got some time on your hands with nothing to do."

Josh didn't respond.

"What?"

"I think you've gone nuts, JB. Seriously."

"So what? If I'm wrong, you get a little vacation in the countryside before you go back to the world."

"You know, I'd actually like to. I'd like to prove once and for all that you're a paranoid schizophrenic and see that you get heavily medicated. But I'll be lucky to find my way back from the airport. How the hell would I track down a bunch of old agricultural projects out in the middle of nowhere?"

"Why don't you just ask Stephen Trent to take you on a tour?"

When Josh didn't answer, a smile spread across Flannary's face. "Because you think I might be right."

"No."

"So to review," Flannary said. "What you're concerned about is getting lost, getting kidnapped by rebels, getting sexually violated by baboons . . . that kind of thing."

Josh knew he was being set up, but after everything that had happened, everything he'd seen, it was hard not to have a little of Flannary's paranoia rub off on him.

"Yeah. I guess."

Flannary slapped the dash again. "Well, my boy, I think I have a satisfactory solution to those problems. In fact, I think I have a solution you're gonna fall in love with."

24

The satellite phone in Josh's pocket began to ring just as the soldier frisking him started up his left leg. Normally the fact that he was scared shitless would have prompted him to let the caller leave a message, but he hadn't been able to reach his sister in two days, and it was killing him. He took one of his hands off the Land Cruiser's scalding hood and dug the phone out.

The rifle butt to the kidneys he'd been expecting didn't materialize, and instead the soldier wandered off to start what would ultimately be a disappointing search of the Land Cruiser. It had been emptied of virtually everything of value at a similar military checkpoint two hours ago.

"Hello? Laura?"

"It's Stephen, Josh. I wanted to call and tell you I was sorry we couldn't talk when I was at the project. I know you must be concerned about what happened there, and I want to explain. Those weren't our crops—Mtiti's government loaned them to us for the shoot. If we had the funds, we would have bought them and had them planted permanently. But the truth is that we don't right now."

"I understand," Josh said.

"Do you? Good. We're hoping the donations we get from the brochure we're putting together will give us the money to get your project going again."

Across the hood from him, Annika grabbed the hand of the soldier frisking her when it got a little too close to her left breast. She said something with a passive sternness that Josh recognized from the first three roadblocks they'd been through that day. It seemed like an impossible balancing act—she had to be forceful enough for the man to take her seriously, but not so forceful as to make him angry. And, miraculously, she once again managed to create the illusion that they weren't completely defenseless.

"It's not my project anymore, Stephen. We—"

"I know, we still need to talk about your sister and about the possibility of you going home—"

"The *possibility* of me going home? You said—"

"Look, we're going to relocate some of the refugees you've been working with to one of our more successful projects. It has enough capacity to absorb them, and we can get them on the road to self-sufficiency. I'm knee-deep in that right now."

The soldier searching Annika tried to duck into the Land Cruiser's backseat, but she grabbed his sleeve and showed him the pictures and maps Flannary had collected.

"Which project?" Josh said, watching the soldier shrug and shake his head.

"What?"

"Which project are you sending them to?"

"It's in the northeast part of the country."

"Really?" Josh said. "I hear it's pretty up there. Maybe I should go check it out. Where is it exactly?"

"I don't think it would be worth the trip—we've got it under control. In the meantime, I need you to come back to the capital so we can get together. There are some things we need to talk about."

"I'm telling you that there aren't, Stephen. It's not that I don't appreciate the opportunity you've given me here, but it's not going to work out. For a lot of reasons."

"Humor me, then. Why don't you come up this afternoon? We'll have a drink and get everything out on the table."

Josh looked up the road and calculated how long it would take to make the drive. "That's kind of short notice. I don't think I can make it that fast."

"Why not?"

He was about to say "car trouble" but then realized that the phone he was talking on had a trackable GPS in it.

"I'm out in the countryside, Stephen. Like I said, I want to see some sights before I leave."

"Okay, when?"

"Give me a couple days. No hurry, right? We've still got a few weeks before my flight."

"Fine. A couple days. But no longer. There are some things we need to resolve."

The line went dead, and Josh jammed the phone back in his pocket. The guard was starting to look a bit annoyed with Annika's interrogation, but their conversation seemed to be getting somewhere, so he just stood back and didn't interfere.

He should have guessed that she would be Flannary's solution to his reluctance to head off on this particular wild-goose chase. In truth, he'd probably have done it anyway—there was definitely something wrong here, and he wanted to know what it was. Annika was a nice addition on a number of levels, though.

The soldier searching the vehicle slammed the back hatch and waved them on. They climbed in, and Josh accelerated up the dirt road while Annika shouted thanks through her open window.

"Did you get anything?"

"We seem to be going in the right direction, but he didn't know how far or where exactly."

Josh glanced in his rearview mirror at the soldiers settling into a narrow strip of shade. "How long did it take you to learn to do all this?"

"What?"

"Speak the language, handle those guys like that."

She thought about it for a moment. "I've been here almost seven years. Since I was nineteen."

Josh tried to wrap his mind around that amount of time, to imagine what it would be like to have spent more than a quarter of his life there. "What did your parents think of that?"

"Oh, the same thing you would imagine. My father was very angry."

"Really?"

"He thought it was too dangerous. And he believes that people have to help themselves. That this is the only path to improving your life."

Josh grinned. "For some reason, that's the exact attitude I would expect from an old Norwegian guy."

"Are you making fun of him?"

"Nope. It's the same principle my country was founded on. We've even got a phrase for it: pulling yourself up by your own bootstraps."

"Like you did. You grew up very poor, you went to jail. And now you have a good education and a good job. You did it without anyone's help."

"Who told you I went to jail?"

"JB."

"JB's got a big mouth."

She shrugged. "Everyone makes mistakes. And everyone can be forgiven. What's important is that we're truly sorry and try to make things right."

He wasn't so sure. If there was a God, He clearly wasn't impressed by the Hagartys.

"You see, I'm different than you," Annika continued.

"Not an ex-con?"

"I was going to say that I grew up privileged. I lived in the small world that money could buy. Do you understand what I mean?"

He nodded.

"The price, though, is that you become a very tiny piece of a machine that works perfectly without you. I wanted more. I wanted to see what else there was in the world. I wanted to help people who weren't born like me. People who weren't born lucky."

━━━━

The sun was moving toward the horizon, and Josh watched its progress as if it were a gas gauge hovering just above empty. "It's going to be dark soon."

Annika was reclining in her seat with her bare feet hanging out the window. "It's cooler to travel at night."

Her nonchalance wasn't as confidence-inspiring as it should have been. He couldn't figure out if it was the result of her belief that it was safe or if it was just the fatalism that permeated all things African.

She seemed to think they were on the right track, but as near as he could tell, they were just penetrating farther and farther into the middle of nowhere. The calendar rolled back with every mile, leaving behind everything the modern world had to offer— electricity, machinery, modern clothing, and building materials.

The jagged, grassy buttes he was accustomed to had been re- placed with endless jungle that swallowed nearly every trace of humanity. He hadn't realized how reassuring the intermittent villages and occasional animal-drawn carts were until they had disappeared.

"In some ways it's better in this part of the country," Annika said, seeming to read his mind. "By the time aid makes its way this far, most everything of value has been stolen by the government. So people rely on themselves and the culture they developed over thousands of years." She pointed to a distant figure moving along the side of the road ahead. He leaned forward and squinted, finally discerning the shape of a woman carrying an enormous jug on her head.

"Pull over. Let's see if she can help us."

Despite having witnessed similar conversations at least ten times that day, Josh sat transfixed by the way the woman immediately responded to the confidence and caring Annika exuded. It was hard not to wonder if he would have ended up a person like her if circumstances had been different. Probably not. But Laura could. She had it in her to do something worthwhile, and he was going to make goddamn sure that nothing got in her way.

The woman began nodding, the jar on her head teetering precariously. The scene continued to deviate from the script he'd become familiar with as the woman began giving what appeared to be detailed directions. Annika thanked her profusely before jogging excitedly back to the vehicle.

"We've got something."

"You're kidding."

"I swear. Go up about three kilometers and turn left."

———

"That's as far as we go."

The dirt track had been right where the woman said, but the farther they went along it, the deeper the ruts became and the more the jungle closed in. Annika threw open her door and stepped out into the gloom, taking a deep breath of the humid air before continuing on foot.

"This doesn't seem like a good idea to me," Josh said, jogging up next to her but keeping his attention focused on the foliage to either side. He imagined hundreds of pairs of eyes staring out at them. Waiting.

"What doesn't?"

"It's getting dark. Maybe we should come back later."

She threaded an arm through his and pulled him along. "Don't tell me you're afraid."

As much as he hated to admit it, he was.

"People say there are lions out here." He swatted a mosquito on his leg. "And I forgot to take my malaria pill this morning."

"If I lived in Norway, I'd be sitting in a tiny office dreaming about adventure," she said, apparently oblivious to the enormous felines that were undoubtedly tracking their every move. "What would you be doing?"

He glanced behind him. Nothing but deepening shadow. "I don't know."

"You don't know? Okay. What would you *want* to be doing?"

"I guess sitting in an office. Not a tiny one, though. A huge one with mahogany paneling and a really soft leather chair. And air conditioning. Lots of air conditioning."

"What would you be thinking about?"

"Probably the kind of private jet I was going to buy."

He'd expected a disapproving frown but didn't get it.

"A plane? Sure . . . a plane would be good. Where would it take you?"

"Dunno. I guess I never really thought that far ahead."

The bugs had found them, and she shook her head, using her long hair to shoo them from her face. "What good is a plane if you don't have anywhere you want to go?"

Despite her good-natured delivery, the question shook him a bit. In a single sentence, she'd made one of the main goals of his life seem like complete nonsense. How was it that it had never occurred to him that a plane wasn't an end? It was a means.

"Could we change the subject?"

"From money?"

"It seems more important if you've never had it."

"And that's how you Americans judge yourselves, isn't it? The more you have, the more valuable you are as a human being."

"I knew it."

"What?"

"You're a closet American hater."

"Oh, no. Definitely not. I love Americans. You're always thinking of something new and better. I just wonder when you're going to stop and enjoy those things you dream up."

They crested a hill, and she pointed, prompting him to slow and finally stop. The hill wasn't as elaborately carved as the one he'd been in charge of, but the terraces were still visible beneath the jungle reclaiming them.

Annika held up a color photo of the project from NewAfrica's brochure. He squinted at it in the failing light, trying to reconcile the image with what he saw in front of him. After a few moments, landmarks began to appear: a saw-toothed ridge to the east, a square depression where the tool shed had once sat.

"This is it," he said, focusing on the smiling faces of the people standing around Stephen Trent in the photo. After watching the presidential shoot at his own project, he saw that the crafting of the illusion was obvious. The angle, the focus, the workers' positions and expressions were all carefully designed to create a sense of progress that had never existed.

"Nothing's changed," Annika said.

"What do you mean?"

"Look at the state of the work in the picture."

She was right. It looked like the project had been abandoned the day after the photo had been taken.

25

This tile is so beautiful! And the water . . . it's so hot!"
Josh laid a pair of his pants on the bed along with a belt that would hopefully keep them from falling down around Annika's ankles.

It had been too late to take her back to her village, and he'd managed to convince her to stay the night at his place with the solemn promise that he'd return her first thing in the morning.

"I can't believe you have a pool here."

"It's more of a hole in the ground lined with plastic, but I'm glad you enjoyed it. They serve breakfast next to—"

The shower curtain rustled, and her face appeared around it. "They serve you breakfast?"

"It's nothing fancy," Josh said, squeezing some toothpaste onto his brush. "Just a little fruit and some cereal."

"I'm glad to see you sacrificing so much to help Africa."

It was hard not to be embarrassed by the way he lived. Despite everything that had happened to his project, to the people who were counting on him, he still had his pool, his breakfasts, and American Movie Night every Sunday.

She was enjoying herself too much to continue scolding him

and instead nodded toward the shelf over the sink. "Is that shampoo?"

Josh held it out, and she snatched it, immediately disappearing again.

"It smells like apples! I love the smell of apples, don't you?"

He finished brushing his teeth and stood watching her vague shadow through the shower curtain. It was impossible not to.

"So what's next, Josh?"

"What do you mean?"

"JB's envelope had information on other projects. What if they're all like the one we saw today? We should try to find them."

"I thought you had to get back."

"I do. But this would just take another day or two. And it will give the women in the village something to gossip about. They feel so bad for me, you know."

"They feel bad for you?"

"Because I don't have a man and I'm so skinny and old, they figure I don't have much chance of getting one." She fell silent for a moment. "Oh, no. The water's getting cold and you haven't showered yet. Just let me get the soap out of my hair. I'll be out in a minute."

He chewed on his thumbnail, uncertain what to do. It was an opening that seemed almost too perfect to pass up.

"You don't have to get out. I mean, we could share."

Her face appeared again, and her gaze ran from his feet upward until their eyes met. "I bet not many girls say no to you, do they?"

He shrugged uncomfortably, and she withdrew behind the curtain.

"I think a cold shower is just what you need."

Josh adjusted the thin blanket separating him from the floor as Annika crawled into his bed and switched off the light. Giving her the bed had seemed like the chivalrous thing to do—particularly in light of the clumsy pass he'd made—but he was starting to regret it. The concrete grinding into his tailbone was bad enough, but now he found himself wondering what African creepy-crawlies skittered from their hiding places when it got dark.

He could hear her thrashing around on the lumpy mattress, obviously having nearly as much trouble getting comfortable as he was.

"Do you get lonely, Annika?"

"What?"

"You know. Living all the way out there by yourself."

"I'm not by myself. I have a lot of friends in the village. They've been good to me."

"Is it the same, though? Do you feel like they've really accepted you?"

In the glow of the floodlights bleeding through the curtains, Josh saw her scoot to the edge of the bed and look down at him. "You mean will they ever consider me one of them? No. I don't think so."

He wondered how many times she had seen some American or European show up in Africa only to leave a few weeks later. He wanted her to think he was different. But was he?

"Will you always do this kind of work? Do you see yourself being in Africa for the rest of your life?"

She thought about that for a moment. "Always is a long time. I—"

The sound of knocking silenced her.

"Josh?" The voice was muffled but identifiable as Katie's.

Maybe it was a trick of shadow, but he could make out just enough of Annika's expression to see that she wasn't happy that there was a woman banging on his door in the middle of the night.

"Katie? What's up? It's after midnight."

"Yeah, could I talk to you a minute?"

"Can it wait 'til morning?"

"I guess," came the uncertain reply. "We were all just wondering what's happening with your people in the refugee camp."

=====

"Did you know about this?" Annika said.

The customary gloom of the refugee camp had turned to a blinding glare. Military vehicles blocked nearly every road, and soldiers directed spotlights at the crowd being herded toward trucks idling in the muddy square.

And in the center of it all was Gideon.

He was standing on the roof of a pickup shouting into a bullhorn as the people from Josh's project milled past, clutching their children and what few belongings they had left.

Josh grabbed Annika's arm and leaned in close so she could hear over the din. "Stephen told me they were going to move them to a finished project. I thought he meant that NewAfrica was going to put them on buses over the next few months—not that the military was going to shove them in the back of trucks in the middle of the night."

A young girl Josh recognized began to cry, obviously lost and largely ignored by people trying to get a place for themselves and their possessions on one of the trucks. He pushed through the crowd and scooped her up, then fought his way back to Annika, who, for all her experience in Africa, was looking a bit shellshocked.

"Has JB told you what he thinks is going on at NewAfrica?"

She nodded numbly. "I thought he was crazy. I only agreed to go with you because I wanted to get to know you. . . . " Her voice trailed off.

Despite everything going on around them, he couldn't help feeling a brief burst of happiness at hearing that.

"I'm going to try to find this girl's mother," he said, wading back into the crowd. "While I'm gone, see if you can find out what's going on."

There was recognition in the faces of the people he passed, but none of the accusation and anger he'd expected. Mostly he saw resignation—to the unknown, to powerlessness, to inevitability.

A woman's shout rose above Gideon's electronically amplified voice, and Josh saw her pushing toward him through the crowd. The reunion was more practical than emotional, with the woman immediately setting her daughter down and handing her a bundle of cooking supplies. After a few grateful words, both disappeared back into the sea of people, the child struggling to keep up, which was undoubtedly how she'd gotten lost in the first place.

It wasn't callousness on her mother's part, he knew. She was doing all she could, but ultimately it was up to the little girl to survive.

Josh fought his way to within twenty feet of one of the cargo trucks his people were being packed into but could get no closer. The bed was covered with an arched green canopy that deflected light, and the people being shoved inside by Mtiti's troops seemed like they'd been wiped from existence.

An old woman fell in front of him, spilling the meager contents of her hand-sewn bag into the mud. No one helped her, instead using the opportunity to push a little closer to the truck.

Josh knelt, using his body to protect her from being trampled and fishing the phone from his pocket. He disabled the ringer and stuffed it into her bag as he helped her recover her things.

When she was back safely on her feet, he headed off toward where he'd last seen Annika, the surging crowd forcing him into a route that took him alongside Gideon's pickup. He was sliding past the passenger door when the bullhorn fell silent and a hand clamped around the back of his shirt. He tried to jerk away, but he couldn't break free and instead twisted around to look up into Gideon's ever-present sunglasses.

"Stephen Trent wants to talk to you."

"I know. I told him we'd get together in a few days."

"No. Now."

Josh pulled back again, but Gideon held fast.

"Where are you taking these people?"

"To another project."

"Which one?"

"One that can support them." Gideon motioned to a group of soldiers who immediately started in their direction.

Josh threw his arms up and slipped out of the shirt, then bolted bare-chested back into the throng. Gideon shouted into the bullhorn, and the soldiers began to chase, swinging their rifle butts at anyone who slowed them down.

Annika's height and blond hair made her easy to spot, and Josh adjusted his trajectory to intercept her as she questioned the people flowing by. She didn't see him coming up behind her and was startled when he grabbed her by the arm and started dragging her back toward where they'd parked the Land Cruiser.

"What are you doing?" she said, nearly falling as he used a momentary gap in the crowd to break into a full run.

He jerked his thumb back at the soldiers twenty feet behind them. "Time to go!"

26

JB Flannary shoved the files to the edge of the desk and sipped coffee full of elaborate flavorings he couldn't identify. Every time he returned to the West, it irritated him a little more. The constant whining about self-inflicted problems, the thousands of choices when one would do, and the endless news reports about the horrible economic suffering being inflicted on the middle class. The current issue of the magazine he wrote for was actually running a story titled "Too Poor to Be Thin" about how it was impossible to buy the food necessary to lose weight without an income of around eighty grand a year. Maybe he'd pitch a follow-up with an article called "Diet Secrets of the Sudanese."

To be fair, though, the Internet ran at the speed of light, power transmission and phone service were 24/7, and he hadn't had to bribe a government official since he arrived. There was just no denying that if you needed something done, Westerners—and Americans in particular—were your go-to guys.

"Do you have everything you need, Mr. Flannary? Can I get you anything else?"

"Thanks, Tracy. I think I'm good."

She was probably twenty-three, slightly plump, red-haired,

rosy-cheeked. And she'd been responsible for shattering his anonymity less than a minute after he'd walked into the magazine's office suite. As he recalled, she'd actually used the word "gosh" when she'd spotted him.

"You know, I've read everything you've ever written. I've really found your commitment to the poorest people in the world inspiring."

"Thanks."

"Anything you need, just let me know, okay? Seriously, anything —I know I have a lot to learn, and I can't think of anyone I'd rather learn it from."

She just stood there, staring down at him as though he were some kind of holy relic. It was hard to know how to react. Clearly any girl who would see him as heroic was deeply disturbed. He slid his letter opener across the desk and out of her reach.

"Flannary!" a familiar voice shouted loudly enough to make him duck involuntarily. "What the hell are you doing in my building?"

"Bobby! It's always a pleasure."

"Shut up."

Robert Page stopped in front of the desk, glared at the files on it for a moment, then fixed his stare on the young woman who was subtly backing away from the managing editor of the magazine she worked for.

"You! What's your name?"

"Tracy, sir."

He stuck a finger in Flannary's face. "Tracy. You're young, so you think his life is glamorous and meaningful. Don't be fooled. You don't want to end up like this."

Flannary expected her to melt into a quivering puddle, but instead her expression turned resolute. "I think he's brilliant."

Page groaned quietly and flicked a hand in her direction, indicating that she was dismissed. They both watched her go.

"You don't work here anymore, JB. You're just some crazy Africa guy who very occasionally does freelance work for us. You can't just walk in here, take over a desk, and start using our interns."

"I'm working on something you'd kill for. The *Times* is drooling all over it, but you and I've got a relationship, so I thought I'd give you first crack."

"The *Times,* huh? So your brother wants it, but you're gonna give it to me."

"Like I said, we have a relationship."

"Give me a break, JB. The economy sucks, the Arabs are going nuts, and the Chinese are taking over the world. No one here cares about Africa anymore. It's the same old crap, year after year."

"You haven't heard my angle."

"If I listen to it, will you go back there? And stay?"

"You have my word."

Page turned and stalked toward his office, indicating that Flannary should follow. He slammed the door behind them and then dropped into a sofa. "Okay. In five minutes or less, what have you got?"

"I have an NGO—"

"Here it comes," Page interrupted. "Here, let me finish for you: 'For reasons that would take seven hundred pages of background to explain, this particular charity isn't being as effective as it could be.' I'm riveted."

"You said I had five minutes. I assume we're not counting the time you spend droning on?"

Page sank farther into the sofa cushions. "Fine. Go ahead."

"I'm not talking about a charity that's naive, or even one that's self-serving. I'm talking about a charity that's operating basically as an organized crime outfit."

"Is this a joke?"

"No."

"I warned you about drinking in the sun, JB."

"I'm serious, Bobby. I don't know why someone didn't come up with something like this sooner. Think about it: Most people assume all charities are right in the middle of the moral high road, right? What little oversight they have doesn't even *consider* the possibility that their basic intentions aren't good. No one's looking for this."

"What the hell would they steal, JB? A bag of food and a thirty-year-old Datsun with no tires?"

"Are you kidding? How about the tens of millions of dollars flowing in from the U.S. and European governments and private donors? And what about the money coming in from mining? Or the money Umboto Mtiti would be willing to pay them to keep the international community off his back?"

"And you have evidence of this?"

"Right now it's mostly circumstantial. But that's why I'm here—to put together something solid."

"I thought you were here to go to your brother's wedding."

"That's just my cover story."

Page gazed disinterestedly out the window behind his desk.

"Stealing isn't complicated, Bobby. This is a simple story about a group of criminals taking advantage of poor, helpless people."

"It's Africa, JB."

"So what are you saying? That the Africans don't matter? That we should just shove them into a corner and pretend they don't exist?"

Page's eyes widened. "What happened to the cynicism, JB? Don't tell me you're going native."

"You have no clue how those people have to live. And the idea that a bunch of assholes from the West would go in there and knowingly contribute to the suffering . . ." Flannary's voice trailed off for a moment. "Look, the NGOs I've written about in the past are a problem, but there's a big difference between being a clueless bull in a china shop and what I'm talking about here."

"I don't know," Page said.

"Come on, Bobby. It's got a strong domestic angle—we're talking about an American charity ripping off American donors and the American government. I also think they may have murdered one of their American workers. A young kid who went over there to help."

Page stared out the window for another minute. "That girl Tracy seems to be able to tolerate you. You can have her for two days. After that, you're going to have to prove to me that this is going somewhere."

Flannary was going to protest getting stuck with a kid barely out of diapers but decided not to push it. "You won't regret this."

"Yes, I will," Page said, pointing to the door.

Flannary got up to leave but paused with his hand on the handle. "Are we still on for dinner tonight?"

"I'll pick you up at your hotel at seven thirty."

27

Josh Hagarty pressed the phone to his ear, feeling a weak burst of adrenaline every time the crackling ring sounded but preparing for the almost inevitable moment when the connection died.

Two rings. Three.

He and Annika were staying at a remote B&B run by a German woman so old she seemed indestructible. A chain-smoking mummy with a vaguely creepy accent and an affinity for vicious dogs. She'd told them that the guesthouse had once been a successful stopping-off point for Europeans on safari but that after Mtiti's rise to power, business had dried up. Despite the hard times, though, the plumbing worked and the electricity was just reliable enough to run a glacial Internet connection and an utterly unreliable phone.

Four rings. A new record. He pulled his back off the bed's headboard and leaned forward.

Come on, babe. Pick up.

"Hello?"

"Laura! Christ, I can't believe I finally got you."

Annika came out of the bathroom wearing only a T-shirt and a pair of panties. Normally Josh would have had to concentrate not to stare, but he'd been trying to get in touch with his sister for two hours, and for the moment, the sound of her voice obscured everything else.

"Are you okay, hon? Is everything all right?"

"I thought you were coming home, Josh."

Her voice was almost unrecognizable, and it wasn't just the bad connection. There was none of the deadpan excitement that was always audible when he called or came home. For the first time in seventeen years, he thought he heard despair. "It looks like I've got a flight out on the nineteenth. That'll put me in Kentucky on—"

"The nineteenth? That's like two weeks!"

Laura had always been fiercely independent. She made a point of constantly reminding him that she wasn't his responsibility— that she loved him but she didn't *need* him. All that was gone now.

"There just aren't any flights right now. If I could get there any sooner, you know I would."

"It's okay. It's just that it would be better if you came home, Josh."

He wiped the sweat from around his mouth as Annika looked on with concern. "What if I could figure out how to send you the money I've made? Could you get an apartment or a hotel or something until I get home?"

"I can't leave Mom, Josh. You don't know what's happening here. It's—"

"You don't have to leave Mom!" he shouted and then paused to regain control of the volume of his voice. "Look, you can spend as much time with her as you want. But you need somewhere else to go. Just until I get there."

He heard a familiar crash that was the trailer's screen door being thrown open, followed by a startled yelp from his sister.

"Laura? What's going on?"

"Stop!" he heard her shout, though she sounded increasingly distant. "Give that back!"

"Laura? Are you—"

"Hey, so is this big brother?"

Even after a decade, he recognized the voice immediately.

"Ernie, put Laura back on."

"I should have known you'd end up in Africa, the way you used to hang around all those coons back when we played football. Seemed like you liked them more than you liked us."

"Ernie, put—"

"Nice family you got here," he interrupted, obviously enjoying himself. "And your sister? Cute kid. You remember how I love blonds?"

"If you fucking touch her, I'm gonna come back there and kill you, you piece of shit."

"You threatenin' me, Josh?"

"I'm telling you what I'm going to do. You take it for what it's worth."

"I'm kinda scared now. I may have to call the cops for protection. They know all about you ex-cons. Or maybe we'll just get your mom to sign a restrainin' order and keep you away from here."

"Just hang up the phone, Ernie." Fawn's voice.

"No!" he heard Laura shout. "Don't hang up! I want to—"

The line went dead, and he just sat there, staring at the phone in his hand.

"What happened?" Annika said. "Is she okay?"

He didn't answer, sinking back into the mattress and letting the phone fall to the floor. He barely noticed when she crawled onto the bed and straddled him.

"Josh?"

"There's a guy living at the house," he said haltingly. "I used to know him. He's . . . he could hurt her."

"What about the police?" she said, bringing her face closer to his in an effort to make eye contact. Her hair brushed lightly against his chest.

He shook his head. "It's complicated. My family's not like yours, Annika. We're . . ." He fell silent. How could he explain to her something that he himself didn't completely understand?

"You've told me how strong and smart Laura is. And you'll be home soon. She can take care of herself, right?"

"I don't know," he said honestly. "She's only seventeen. And I left her. I left her when I went to prison, then I left her when I went to school. And now, for the thousandth time, I'm not there when she needs me."

"You came here for her, Josh. NewAfrica was going to send her to university, to give her medical insurance. They were going to pay you enough money to take care of her."

"But it didn't work out that way, did it?"

"Sometimes things don't. But you did everything you could. That's important."

When he didn't respond, she leaned forward and pressed her lips against his. He knew he should push her away, but instead he slid a hand along her bare thigh.

Just for a little while. He could forget about NewAfrica and Ernie Bruce. About his past and JB Flannary. For a few minutes he could pretend to have something good in his life.

28

L ook at that," Annika said, pointing down at the rutted path they were walking along.

It had been ten hours since they'd left the guesthouse, most of which had been spent lost, hammering the Land Cruiser over increasingly remote dirt roads. But now there was finally evidence that they were on the right track.

The afternoon rains had left the story of the people they were trying to find etched unmistakably in the ground. Deep furrows made by the tires of overloaded trucks had been first, followed by indentations made by people jumping out of those trucks, and now the unmistakable pattern of a tractor tread crossing the carpet of footprints extending into the distance.

Josh knelt and ran a hand over the impressions in the damp earth, allowing himself a rare flash of optimism. They were going to find a well-equipped agricultural project run by someone capable of helping the people he'd so badly let down.

"I think we're finally gonna be able to prove that JB's nuts," he said, looking up at Annika. "Too much drinking in the sun."

The uncertainty behind her smile was obvious, but he chose to ignore it.

"Come on," she said holding out a hand and helping him to his feet. "We could have a long way to go."

He'd never been particularly claustrophobic, but the way the jungle encroached on the narrow track and spread itself out above created a world of impenetrable shadows, unfamiliar sounds, and suffocating humidity that was starting to get to him.

The Land Cruiser had made it a few miles past where the trucks had gotten bogged down, but they'd had to abandon it when the rock ledges became too steep to negotiate.

"You look better," Annika observed.

It was the first time that day either one of them had said anything even remotely personal. For the most part, their trip had consisted of long silences punctuated by brief comments about the map Annika had printed showing the location of Josh's sat phone and, presumably, the old woman whose bag he'd hidden it in.

Neither one of them seemed to know how to deal with what had happened the night before. It was amazing how sex could change things. But kind of wonderful, too.

"I feel better," Josh responded. "You know, when you think about it, there isn't a single thing that's happened that can't be explained by Africa's normal state of insanity: the abandoned project we went to, the way they carted my people off. Even Gideon getting those soldiers to chase me. And Laura? What you said is exactly right. She's smart, and she's strong. She can handle Ernie and Fawn until I get home. It's only a little while longer. Everything's going to be okay. It's going to work out."

His newly improved attitude sounded a little forced, even to him. But why couldn't it all work out? Why couldn't things go his way for once? The way he saw it, he had a little good luck coming.

"If you're so certain, maybe there's no reason for us to be here, Josh."

He looked at her, unsure how to interpret the statement. The construction seemed vaguely sarcastic, but the delivery wasn't. The closer they got to finding what they'd been looking for, the more nervous she became. In fact, she was starting to look a little ill.

"Are you okay?" he said, putting a hand on the back of her neck and squeezing gently.

"Sure. Of course I am. It's just the heat."

An obvious lie, but not one he wanted to think about.

"I just need to be sure that my people are doing okay, Annika. That NewAfrica's just self serving and not—" He paused for a moment, trying to find the right word, but she beat him to it.

"Evil?"

"Yeah, I guess."

"And then you can leave here with a clear conscience and never think anything about it again."

He wasn't sure what to say. It seemed ridiculous to be feeling about her the way he was—they hardly knew each other. Why had he spent most of the day fantasizing about a life together? A life lived all over the world, full of adventure, with never a moment behind a desk or worrying about keeping up with the Joneses.

"I'm sorry," Josh said finally. "If you—"

"I understand. You have a lot of responsibilities. And there are many things beyond your control. It's a hard thing for us."

"Us?"

"Whites. We think we have power over everything, and when we don't, we think it's a failure. But sometimes it doesn't have anything to do with us."

Her words were oddly off subject and had the vague sound of a warning. He told himself it was just his imagination.

The path they were on began to widen, finally opening into a large clearing hacked from the jungle. The dirt had been churned up, and there were downed trees pushed into piles at the edges. At its center was a single shovel, standing upright.

He tried to continue forward, but Annika grabbed his arm.

"There's nothing here, Josh. Let's go."

He looked behind him at the thousands of footprints pressed

into the ground and shrugged her off, walking to the shovel and taking hold of it. She followed but stopped a good ten feet away when he began to dig.

It took less than a minute for him to strike something. Not rock or wood. He dropped to his knees, digging with his hands, feeling increasingly nauseated. The first thing he uncovered was a dirty piece of cloth. He recognized the pattern and dug faster, throwing the debris behind him and revealing the motionless form beneath.

He rose and took a few stumbling steps back. It was the old woman he'd helped in the refugee camp. But now her open eyes and mouth were filled with dirt, as was the deep gash across her throat.

He looked around him at the churned dirt covering an area half the size of the football field where he'd spent much of his youth.

"Josh," Annika said. Her voice was steady, but the sun was reflecting off the tears on her cheeks. She approached and reached out to him, but he backed away.

"You knew," he said. "You knew what we were going to find here."

"I wasn't sure. I—"

"Why didn't you say anything?"

"Like what?"

Josh had never been prone to panic, but now he could feel it creeping up on him. This wasn't a misunderstanding or an accident. He was standing over the rotting bodies of a hundred people who a few nights before had been living, breathing human beings. He looked into the dirt-covered eyes of the old woman and imagined that the rest were staring up at him, too. Blaming him. Thirsting for revenge.

"Everything JB said was right," he stammered. "It's all bullshit. Stephen Trent, NewAfrica. They've never built anything or fed anyone. They're helping Mtiti get rid of the other tribes and keeping his image polished for the rest of the world. Why? Why would they do this?"

"For money," Annika said. "You look at the poverty here and you think there is no money. But that's not true. It's everywhere."

Money. For some reason the word cleared the fog from Josh's head. Everything he'd seen since he'd arrived in Africa was so complicated, it had never occurred to him that the answer to any question here could be as simple as that.

It all made perfect sense. Dan had found out what was going on and started to investigate, so they'd gotten rid of him. But he had to be replaced, preferably by a very different kind of employee. Someone desperate, someone who didn't care one way or another about charity or Africa or breaking a law or two.

He looked down again at the old woman. The handmade wooden jewelry she'd been wearing when he'd helped her was gone—stolen by the people who had killed her. Why would they leave a perfectly good shovel? And not only leave it but leave it right above that particular woman's grave? He dropped to his knees again and began pawing through the dirt. It took less than a minute to turn up his sat phone, no longer in her bag but buried beneath one of her stiff arms.

———

Gideon stood in the shadow of the jungle watching the scene playing out in front of him: Josh Hagarty using the shovel to uncover the old hag, his shock, his weakness. And even more intently, he watched the woman. Annika Gritdal, his informants told him. She was a missionary working in a remote village to the north—one Josh had visited a number of times. By all reports, her language skills were excellent, and it seemed almost certain that she was the one who had translated the threat to Tfmena.

By European standards, she was quite beautiful. And here she was quite exotic. He knew people who would pay handsomely for a woman with pale skin and blond hair, though it was impossible.

Trent would find out, and what he knew Mtiti knew. The president would tolerate nothing that could generate negative press in the West, and Gideon knew he was already on the verge of falling out of favor with his brother-in-law—something that had proven fatal to many before him.

But now he had turned things back to his advantage.

His people had found the phone when they were divvying up the belongings of these Yvimbo dogs and brought it to him. His initial reaction had been to bury it far to the south, leading Hagarty deep into dangerous rebel country. But then he'd changed his mind. This arrogant American had caused him to shut down his store and with it much of his livelihood. Gideon had found himself belittled in the eyes of Mtiti and his position with NewAfrica threatened.

So he'd left the phone and the shovel. And he'd waited.

Now there could be no dissent from Stephen Trent. Hagarty and his woman knew too much and would have to die. But not quickly. No, this was something Gideon had looked forward to for some time. They would suffer greatly first. They'd beg for death.

He pulled a pistol from his waistband and crept through the foliage, watching Hagarty dig through the dirt around the old woman's body. There was more than fifty meters between them, and before he showed himself, Gideon needed to be in a position to cut off their escape. He was in no mood for a chase.

Hagarty found the phone and immediately began pushing buttons on it, though instead of putting it to his ear, he let it hang loosely from his hand while he scanned the edges of the clearing. A moment later, the phone in Gideon's pocket started to ring, cutting through the still air and causing the birds in the trees above him to take flight.

By the time he managed to turn it off, Hagarty and his woman were sprinting back the way they had come.

29

JB Flannary stood huddled against the apartment building, using the stairs to block the wind but still shivering in his borrowed coat. It was one of the things he hated most about America—the crushing cold and darkness that closed in so quickly in the winter.

The NewAfrica plaque on the building across the street flashed in the headlights of passing cars, and Flannary tried without success to catch a glimpse of what was beyond the darkened windows. No one had gone in or out in the fifteen minutes he'd been standing there, but that wasn't surprising. Charities—even twisted, evil ones—tended to be nine-to-five affairs.

"Sorry I'm late!"

For some reason the piercing cheerfulness of Tracy Collins's voice had an ability to startle him that the sound of machine-gun fire had lost. He looked into her smiling face as she approached, a backpack slung over her wool-clad shoulder.

"Do you have everything?"

"Of course, JB! Absolutely."

He tried to work up a little cynicism—or at least a little skepticism—but it felt artificial. Over the last two days Tracy had demonstrated that youth and stupidity didn't always go hand in hand. While he'd been drinking himself into oblivion at his brother's increasingly inane prewedding festivities, she'd been channeling Woodward, Bernstein, and Steve Jobs in roughly equal amounts.

Tracy pushed past him and buzzed one of the apartments, bouncing slightly on her heels. Whether it was from the cold or excitement, he wasn't certain.

"So what made you want to be a reporter, JB?"

"Huh?"

"For me, it was seeing so much injustice that wasn't reported on, you know? The media's gotten so lazy. Not like your generation."

A voice from the speaker saved him from having to answer.

"Yes?"

"Hi, it's Tracy Collins. We talked earlier?"

The lock buzzed, and Flannary followed his young assistant as she headed for the stairs.

"I know it sounds naive, JB, but I still believe the press can make a difference in people's lives. We've just gotten off track. Instead of challenging people, now we just reinforce their beliefs, you know? But I think that's going to change."

"Really?"

His hangover seemed to be getting worse, but that was biologically impossible, so it had to be his proximity to this untainted ball of positive energy. Hopefully they'd do what they needed to do fast enough for him to get a little hair of the dog on the way back to his hotel.

Tracy's knock on the third-floor door was immediately answered by a woman in her midfifties.

"Hi, I'm Tracy, and this is my boss, JB Flannary. JB, this is Ms. Jones."

"Nice to meet you," he said, shaking her hand and examining her vaguely nervous expression with suspicion. He didn't trust people named Jones. Sounded too much like an alias.

"So this is it, here?" Tracy said, pointing to a dark window.

"Yes," the woman answered. "The fire escape is just outside. You said a hundred dollars a day, right?"

"Yup. That's right."

Flannary's jaw tightened, but Tracy was already pushing the window open and slipping through.

"So, Paris Hilton, huh?" the woman said.

"Crazy, isn't it?" Flannary responded, slipping a leg over the sill and feeling the cold outside air blow up his leg.

Through Internet wizardry he didn't fully understand, Tracy had found the phone numbers and basic background on all the people with apartments facing the NewAfrica building. After selecting Ms. Jones as the best candidate, she'd called and offered to pay her to let them put a camera on her fire escape. The cover story was that Paris Hilton was sleeping with someone who worked across the street.

"This thing's super-cutting-edge," Tracy said as Flannary pulled himself out onto the fire escape. "It's got great optics, a huge zoom, and amazing resolution, and it automatically adjusts to ambient light. It even works in the dark. No one will be able to walk in or out of that building without us getting every detail."

He nodded and wrapped his arms around himself, noticing for the first time that she was dressed entirely in black. An amiable, chubby cat burglar.

The more they looked into NewAfrica, the stranger things became. The board members seemed to be generally on the up-and-up—mostly wealthy New York women of leisure who were involved in various charities around town. They didn't seem involved on a day-to-day basis, though, and as near as they could tell, none had ever been to Africa. Employees were similarly mundane and also rarely left the United States. Pure bureaucrats well-versed in the theory of aid, if not its unfortunate details.

Stephen Trent, though, broke that mold. A cursory glance at his background suggested he came from the world of real estate development and venture capital. A little digging, though, turned up the fact that it had been mostly fraudulent real estate development and venture capital. He'd managed to stay out of jail, but that seemed to be more the result of fancy legal footwork than innocence. The bottom line was that a lot of people had lost a lot of money on his scams, and someone had gone to great lengths to bury that information.

Another intriguing fact was that Trent had no history of charitable work or world travel. The idea that some Midwestern con artist would be able to suddenly ally himself with Umboto Mtiti and insinuate himself into the politics of Africa seemed far-fetched to the extreme. Flannary had met him on no less than three occasions and he was clearly a lightweight. Slick? For sure. But not a man with the knowledge or resolve that it would take to get an operation like NewAfrica off the ground.

Flannary's gut told him someone else was pulling the strings. And that had inspired Tracy to come up with the camera idea.

"So we just come and pick up the tape in a couple of days?" Flannary asked, trying not to think about how much all these fancy optics were costing him.

She looked back and cocked her head. "What do you mean?"

"To watch it."

"Oh, right. Then we can put some ABBA on my eight-track and watch it on my black-and-white TV." A bemused grin spread across her face. "We're going to link to Ms. Jones's wireless, and then we can connect to it over the Web, JB. It'll download into files that we can fast-forward, rewind, enhance, or whatever. It'll all be right at our fingertips—archived and date-stamped."

One last turn of her screwdriver, and the camera was mounted. She grabbed her bag and ducked back through the window. "Come on, we'll pull this thing up on my laptop and see what we've got."

"I'll be in in a second," Flannary said.

"You sure? Kinda cold out here."

He nodded and slid the window shut after her.

He'd been trying to contact Josh for the last two days, and the best he'd gotten was a prompt to leave a message. Every time he couldn't get through, the knot in his stomach tightened more. Had something happened to the kid? Or worse, maybe his reporter's insight into people had misfired and Josh wasn't as innocent as he seemed. If that was the case, what had happened to Annika?

Flannary dialed the number for Josh's sat phone and listened to the familiar recording in its entirety before hanging up.

30

A barrage of machine-gun fire tore the limbs from the trees just ahead and sent Annika sprawling to the ground. Josh managed to get a hand under her arm and jerked her to her feet before she'd even stopped sliding.

A glance back placed Gideon in the middle of the narrow dirt road about seventy-five yards away. He was motionless, taking careful aim this time. He wouldn't miss again.

Still gripping Annika's arm, Josh made a sudden left turn, crashing into the jungle at a full sprint. Rounds pulverized the wide leaves above them, turning the air to a hazy green as they searched for cover.

They stopped behind the broad trunk of a tree, both breathing hard and Annika wiping at the spiderweb of blood covering her face.

Josh held her head steady, examining the gash across the bridge of her nose. It didn't look all that serious, but her eyes were a little cloudy. Her impact with the ground must have been harder than he'd thought.

"Are you all right?"

She nodded as Gideon's shouts penetrated the dense foliage.

They were in Xhisa, but no translation was necessary. The African wanted to tear them apart.

"We can't stay in the jungle," Josh said. "We've got to get to the car. Can you still run?"

She closed her eyes tightly for a moment, and when she opened them again, they had cleared. "Faster than you."

They burst back out onto the road, partially crouched and going hard. No shots this time, but Gideon had closed to fifty yards in the time they'd been stopped.

The heat and exertion were making Josh increasingly light-headed. It had been a long time since those high school football practices beneath the Kentucky sun. Annika, on the other hand, hadn't spent the last six years lounging around in air-conditioned libraries, and she was already ten feet ahead, giving him something to focus on as he stumbled down the steep track toward the Land Cruiser. Even with that carrot, though, she was steadily pulling away.

"Annika!"

She looked back, and he threw the ignition keys to her. It wasn't until she caught them that he realized she'd been holding back. In less than a minute she was disappearing into the failing light.

Gideon obviously didn't want to lose sight of her, and more shots rang out, but they went wide. It seemed that the African was unwilling to stop running in order to line up his shot, and Josh knew that reluctance was the only thing keeping them alive.

By the time he made it through a hard right bend that briefly obscured him from Gideon's view, he wasn't running so much as lurching down the road trying not to throw up. The adrenaline and horror that had fueled his escape so far were running out, and he could barely keep his legs moving. The darkness had become deep enough that his footing was obscured, and every pebble he stepped on conspired to rip his feet out from under him.

The crunch of Gideon's boots was now audible, but even that

failed to give him the strength to go faster. The gloom stretched out forever, and his death suddenly seemed inevitable. He wondered if this was how Dan Ordman had felt and if it was Gideon who'd actually done the killing.

Thoughts of death cleared his mind, and he decided that if he couldn't get away, maybe he could tie Gideon up long enough to help Annika. The question was, how?

The darkness ahead was suddenly pierced by two red dots suspended in space. It took a moment for him to decipher what they meant, but when he did, he felt a burst of adrenaline that he didn't know he had left. The Land Cruiser's brake lights.

Josh put his head down and forced himself forward. The lights were probably no more than a hundred yards away, but the sound of Gideon's footfalls was getting louder every second. A hundred yards might as well have been a hundred miles.

The lights were replaced by the sound of the engine and spinning tires, but instead of fading, the noise got louder. A moment later, the outline of the vehicle became visible, as did the shape of the open passenger door.

He aimed for it, nearly falling beneath the wheels as his right arm stabbed through the open window. He hung there, coughing and gasping as Annika shifted into drive and slammed the pedal to the floor. The force of the acceleration caused the door to swing closed, and he was slammed painfully between it and the jamb.

Behind him, Gideon dove, but with most of Josh's body protected by the door, all the African could get hold of was the collar of his shirt. It immediately tore away, and Gideon hit the ground, rolling uncontrollably until he finally came to a stop at the edge of the jungle.

Annika used her free hand to pull Josh inside, and he lay across the seats trying to gulp enough air to keep him conscious. He barely reacted when Gideon shot out the rear window, managing only to look up at Annika as she hunched over the wheel.

A second volley missed entirely, and Josh was nearly thrown to the floor when Annika skidded the vehicle into a turn. A moment later he could feel himself being pressed deeper into the seat as she accelerated.

They were going to make it.

———

"There! I see him."

Josh was on his knees in the passenger seat, pointing to a distant glow visible through the shattered rear window.

"How far back?" Annika said, unable to look for herself. She had the Land Cruiser's headlights turned off and was navigating by the light of a three-quarter moon.

"I don't know. A few miles? But he's closing on us quick."

"I can't go any faster."

She was right. They couldn't afford a flat tire or broken axle, but at the rate Gideon was gaining, it would only be a few minutes before he was leaning out his window shooting at them with that goddamn machine gun.

They could turn on their headlights and floor it, but what if Gideon had people in the area? The arrogance that had made him wait in that clearing alone was probably gone now.

"Is there anywhere to turn off?"

"I've seen a few places we could squeeze into," she said. "They've all been pretty steep and narrow, though, and I don't know if we'd ever get back out."

Josh laid his head in her lap and used the penlight on his keychain to search through the fuse box. Her legs were covered with a thick film of sweat, and he had a hard time not slipping off them as he worked.

"What are you doing?"

"Killing the brake lights," he said, pulling the appropriate fuse. "Next time you see somewhere we can get into, do it."

It took a few minutes of vetting every break in the foliage, but they finally found something workable. She pulled in carefully, making it no more than fifteen feet before a series of boulders stopped their progress. They immediately jumped out and began bending thick fronds in front of the opening to camouflage it.

After a few minutes, the strengthening glow of Gideon's headlights forced them back into the Land Cruiser. Annika put a shaking hand on the key, ready to ram the side of Gideon's truck if he stopped.

But he didn't. He careened past at a barely controllable speed, his vehicle making a metallic grinding sound that Josh recognized well from his years working in auto shops. The African had pushed too hard. He'd be broken down by the side of the road within the hour.

They sat in silence for a good ten minutes before Annika eased out onto the road and headed back the way they'd come.

"Where are we going?" she said.

"I don't know. I was hoping you'd have an idea."

"Back to my village?"

"It seems like that's the first place they'd look."

"Do you have any money?"

He shook his head. "A few bucks. I used most of it last time we gassed up. You?"

"No."

It was a situation that seemed almost laughably absurd—that a lack of cash in hand could become a death sentence. Where would they get food? Shelter? Fuel? How would they stay hidden from Mtiti's soldiers when their white skin was basically a neon sign blinking over their heads?

"That's the first time I've seen Gideon, and I'm sure it's the first time he's seen me," Annika said. "How would he know who I am and where I live?"

"Are you kidding? How many six-foot-tall blond women are there wandering around in this country? And you were at the compound with me a few days ago. All he'd have to do is ask."

"Why would he? There still may be time."

Josh thought about it for a few moments, but the truth was that having absolutely no alternatives made the decision easy.

"Fine."

He pulled his phone from his pocket and turned it back on, disabling the GPS function while it acquired satellites. There were four messages—all from JB, he discovered as he listened to them.

"Josh. Call me."

"Hey, Josh. I haven't heard from you. Call me as soon as you get this, okay? It's important."

"Josh, I'm starting to get worried. Where are you?"

"Goddamnit, Josh. If you're working for these sons of bitches and anything's happened to Annika, I'm going to cut you up and throw you to a pack of wild dogs. I swear I will."

"Who was it?" Annika asked, concentrating on the dark road ahead.

"JB, JB, JB, and JB."

Josh dialed and listened to the phone on the other end ring, enjoying the relative clarity of it after dealing with the local landlines.

"Hello?"

"JB, it's Josh."

"Where the hell have you been? Why haven't you been returning my calls?"

"I've been doing what you told me to, which, as it turns out, involved dodging fucking machine-gun bullets."

"Is Annika all right?"

"She's fine. And I am, too, thanks for asking."

"What happened?"

"We went to the project you had the most information on, but it looks like it was abandoned before it was even half done."

"I knew it!"

"There's more. They picked up the people from my project to relocate them to one that was supposedly finished."

"And?"

"They're all dead, JB. Gideon and his people used a bulldozer to bury them in the middle of the jungle, and then he waited there for us. It's pretty much just luck that we're still breathing."

Silence.

"JB? Are you still there?"

"You've got to get out of there, Josh. Find a border and drive over it. No, wait. If Gideon's involved, so is Mtiti. The first thing he'll do is cover the borders and consulates."

"I'm looking for ideas, JB."

There was another long silence before Flannary spoke again. "I'm working on this, Josh. Once it blows open, Mtiti and Stephen Trent are going to have a hell of a lot more to worry about than you. Until then, though, there isn't anything they wouldn't do to shut you up."

Josh sank back into his seat and looked at Annika. The light from the gauges gleamed off her hair as it blew around her face.

"How long?"

"I'm not going to lie to you, Josh. I found out that Stephen Trent is a former con man, but that's not proof of anything. And getting information out of Africa is damn near impossible. I'm trying to figure out who's pulling NewAfrica's strings, but they don't exactly advertise, you know? And then there's the magazine's publishing schedule—"

"The magazine's publishing schedule? Are you kidding me?"

"Calm down, Josh, I—"

"We're on the run in the middle of Africa, JB. Don't tell me to calm down. Tell me you've figured out a way to get us out of here and back to the States."

"Why would that help? NewAfrica's based here."

Josh fell silent, suddenly thinking about Stephen Trent's interest in Laura and his insistence that they get together to discuss her.

"Shit!"

"What?" Flannary said. "What's wrong?"

Josh hung up without responding and immediately dialed his

sister. "Come on," he said, tapping his hand nervously on his thigh. "Pick up the goddamn phone."

"Hello?"

"Laura!"

"Josh! I'm so glad to hear from you! I'm sorry about—"

"You've got to get out of there right now."

"What about Mom? I thought you were—"

"Shut up, Laura! You're going to do exactly what I tell you. Do you hear me? *Exactly*."

31

JB Flannary walked unsteadily into the office, barely feeling the coffee cup burning his hand and ignoring the greetings of the people around him. The good news was that his brother's wedding was finally over. The bad news was that he'd used it as an excuse to see if he could still drink himself into oblivion. The answer turned out to be no, and now he was paying for the attempt with a hangover that might actually prove terminal.

"JB!"

He winced and kept walking as Tracy ran up to him.

"Why haven't you been answering your phone? I've been trying to call you all morning!"

He watched her out of the corner of his eye, unable to turn his head without it feeling like someone was driving an ice pick into it. Her cheeks were rosy. Honest-to-God rosy.

"Gosh, you look awful, JB."

"What did I tell you about saying 'gosh'?" he managed to get out as he entered the cubicle Robert Page had set him up in and eased into a chair.

"To always replace it with 'fuck.' But—"

He put a finger to his lips, silencing her. "Not now, okay? I just need to sit here in complete silence for a while."

The truth was that he'd skipped his brother's wedding ceremony and stayed at the reception only until the band launched into "The Wind Beneath My Wings." Improbably, things had gotten progressively worse after that. He'd returned to his hotel and ended up spending the night with a bottle of tequila obsessing over his involvement in putting Josh and Annika in danger.

Another failure in a long line of failures. If he had any gift at all, it was escaping unscathed from things that killed people more worthy than him.

"But, JB, I need to—"

He waved a hand, silencing her again, and concentrated on taking the top off his coffee.

While he'd never say it aloud, he'd originally gone to Africa for the same reason as so many others before him—to save the noble African. Then, also like so many before him, he'd discovered that the noble African didn't want to be saved. Most people who had that particular epiphany went home, told stories about their adventure, and buffed the memory until the tarnish faded. Not him, though. He'd stayed. Why? What had he hoped to accomplish? It was a question he'd never been able to answer but that always resurfaced when he drank Western booze.

"Seriously," Tracy said, "we need to talk."

He finally got the lid off his coffee and peered down at the dark fluid. "No cream. There are a hundred different coffee drinks on the menu, and you can't get cream. Tracy, would you mind—"

"I'm not getting you any damn cream!" she shouted.

He jerked back in surprise, snagging the wheels of his chair in the carpet and nearly tipping over backward. The entire office went silent.

"Now, you're going to just sit there and listen to me, JB."

He opened his mouth to protest but didn't manage to get any sound out before she jabbed a finger in his face. "Shut it!"

He did, and she slapped an eight-by-ten photo on the desk in front of him. It depicted a man in a long wool coat glancing back over hunched shoulders. The background had been erased, so there was no context. Just the man.

Flannary leaned in a little closer, examining the slightly blurry features of the face. The eyes had a subtle slope that suggested Eastern Europe to him. The skin was pale and the expression angry, but not at anything specific as much as life in general.

"This came in from the camera we set up," Tracy said. "He went into the NewAfrica building last night."

"So?"

"He's not an employee—"

"Maybe he's a donor. Or a delivery man. Or he was lost and needed directions."

"It was after hours, and he was in there for quite a while."

"Can't say I know him."

"Me either. So I posted his picture to some of the Internet crime forums."

"You did what?"

"Don't worry, I did it in a way that no one can trace the post back to us. And I took out the background so there's no way to locate it."

"I'm not sure that was a great idea, Tracy. We—"

"It *was* a great idea," she protested. "In fact, it was a *fantastic* idea. If two heads are better than one, then a thousand heads are better than two, right?"

It depended on how hard they were pounding. "And what did your thousand heads tell you?"

She grinned and slapped a copy of a newspaper article on top of the picture. The accompanying photo was a grainy copy of a bad original, but there was no doubt it was the same man. A little younger, perhaps, but the same tilted eyes and pissed-off expression. Flannary squinted at the text but couldn't make anything of it.

"It's in Czech," Tracy said. "The translation's on the back."

It was in her handwriting, with numerous scratch-outs and notes written in the margins. Obviously, she'd done the work herself.

"His name is Aleksei Fedorov," she said, saving him from having to decipher her writing. "He's a Russian businessman who everyone thinks was heavily connected to international drug and weapons trafficking. The Czech government thought they had him on a tax-evasion charge, but he managed to get out of it. After that the Europeans really turned the heat up on him. One prosecutor basically said he was going to make it his life's work to see Fedorov behind bars."

"This article is over ten years old. How'd it go?"

"Not so well. They found the prosecutor hanging from a tree."

"Suicide?" Flannary said hopefully.

"Only if he also managed to set himself on fire before he died."

"Great."

"After that Fedorov pretty much disappeared."

"But now you've found him."

She nodded. "I think you'll find this interesting: There was a lot of speculation that he was routing cocaine through African countries with corrupt governments. The idea was that law enforcement and the military would work for him instead of against him, and most of the people in those countries wouldn't know a bag of cocaine from a hole in the ground."

"So we have our connection to Africa," he said, feeling his hangover subside a bit.

"It gets better. Can you guess when NewAfrica was first chartered?"

"Right around when Fedorov disappeared?"

"Exactly. He lost his anonymity, and the government was

starting to close in on him in Europe. So he relocates to the U.S. and uses his contacts in Africa to start a bogus charity."

"But he needed a slick front man," Flannary said. "So he found Stephen Trent."

She grinned widely and lowered her voice. "Congratulations, JB. This is an incredible story—a known criminal causing incredible human suffering. And now you have the chance to blow it wide open. To make a real difference to the people this guy's victimizing."

"*We* have the chance, Tracy. We."

32

W hat do you think?" Annika said.

They were parked on top of a hill that gave them an unobstructed view of her village. The rising sun had turned the eastern sky into an orange ribbon that cast an ethereal glow over the tiny dwellings and whitewashed church below.

A few stovepipe chimneys had smoke rising from them, and a lone woman was walking toward the river for water, but everything else was still and silent.

"There could be an entire army waiting for us in those huts," Josh said. "We're about to bet our lives that Gideon's too stupid to have figured out who you are."

"Or that he thinks we wouldn't be crazy enough to come back here."

"Thin. Very, very thin."

The ascent of the sun dissipated the shadows, but, for the first time since he'd arrived, he took no comfort in seeing them go. "I'm sorry I got you into this, Annika."

"It's what I came here for, isn't it? To try to help people?" She smiled but wasn't able to completely mask her fear. "Besides, this is JB's fault. And I'm going to give him a hard kick when I see him next."

Josh fired the Land Cruiser's motor and glided down the hill, pulling up in front of the church and getting out.

They didn't speak as they crept through the gate protecting Annika's garden and entered the room that had been her home since she'd arrived in Africa. It was even more austere than he'd imagined—a twin bed neatly made with threadbare blankets, an old armoire, and a desk with a cross hanging above it.

"Give me some help," she said, kneeling next to the armoire. They slid it away from the wall, and she began prying up the loose floorboards that had been beneath it.

"What's that?" Josh said, catching a glimpse of gray metal. "You've got to be kidding me. A safe?"

"My father was afraid for me when I came here. He sent it."

"Did he send the concrete it's set in, too?"

She shook her head seriously and spun the combination dial. "I believe that you should put your faith in God. But a little cement doesn't hurt, either."

A moment later she had retrieved a pouch containing her passport and a stack of money about an inch thick.

"I don't suppose you have a gun in there."

"No guns," she said, hanging the pouch around her neck and slipping it beneath her shirt. Her expression melted into one of resigned melancholy as she looked around the room. "I'll never be back here."

With his mind occupied entirely by staying one step ahead of Gideon, Josh hadn't considered the effect all this would have on her. The village was her home. And not only that, it was the place she had devoted her life to. The people here were as much a family to her as the people she'd left in Europe.

And now it was over. No good-byes. No standing back and reflecting on everything she'd accomplished. No celebration of the village's bright future. She was just going to disappear forever.

"I'm so sorry Annika. I . . ."

His voice faded when the sound of an engine became audible, so close that it seemed as though it had been there the whole time and they just hadn't noticed it.

"Come on!" he said, grabbing her arm and pulling her toward the door that led to the garden. He threw it open, but instead of running for the jungle, he dragged Annika to the floor. They hit hard, but he still managed to kick the door shut just as a staccato burst of machine-gun fire sounded. Annika threw an arm over her face, protecting it from the splintering wood as the bullets penetrated the room. A moment later, the guns went silent, replaced by the sound of laughter.

Josh dragged the armoire into a position barricading the rear door while Annika crawled toward the one leading to the main part of the church. She peered through it for a moment and then motioned for him to follow as she ran crouched through the tightly packed benches. Angry shouts and terrified screams penetrated the gaps in the walls, echoing eerily around the structure.

Josh kept up for a few seconds but then slowed when it occurred to him that this was exactly what the men who had shot at them wanted—to flush them out the front of the church and into the square where their comrades were waiting.

Ahead of him, Annika slid up to the edge of a window and looked outside. The morning light illuminated her face, and he actually had to turn away when he saw the horror there. This was his fault. He'd killed them both.

In the small plaza, men in dirty fatigues were making a game of dragging terrified, half-dressed villagers from their homes. Children wailed, women struggled, and men were beaten with rifle butts at the slightest hint of resistance.

Josh counted six soldiers, all teenagers and all staggering drunk despite their tender age. The only adult stood in the shade of the machine gun mounted in the bed of the rust-eaten pickup he and his team had arrived in. He was unsteady but didn't seem quite as hammered as the others. His uniform, consisting of a pair of gray camouflage pants and an unbuttoned olive drab coat, was clean and untorn. There was a flash of pink and yellow whenever the jacket swung open, and Josh found himself mesmerized by the odd familiarity of it.

He moved closer to the window, concentrating on the man. Without the ubiquitous grin and subservient gait, he was transformed. But still there was no mistaking the Hawaiian shirt or bulging cheeks. Luganda.

Josh was too preoccupied with his bartender's betrayal to notice the quiet whimper that escaped Annika when a bawling child was thrown to the ground in an effort to shut him up. But he wasn't so distracted as to overlook her breaking for the church's front door. He chased her down before she could reach it, grabbing her around the waist and clamping a hand over her mouth as she fought against him.

"What are you going to do?" he whispered. "Throw rocks?"

She got an arm free and pulled his hand from her mouth. "This is about us, Josh. Not them."

He knew she was right, and he was disconcerted at how easy it was to hide from the realization. Everything in this country seemed vaguely like a movie to him—real enough to look at, maybe even interact with on some superficial level, but not an actual part of his reality.

When he was certain she'd stay put, he released her and went to the window again. Despite the lack of military discipline, Luganda's soldiers worked with impressive efficiency. The huts were all empty now, and the entire population of the village was kneeling in the square. It wasn't a movie. These were real people. And real guns.

"Is there any other way out of here?"

She didn't seem to hear him.

"Annika!"

She blinked a few times. "No. Just the front and back doors."

Outside, Luganda had one hand on the shoulder of what seemed to be his youngest soldier and was pointing at the church with the other. The kid, probably no older than thirteen, nodded reluctantly before heading their way. The other boys cheered him on drunkenly as he thrust out the machine gun hanging around his neck.

Josh looked behind him at the empty church, trying to quell the panic rising in him. The makeshift barricade of the back door seemed to have held, but judging from the silence coming from that part of the building, it was due more to a lack of interest than the strength of the barrier. Those men were just there to keep them boxed in.

"Is there anywhere we can go? Somewhere to hide?"

He let himself feel a small glimmer of hope when she took his hand and led him back down the aisle. She'd put in a safe, maybe she'd built an escape hatch of some sort. Or maybe she really did have guns and hadn't wanted to resort to them until it was absolutely necessary.

When they got back to her room, though, she knelt down in front of her desk and looked up at the cross.

"Annika, what the hell are you doing?"

"Praying. I know you say you're not religious, but I think you should pray with me. You might—"

"Are you fucking kidding me? There's a time and a place for praying, and this sure as hell isn't it."

"No? Then when?"

The sound of the front door to the church opening reached them, followed by the echo of approaching footsteps. He picked up one of the boards she'd removed to expose the safe while she looked on passively.

"What are you going to do with that, Josh? There are too many of them. And they're armed with more than sticks."

"I can't die here, Annika. I have a sister at home who needs me. I have things I want to do. . . ."

"Sometimes things are beyond our control."

He suddenly became aware of the weight of the sat phone in his pocket, and he clawed it out, dropping the board.

"Who are you calling?"

"Trent. I'm going to tell him that none of this is any of our business. That we just want the hell off this continent."

The footsteps on the other side of the closed door slowed, becoming more cautious.

"I'm going to tell him that if he calls these guys off, we'll never say anything about this."

Trent's office phone started to ring, and he thought about Laura. About how she'd take the news that he'd been gunned down in middle-of-nowhere Africa. About what would happen to her when she had no one to turn to—no one to shove her out of the life she'd been born to.

It was still ringing when the boy kicked the rickety door open. He started screaming in Xhisa, jerking the barrel of the gun from Josh to Annika and back again every second or so.

Josh put the phone slowly back into his pocket and retreated a few steps, holding his hands out in front of him. "Take it easy, kid. Okay?"

Annika looked around the room with an expression of sad nostalgia. She barely seemed to notice the shouting, gun-waving child.

"Talk to him," Josh said. "Say something!"

She shook her head. "They don't send children to negotiate, Josh. They send them to kill. We're his initiation into manhood."

"I'm not going to just stand here and let this little bastard shoot us."

"It happens every day here. To people more innocent than us."

The boy was shaking visibly, trying to conjure up enough rage to do what he had been told. Around his eyes, though, it was clear how far from home he was. And how much he wanted to be transported back there.

He swung his gun toward Annika yet again, but this time something in him had changed. He was ready.

Josh lunged, but it was too late. There was the deafening crack of the gun, Annika falling backward, the warm spatter of blood.

His momentum carried him into the boy, slamming him hard into the wall. The gun fell from his hands, and Josh grabbed for it, already fantasizing about using the butt to cave the kid's skull in and then going out the front door shooting. He might not ever leave this village, but he was going to make sure Luganda didn't, either.

The fury that was blinding him started to subside when he noticed that the boy wasn't fighting back. It was only then that he saw that part of the kid's head had been ripped away. Josh released him and watched him slide to the ground, finally comprehending what had happened. The rusted old Russian gun had blown up in his face.

He turned and dropped to his knees next to Annika's motionless body, yanking her T-shirt up and finding nothing but smooth, unbroken skin. The only blood on her was in her hair, a matted section above her left temple about the size of a silver dollar. He put a hand on her chest and felt the rise and fall of her breathing. She wasn't shot. She'd just hit her head on the bedpost when she'd fallen.

More shouting drifted in from the front, and he pushed closed the door leading to the church before opening the armoire and shoving the clothes hanging in it under the bed.

He dragged the boy's body across the floor, trying not to think about the mangled head nestled against his chest. His shirt was soaked with blood by the time he had crammed the body inside the armoire and closed the door.

When the urge to vomit subsided, he pulled Annika to the crimson puddle that the boy had left by the door, splaying her limbs artistically before lying down next to her.

Less than a minute passed before the door was thrown open.

He didn't move, looking through his nearly closed eyelids at the boots that passed by. Annika's right hand was beneath his leg, and he tried not to tense when it twitched. He hadn't prayed since he was a kid, but she was right. If not now, when?

Okay, God. I can understand why you might not want to help me out. But Annika's lived her whole life for you. Please don't let her wake up.

From what he could see from his position on the floor, there were three soldiers in the room, one of whom was Luganda. Even in Xhisa, Josh could confirm that his speech was slurred by alcohol.

"Agabezi!" Luganda shouted.

Probably the name of the kid leaking into the armoire. For obvious reasons, there was no answer, and the man said something that elicited guffaws from the other soldiers in the room. Maybe they thought that the boy had run off and hidden after killing them. If so, they obviously found it hilarious that an act as trivial as cold-blooded murder would bother the average adolescent.

Josh focused on staying completely relaxed and controlling his breathing, but what were the chances that no one would open the wardrobe or check to make sure they were really dead? When they did, though, he'd be ready. The board he'd dropped earlier was within reach, and with the element of surprise he still had a chance of cracking open Luganda's lying, back-stabbing skull before they shot him. Surely Annika's God wouldn't deny him that.

Luganda's dusty boot prodded Josh's shoulder and then delivered a hard kick to his stomach. He'd seen it coming and managed not to react, keeping his muscles slack as the pain flared and Luganda shouted down at what he assumed was a corpse.

Once again Josh cursed his inability to understand. He thought of the dismissiveness with which JB had treated Luganda and how he himself had fallen into that trap. He realized that he didn't know the first thing about the man—how old he was, if he had a family, how he'd come to work at the compound. The African had just faded into the background—a provider of drinks and maker of arrangements.

Luganda kicked him again, this time nearly falling over from the effort. When he regained his balance, he gurgled a few orders and Josh was lifted from the floor.

═══

The soldiers swung him back and forth a couple times, and then Josh felt himself floating in the air for a moment before slamming down in the bed of the pickup truck. Something metal jabbed into his back, but he managed to keep from grimacing. Not that it was likely the two soldiers would notice. They'd dropped him three times on the way through the church to hit off a jug of African moonshine and were well on their way to not even being able to stand.

Luganda could still be heard shouting the dead boy's name as Annika was thrown into the truck on top of him. Josh waited a few seconds before allowing himself to partially open one eye. From his position, no one was visible, and he dared a glance up at the belt-fed machine gun above him.

It was almost unbearably tempting. He'd never fired a gun like that, but it seemed simple enough. Jump up, throw the bolt, and a second later you were cutting people in half. The problem was, which people? It didn't exactly have the look of a surgical tool, and while he didn't have as big a problem as he should with leaving Annika's villagers to their own devices, shooting indiscriminately into them in an attempt to save his own skin was another matter entirely.

He shifted his head subtly to look over the truck's back gate as muffled shouts erupted from inside the church.

"Agabezi! Agabezi!"

It was a familiar theme, but with critical differences. The voice was unfamiliar, and the tone was panicked.

They'd found him.

Josh shoved Annika's limp body off him and leaped over the side of the pickup, spotting two soldiers running out of the church as others ran to meet them. No one was looking in his direction when he slid into the driver's seat and reached for the keys hanging in the ignition. That changed when the truck's sickly starter began to turn. The first shots sounded just as the engine caught. He slammed his foot to the floor, feeling the pickup's sluggish acceleration and watching the young soldiers grow larger in his rearview mirror.

He waited for the bullet that would kill him to penetrate what was left of the back of the cab, imagining it puncturing his lungs, leaving him to drown in his own blood while they pulled Annika from the back and beat her to death. Or worse.

But the bullet never came. There were shots—seemingly thousands of them—but the soldiers were too young and too drunk to hit anything.

Just before Josh rounded the corner and disappeared behind a low ridge, he stuck his arm out the open window and raised his middle finger.

33

Stephen Trent didn't rise from his desk when Gideon entered but jumped to his feet when Umboto Mtiti followed. He glimpsed soldiers taking up positions in the hallway before Mtiti slammed the door shut behind him.

"Mr. President," Trent stammered, feeling the sweat break cold at his hairline, "why didn't you tell me you were coming? We aren't prepared—"

"Yes, that's obvious, isn't it?"

Gideon's ubiquitous sunglasses were gone, revealing yellow-and-black eyes. The casual arrogance of his stride had disappeared, too, replaced by the awkward gait of someone completely consumed with not doing or saying the wrong thing.

"To what do I owe this honor, Excellency?"

Mtiti sat in one of the chairs in front of Trent's desk, the medals on his uniform rattling ominously. Gideon stood well behind him, partly out of subservience and partly in an attempt to disappear.

"Your new man found the bodies of the people we relocated," Mtiti said.

Trent didn't answer immediately, trying to focus on what he

had heard and not on how vulnerable and far from home he was. "I don't understand, sir. How could that be possible?"

"I'm told that he hid the phone you gave him in some old hag's belongings. Apparently there is a GPS in this phone?"

Trent's legs were in danger of failing him, and he sank into his chair. He looked past Mtiti at Gideon. "How could you and your people not know that?"

Gideon had never made any bones about the fact that he considered Trent weak and pathetic—good at cleverly carrying out Mtiti's will but of little use otherwise. In a world where one was judged on physical strength, courage, and willingness to do violence, Trent knew he came up far short.

"This is your fault," Gideon said. "You should never have given him the phone."

That prompted Trent to return his slightly averted gaze to the president. As usual, Mtiti's face was a thick mask, equally likely to break into insane laughter or homicidal rage at any moment.

"We gave him the phone so Gideon could keep track of him. Just like Dan. Just like everyone."

Mtiti didn't react, but out of the corner of his eye, Trent could see Gideon glaring defiantly. It infuriated Gideon to have to explain himself in the presence of the soft, pale man in front of him—to know that Trent's business relationship with the president could eclipse Gideon's own blood connection. He understood his position well, though, and was smart enough to be careful.

"I don't understand how this happened," Trent continued. "How do you know he used the phone to track those people? Did you see him at the gravesite? Did you just stand there?"

"If it weren't for me, we wouldn't have discovered any of this," Gideon said, the volume of his voice rising, but not quite to his normal shout. "He would be on his way to America, knowing everything."

Trent was about to fire back but held his tongue. It seemed likely that Gideon had indeed known about the phone and had left it where it was, salivating over the thought of exacting his own personal revenge against Josh Hagarty. And then he'd let him get away.

But making that accusation any more forcefully could be dangerous. Just as Gideon had to acknowledge the power of business relationships, Trent had to acknowledge that family relations represented a bond too strong and complex to be trifled with by an outsider.

"Enough of this," Mtiti said. "Where are they now?"

"'They'?" Trent said.

"He's with a white woman," Gideon replied. "They went to the village where she works. I sent soldiers, but they escaped."

"They escaped?" Trent said incredulously. "Two unarmed whites—one of whom is a woman—escaped your soldiers?"

Gideon stared silently back at him.

"Who has the phone now? You or them?" Trent asked.

"They do," Mtiti said. "Find them. Now."

Trent reached for his laptop and pulled up the website used to track the location of the sat phone. He entered his user name and password and waited for the screen to respond.

Invalid log-in.

He typed them in again, more carefully this time, but knew it was futile. Josh Hagarty was many things, but he wasn't an idiot.

"They've changed the password."

"Change it back," Mtiti said.

"It's not that simple, Excellency."

"Why is it not simple? It's your phone, isn't it? Didn't you pay for it? Didn't you buy it from a company in your country? Maybe you don't want to change it back. Maybe you're working for this phone company? Maybe they want to take over the communications in my country and give them to the Yvimbo."

"Excellency," Trent said, struggling to maintain a soothing tone, "it's the same security system that's used all over the world. I can have the phone shut off, but it's going to be very complicated to—"

"So once again, *I* have to do this. I have to clean up your problems. Like I did with your last man."

"We can have this taken care of quickly and easily, Excellency. You just need to have your people watch the airports and—"

"Are you telling me how to find two whites in my own country?"

"No. I'm just saying that we need to coordinate—"

"What do we need to coordinate? Why do I need you? You and your people are the cause of these problems! And now you're going to tell me how to solve them? You're going to give me orders?"

"I wouldn't presume—"

"But you already have, haven't you? That's what you people do. You presume."

━━

Stephen Trent made himself a drink and looked around the empty office. Mtiti and his people had been gone for almost fifteen minutes, but the tension remained. He could hear the staff outside, chattering nervously and working as if their lives depended on it. As if Mtiti was deciding whether their contributions to his country were worth the food and air he wasted on them.

Trent supposed that bargains with the devil always seemed good at first. He had avoided not only prison but also a criminal record and gotten a well-paid job in New York running Aleksei Fedorov's new pet project. But when it had become apparent that the potential profits and lack of oversight were beyond even Fedorov's most optimistic estimates, the freedom that Trent had been so grateful for began to look more like slavery.

At first Mtiti had been lukewarm to Fedorov's proposal, but it hadn't taken long for NewAfrica to prove itself. Whenever it was involved, the world was blinded by the fundamental assumption that all intentions were good and that the charity itself would police any problems that arose. And even when reports of serious issues did surface, the reaction was generally to downplay them for what the aid industry assumed was the greater good.

Soon greed had overtaken caution. The diversion and sale of donated goods was combined with narcotics trafficking. And when that proved successful, they had added arms dealing, and finally the genocide that Josh Hagarty had discovered.

Now Mtiti not only expected to be able to butcher his enemies in broad daylight, he expected NewAfrica to get him a humanitarian prize for it. And for Aleksei, there wasn't enough money in the world.

So at a time when every indication was that they should be pulling back and taking fewer risks, they continued to recklessly expand. And it was that blind ambition that had created the situations with Dan and Josh.

Trent dialed the phone on his desk and cradled the handset between his ear and shoulder. His hand didn't shake when he put his drink to his lips. The sense of inevitability made fear seem increasingly pointless.

"What?" Fedorov said by way of greeting.

"Josh Hagarty saw the new project, Aleksei. He saw the graves."

There was a brief silence before he exploded. "What the fuck are you talking about? How could he find the dump site? How would he know anything about it?"

"I—"

"Where is he now? You have him, right?"

"No. He ran. He—"

"Does Mtiti know?"

"Yes. He just left my office."

"You told him? You told that stupid piece of shit without calling me first? Are you fucking crazy? Do you have any idea what you're putting in jeopardy, Stephen? Do you?"

It was pointless to protest or try to set the record straight. Fedorov knew damn well that Trent wouldn't go to Mtiti without his approval. But he believed whatever best fueled the fury that kept him going. "I understand very well, Aleksei. I'm the one who's here. I'll be the one Mtiti comes for if things go wrong."

"So what you're saying is that it won't have any effect on me at all if you collapse everything I've built? Everything—"

"We can take care of this, Aleksei. And there's no way Josh Hagarty could know about you."

"Are you willing to bet your life on it?"

Trent knew he already had. It could be a few weeks from now or a few years, but he didn't doubt that he would die a violent, drawn-out death. Whether it would be savage and primitive at the hands of Mtiti or the colder, more precise suffering that Fedorov would inflict was unimportant.

"We have another problem, Aleksei. One that Mtiti doesn't know about. JB Flannary is back in the United States."

"The reporter? So what?"

"I find it suspicious that after only a few weeks Josh is behaving like Dan did after being here over a year."

"You think Flannary's behind it?"

"I don't know, but he didn't always write sunny stories about the benefits of foreign aid. In his day, he burned a few charities pretty badly."

"And you let him out of Africa, where he could have been dealt with at the snap of a fucking finger?"

"I can't track everyone in the country, Aleksei. I don't have the manpower."

"And so you sit over there in your villa with all your servants and call me when you've completely fucked things up?"

It was an interpretation of the situation that Fedorov undoubtedly believed wholeheartedly. "I'm sorry, Aleksei. I'm doing my best, but you have to understand that it's barely controlled chaos here. I—"

"Shut the fuck up. Just shut up!"

"Aleksei, please. Josh still has the phone we gave him. I can't track him with it, but I *can* use it to contact him. You need to send people for his sister. Once we have her, we'll have control of the situation again."

Fedorov let out a long string of expletives in his native language as Trent drained the Scotch from his glass. Josh's close relationship with his sister and the relatively easy access to her was one of the reasons they'd picked him. It had been something Fedorov had insisted on after the problems with Dan Ordman, but not a card Trent had ever expected to play. She was an innocent seventeen-year-old girl. But, like her brother, she would never get a chance at the life she'd so recently started.

"Where's Flannary?" Fedorov said finally.

"I don't know exactly. He has family in New York and connections to a magazine there."

"So I guess you want me to handle that, too, don't you, Stephen?"

34

"Mom!" Josh shouted into the sat phone. "This is important. When was the last time you saw Laura?"

"I don't know. Maybe yesterday?" She sounded relatively lucid —he must have caught her in that critical time between creeping hangover and early buzz.

Josh scooted back a few inches, pulling Annika out of the encroaching sun and letting her head settle in his lap again. She'd regained consciousness about an hour after they'd escaped the village, but then immediately went out again. The blow to her head had been harder than he'd originally thought, but he had no idea what to do about it. Help was absolutely not on its way.

"What about last night, Mom? Did you see her then?"

"Where are you, Josh?"

"I'm in Africa, remember? Now, concentrate. Did you see her last night?"

"I don't think she was here. I don't know where she is. Do you want me to have her call you?"

Annika stirred, and he ran a hand through her hair, trying to will her eyes open. It didn't work.

"Mom, you need to listen to me. You can't have Ernie Bruce
... Mom? Are you there?"

The connection had gone dead.

A quick glance at the battery indicator showed half a charge,
and he dialed again, only to get a recording saying that the service
had been cut off.

Trent.

He sagged against the tree behind him and stared up at the
endless blue of the sky. How the hell had all this happened? A few
months ago, he'd been sitting around eating nachos with his friends
and worrying about getting a B-plus in Quantitative Methods.

"Josh?"

Annika was looking up at him with reasonably clear eyes and a
symmetrical expression that didn't seem to indicate brain damage.
He let out a long, relieved breath. "Jesus, Annika. I was really
starting to worry. Are you okay? How are you feeling?"

"I don't understand. What happened?"

Based on the last thing she'd seen before she was knocked out,
she'd probably expected to wake up at the pearly gates, not lying in
the dirt next to a stolen truck.

"We got away."

He helped her into a sitting position and kept her steady while
her light-headedness passed.

"How?"

"It's a long story."

"What about the village?"

"I don't know."

He tried to prevent her from standing, but she shook him off
and walked unsteadily away, stopping after twenty-five feet to
look out over the sweeping landscape below. They were a good
seven hours from her village, parked on top of a steep hill surrounded by rebel territory. He figured Mtiti's men would think

twice about penetrating this far into Yvimbo-controlled land, but if they didn't, at least the elevated position would allow Josh to see what was coming.

"Were any of the soldiers hurt when we escaped?" Her voice was getting stronger, but he wasn't sure that was a good thing.

"The kid who tried to shoot you is dead. His gun blew up on him."

She put her face in her hands, and for a moment he thought she was going to fall.

"I didn't have anything to do with it, Annika. It just happened."

"We weren't supposed to get away."

"What do you mean?" he said, though he knew perfectly well.

She turned toward him. "I'm talking about how angry our escaping would make those soldiers. I'm talking about what they might have done to my friends because of that anger."

"I saw the opportunity, and I took it, Annika. What did you want me to do? Watch them gang-rape you and then hack you apart with a machete before they staked me out and set me on fire?"

"Yes!" she said. "We're two people, Josh. There are sixty people living in that village. Sixty people who had nothing to do with any of this."

"Nothing to do with any of this?" he said, jumping to his feet. "Are you kidding? This is *their* country. Mtiti is *their* president. Those soldiers are *their* children. Not yours. And sure as hell not mine."

"They have no control—"

"Bullshit! That's all I hear from you aid people. Everybody's the saintly victim of a few bad apples. What would happen if the Yvimbo took over? Would they start the first honest government in Africa? Or would they start a genocidal war against the Xhisa? There are no victims here, Annika. There are just people who aren't well-armed enough."

"Just another bunch of Africans," she responded, the tears now visible on her cheeks. "That's what you're saying, isn't it? It doesn't matter if they live or die, right?"

"That's not what I mean—"

"But it's not your fault," she said, her words no longer seeming to be aimed at him. "You just got here. You didn't know any of the people in that village. Why did I go to the window to look out? I knew what was happening. Why didn't I go straight through that door? Those people have been my family for most of my adult life. It was my home."

"For Christ's sake, Annika. You'd just been shot at with a machine gun—you weren't thinking straight. You got scared. You're allowed."

She turned and walked away again, disappearing down a steep slope before he could think of something to say.

He didn't understand any of this—not the country, not the people who populated it. Not even his own motivations. Would he have done the same thing if that village had been full of American women and children? And if so, would it have been as easy?

———

She returned a half hour later, just as he was getting worried enough to go after her.

"Annika, I'm sorry. This was my fault. I stopped you when you tried to go out and help those people. And when I saw a chance for us, I took it without thinking about the consequences."

"It's done," she said, though her tone was ambiguous. No anger but also no forgiveness. For either of them. "Are we in rebel territory?"

"Yeah."

She nodded toward the truck. "What do we have?"

"Not much," he said, grateful for the change in subject. "There's about fifty rounds of ammunition for the gun. A few tools, five gallons of water, and a bag of half-melted candy bars I bought when I stopped for gas."

"How much money do we have left?"

"There wasn't that much to begin with," he said, pulling her pouch of cash from around his neck and holding it out to her. "About three hundred euros."

"This isn't exactly what I had in mind when I decided how much to put in that safe."

"I know," he said. "What do you think we should do?"

She considered it for a moment, avoiding looking at him. "I think we should save my village if it isn't already too late. I think we should send Umboto Mtiti to hell. And I think your friend Stephen Trent should go with him."

Based on her expression, she was dead serious.

"I was thinking on a less grand scale . . ."

"Well, we can't stay here. The food and water you brought aren't going to last more than a few days."

"What, then?"

"We have no idea when JB's story is going to get published, isn't that right? Or even for sure if it ever will. And it's very hard for us to hide because of our skin."

"What about a rebel village? They hate the government. Maybe they'd help us."

"Mtiti doesn't control this area, but he has informants everywhere."

"What do you figure our chances would be?"

"Not very good."

"I was looking for a number."

"Maybe ten percent?"

He let out a long breath. "Jesus. I thought you'd at least say fifty-fifty. Okay, what if we were to split up?"

"Split up? Why?"

"If we both get caught, we're dead. But what if they only got one of us? It seems like they'd try to use us against each other. It might buy us the time we need for JB's story to come out."

"I don't think that makes any sense."

"You know your way around here, Annika. You speak the language, you know the culture. Maybe you could find someone who could help the people in your village—or at least find out what happened."

She obviously hadn't considered that, and her expression turned thoughtful. "What about you?"

"I'd just be in your way."

"And where wouldn't you be in my way?"

"Back in civilization. I can try to contact the U.S. Consulate and maybe get the sat phone turned back on. Maybe I could get in touch with JB and find out exactly what his time frame is. He might even know someone who can help us."

"Your sister. Isn't that what you mean? You need to know what's happened to her."

He looked at the ground, not sure what to say. She was in the same position, but instead of one girl, she had an entire village to worry about. More and more it seemed like his every act was motivated by selfishness.

"I have to get in touch with her," he admitted finally. "I have to know if she's okay."

"I understand."

"I'm not a bad person, Annika."

"I know. Neither of us is. I just can't decide if we're good ones."

35

JB Flannary squinted into the refrigerator and focused on a lonely jar of olives. Robert Page's country home was typical of the New York set: It was neither in the country nor homey. Nothing more than an expensive and generally useless bauble expected in the circles he traveled in.

"There's nothing in there," Page said, poking his head through the door to the dimly lit kitchen.

"You're the master of the obvious."

"I don't need a bunch of your attitude, JB. Get yourself a drink, and the pizzas I ordered will be here before you even have a good buzz on."

The bar was better-stocked than the refrigerator, and Flannary poured himself a tall Scotch as Page disappeared back into the living room. The snowball that he had nudged downhill was now picking up speed and mass, careening out of control, threatening to crush everything in its path. The messages left on Josh's phone about Fedorov had gone unanswered, and now that phone was out of service. A call to Katie confirmed that Josh hadn't been seen at the compound in days and that his project had been shut down.

Now everyone was trapped. If he backed off and didn't publish the article, Mtiti would eventually find Josh and Annika, and they'd be dead. On the other hand, if he did publish the article, there was no telling what would happen to Mtiti and his country. Based on the history of the area, his best guess was a bloody tribal war that would kill tens of thousands and create a refugee crisis that could drag surrounding countries into the conflict. And from that would come . . . nothing.

He downed the Scotch, standing straight and examining his face in the dark window over the sink. The sun-damaged skin and lack of hair made him look older than his birth certificate indicated. As far as he was concerned, the birth certificate was wrong—he'd lived three lifetimes. Or at least seen three lifetimes' worth of the horrors men could unleash on each other.

The Scotch was doing its job taking the edge off, and he returned to the living room. Tracy was sitting at a table typing on her laptop while Page organized stacks of paper on the floor.

"Have you looked at these numbers?" Page asked. "NewAfrica has administered more than seventy-five million dollars in USAID and UN programs. How much of that do you think found its way into their pockets? The oversight reports we've got give them glowing ratings."

Flannary shrugged. "Oversight's looking for competence and efficiency. If your main goal is to create that illusion, it wouldn't be hard to fool them."

Tracy glanced up from her computer. "If the inspectors are assuming that NewAfrica's an honest, good-intentioned charity, they'd be completely blind to this kind of thing. As sick and twisted as he is, you almost have to admire Fedorov for coming up with it."

She was almost giddy. It was the story she'd been dreaming of her entire life—all twenty-odd years of it. In her mind, she would become the hero every journalism student dreamed of being. She would bring down a vicious organized crime figure and snatch millions of helpless Africans from the clutches of an evil, corrupt government. JB tried to remember if he'd ever been young enough to see life in such simple terms.

"Did your guy get photos of the mass grave?" Page asked.

"My guy? He's not my guy."

"You sent him there, didn't you?"

"Hell, no, I didn't send him there! I asked him to go check out one of NewAfrica's old projects. Nothing more."

His tone made Tracy look up from her computer and Page put his hands up submissively. "Take it easy, JB. I'm not accusing you of anything. I just want to know if we have any photographic evidence."

"I think they were busy being shot at."

"Is there any way they could get back there and get pictures? Shit, if we could get something of them moving those bodies, we could—"

"Are you fucking crazy, Bob? They're probably already dead. And if they're not—"

"Don't shout at me, JB. I'm on your side, remember? I just want this piece to be as strong as possible. I want it to be a bomb going off in Washington. And so do you. I'm prepared to give you basically as much space as you need and maybe even some latitude to talk about the failures of the aid industry in general. But we need reaction from USAID and the UN, we need to talk to Mtiti's opposition in country, and we need to try to figure out where all this money's gone. If we put in the time, I see this as a cover. What would you think of that, JB? A cover story."

His smile faded as Flannary stared dumbly at him.

"Have you not been listening to what I've been saying, Bob?"

"We might be able to make month after next. I'd be willing to bump—"

"Josh and Annika might not make it to next week! We put together whatever we can by the deadline for this issue and get it out there. Or I go to the *Times*."

"The *Times*?" Page said. "With what? A picture of Aleksei

Fedorov walking into a building and a phone call from a guy you can't even get in touch with anymore? Yeah, I'm sure they'll jump right on that."

"If I take this to my brother—"

"He'll tell you the same thing I'm telling you. The *Times* isn't the *Enquirer,* and neither are we."

The doorbell rang, and Tracy stood, clearly happy to have an excuse to leave the room. "That's the pizza. I'll get it."

Flannary ignored her as she hurried down the hall. "Then maybe I should go to the *Enquirer*. Maybe they'd show some guts."

"Guts? You mean the courage it takes to run a bunch of bullshit speculation when you have the ability to write a Pulitzer-worthy piece that could do some real good? What kind of impact . . ." His voice trailed off, and his gaze fixed over Flannary's shoulder.

"Don't let us interrupt."

The voice was only lightly accented but still recognizable as Eastern European. Flannary turned slowly, careful not to make any threatening moves.

Tracy was being held by a man who was nearly ripping the hair from her scalp with one hand and covering her mouth with the other. A second man pulled the shades down and then crossed the room, stopping with the barrel of his gun hovering an inch from Robert Page's temple.

The man at the center of it all was easily recognizable from the video they'd taken. Same expression and, as near as Flannary could tell, the same clothes.

"Clever," Aleksei Fedorov said, holding up the webcam Tracy had set up across from the NewAfrica office. Flannary barely had time to raise an arm to protect himself when Fedorov suddenly threw the camera. It shattered against his elbow, knocking him off balance long enough for Fedorov to rush him and slam him back against the wall.

He'd miscalculated, though, not taking into account the fact that he wasn't dealing with a typical middle-aged American reporter. Flannary had spent his life in some of the most violent places on earth, and, without thinking, he swung a fist at the European's head. The force of the blow drove Fedorov to his knees, and Flannary realized that with one well-placed kick, he might just be able to separate this piece of shit's head from his body. To avenge all the helpless people whose meager lives he'd destroyed.

Flannary swung his foot with everything he had, his whole body going tense as he focused on his target. He was six inches from smashing that dead expression right off Fedorov's face when the man who had been covering Page tackled him.

As they hit the floor, the familiar sound of a gunshot filled the room, accompanied by a less familiar ache in his stomach. The lights above seemed to fade for a moment and then became too bright. Flannary squinted up at them, only vaguely aware of Tracy's screams or of Fedorov dragging the man off him.

A moment later, Tracy was next to him, pressing her hand against his stomach, crying soundlessly. He glanced down at the blood gurgling around her fingers and then back at Fedorov, who was bringing a gun butt down repeatedly on the head of the man who had shot him.

36

Much of the capital city was dark, the power outages that occasionally swept across the country having become chronic over the last few days. Josh was standing just inside a small alley in one of the few neighborhoods that had power. Bare bulbs hung from wires strung between buildings, illuminating the well-armed men patrolling the streets. They seemed unusually vigilant, probably worried that the loss of electricity would embolden the rebels, who were becoming increasingly aggressive in their attacks.

Josh had done everything he could to avoid coming into the city—stopping at no fewer than ten villages and towns to find a working phone or Internet connection, with no luck. The consensus, delivered with that unwavering African fatalism, was that the problems were likely to persist for the foreseeable future.

That had left him no choice but to drive his stolen pickup right into Trent and Mtiti's back yard, aiming it at the still-powered business district before parking and covering the last half mile on foot. Jeans, a hooded sweatshirt, and hands in his pockets, provided him with enough anonymity to make it to a tiny storefront with "Phone and Internet Here" graffitied over a well-lit window.

Josh had a lot of regrets in his life but few moments that he would say actually haunted him. Laura crying at his sentencing was one. And now he could add the image of Annika standing on an empty roadside, receding in his rearview mirror. He'd actually skidded to a stop a few miles later, overwhelmed by the need to go back for her but fully aware of the pointlessness of it. Staying together didn't make sense. She was better off where she was. Better off without him.

There were very few people in his life who really meant anything to him, and now he'd managed to put two of them in mortal danger. It was time to stop playing the helpless foreigner and make sure they were safe. What happened to him wasn't important anymore.

A burst of gunfire sounded for what was probably the tenth time in the last hour, and the soldiers drinking in the middle of the intersection across from Josh began jogging halfheartedly toward it. When they were out of sight, he started nervously across the street and entered the store he'd been staking out.

It was crammed with a little bit of everything—Western and African medicine, used clothing, videotapes, canned food. There was a dirty computer at the back, and when Josh pointed to it, the man behind the counter nodded.

Josh sat on the upended log that functioned as a chair and looked skeptically at the screen. Improbably, the Internet connection was functioning, and even more improbably, it was relatively fast. He glanced behind him every few seconds, but the store remained empty, and the man at the counter appeared to be mesmerized by the black-and-white image of Umboto Mtiti on a minuscule television. The distorted, angry sound of his speech filled the store, evoking the same sense of dread as the hum of a nearby hornets' nest.

Josh knew he needed to get out of there as fast as he could, but he had a long list of tasks he had to accomplish first. He had to see if he could contact the U.S. Consulate, since his effort to drive there had been stymied by military roadblocks. He also had to see if he could get the sat phone he'd left with Annika turned back on. But first things first. E-mail.

He felt a wave of panic that there was nothing from Laura but managed to fight it off. It didn't mean anything. In fact, it was exactly what he should have expected. Right?

Nothing from JB, either, but there was something from someone named Tracy Collins with the subject line: *Important Info from JB Flannary!!*

He clicked on one of the linked files and waited for the overtaxed processor to bring up a scan of an old newspaper article. It was in a foreign language, so he concentrated on the photo for a moment. The wavy-haired man had an Eastern European look, thin and intense. The overall impression was that he was someone not to be fucked with. Unfortunately, Josh had a sinking feeling that that was exactly what he'd done.

He paged down to a handwritten translation of the article and began to scan it, becoming so engrossed that he didn't notice the quiet footsteps approaching from behind until the stained blade of a machete was pressed against his throat. He was dragged backward and slammed to the ground, the position of the machete making it impossible to fight back. His hood was pulled back, and the pressure of the blade increased until it broke the skin, causing blood to mingle with the sweat on his neck. Josh remained perfectly still, taking rapid, shallow breaths and watching his reflection in Gideon's sunglasses.

Stephen Trent appeared a moment later, righting the log and taking a seat on it. He motioned toward the door, and a young African man appeared. A moment later, he was kneeling in front of the computer tapping on the keyboard.

"I can't imagine what you were thinking," Trent said.

Josh didn't respond, afraid that any movement of his neck muscles would cause the machete to dig deeper. Out of the corner of his eye, he could see the shopkeeper locking the door and pulling tattered curtains.

"Do you know how much trouble you've caused us?" Trent said, nodding toward Gideon, who reluctantly eased up on the blade.

"A lot, I hope."

Trent shook his head sadly. "Not as much as you probably think. You've been a real irritation, though, I'll give you that. Do you know that Mtiti had to cut off phone, power, or both everywhere except for a few blocks here in the capital? He had to pull soldiers from other assignments to track you when you entered the city and make sure you didn't get anywhere you could do more harm. And I'll tell you right now that he's going to bill us for every dime of this operation."

"Maybe you could do a telethon."

Trent grinned. "I like you, Josh. I'd hoped to bring you along slowly, let you in on what we're doing here. But you didn't need me to say a word, did you? You figured it all out on your own."

The man at the computer stood and turned toward them. "Done."

"You got everything?"

He nodded, and Trent returned his attention to Josh. "We wouldn't want anything to happen to you with a bunch of information on Aleksei sitting in your inbox, would we?"

"Fuck you."

"Don't be belligerent. You had to know this was going to happen. Why go looking for trouble? Why get involved? You don't owe these people anything. Not one of them gives a shit whether you live or die. You're just another white face with money they want to get their hands on." He became increasingly agitated as he spoke, but Josh wasn't sure why. "If you'd just kept your nose out of things, you'd have been living in an air-conditioned villa making more money than you can imagine in a few years. And your sister would be driving a Mercedes around Harvard."

Josh tensed at the mention of Laura, and Trent noticed. "I'm sorry," he said, pulling a phone from his pocket and beginning to dial. "You must be worried sick. Would you like to talk to her?"

Trent put the phone to his ear and waited for the person on the other end to pick up. "We've got him. Uh-huh. He was in his e-mail account when we got here. Everything's been erased. Yeah, he's right here."

Trent held the phone out, and Josh concentrated on not reacting as a thin voice emanated from it. "Josh? Who are these people? You have to help me! They say they're going to—"

Her voice was suddenly cut off, and Josh laid his head back on the floor, his heart pounding uncontrollably. Gideon pulled him to his feet and forced him out into the humid night. Trent followed, still talking on the phone.

"We don't know yet, Aleksei. Yes. It's not going to be a problem. We'll find out."

Gideon opened the rear hatch on Trent's Land Cruiser and shoved Josh inside. There was already someone there, reclining against the back of the seat, face in shadow. His profound stillness left no doubt that he was dead, but it wasn't until the vehicle started moving that Josh caught a glimpse of a blood-stained Hawaiian shirt beneath the green jacket.

Luganda had paid the price for displeasing Umboto Mtiti and NewAfrica. Now it looked like it was Josh's turn.

37

Aleksei Fedorov slapped the duct tape back onto the girl's mouth and went back to screaming into his phone. "Where's Annika Gritdal? This is your responsibility! Do you understand me? Your goddamn responsibility."

Flannary watched, blinking hard in an effort to keep his vision clear.

They didn't have Annika.

He tried to concentrate on that, but it was too thin a victory to hide the defeats. To make him forget his own stupidity and the lives it was about to destroy.

He was lying on a concrete floor in a warehouse full of unmarked crates, the only heat provided by the growing puddle of blood leaking from his belly. Page and Tracy were twenty feet away, secured to chairs next to the wide-eyed blond girl Fedorov had just silenced.

Flannary scooted weakly to his right until he was pressed up against the woman next to him. Her dead eyes stared at the lights hanging high above them, and he tried to recall what she'd said her name was when she'd allowed them to set up that camera on her balcony. The memory was gone, though, so he just lay there stealing what heat was left in her body. Because of him, she didn't need it anymore.

"Are you in?" Fedorov said, leaning over the shoulder of a young man with the distinction of being the only person in the warehouse sitting without the assistance of a roll of duct tape. He had a portable computer on his lap, and his eyes kept flicking nervously from the blood gurgling past Flannary's unfeeling fingers to the dead woman he'd cuddled up with to the three panicked people struggling to free themselves.

"With the managing editor's password, I have access to their entire system. I've deleted all the obvious references to NewAfrica, and now I'm running a search with as many keywords as I can think of to make sure I got everything. I'm pretty sure I did, though."

Page grunted as he pulled against his bonds, and Flannary let his head loll in the editor's direction. He was virtually unharmed— nothing more than a red mark on his cheek in the rough shape of Fedorov's hand. It was all that had been necessary to get him to give up everything he knew in a breathless stream peppered with pleas for mercy and promises to keep his mouth shut. Tracy had been tougher, but what was a girl to do when an Eastern European psychopath threatened to skin her alive?

Fedorov turned toward Flannary and smiled. "So that's about it isn't it, JB? All your notes were at that house, and now they're a pile of ashes. Everything about this in the magazine's archive, all the phone messages, and virtually all the e-mails have been erased—even your friend Josh's. He was in his account when my people found him."

Flannary stared back at him, but the image was starting to swim. Probably just another milestone on his slow journey to bleeding to death. At this point, sooner would probably be better than later.

"Are you thinking about your Swedish Jesus freak, JB? Are

you? Because I guarantee she'll be dead by tomorrow." He thumbed to the blond girl behind him. "You've never met Laura Hagarty, have you? I understand that your friend Josh practically raised her from a baby. So when it comes down to her or Annika Gritdal, who do you think he'll choose?"

Flannary turned his attention to the blond girl for a moment. Laura Hagarty. Of course. He was losing his ability to think.

"That's right," Fedorov continued. "He'll give up your little Swedish bitch in a second."

"Norwegian." Flannary managed to get out.

"What?"

"She's Norwegian, you sociopathic Eurotrash prick." The act of getting out an insult that long left him feeling like he'd run a marathon.

"I don't think her nationality will matter much to the Africans I hand her over to, do you?" Fedorov said, walking behind Page and tossing a rope over a rafter above him. He began casually tying a slipknot in one end as he spoke. "Just one more thing to do, eh, JB? I need the password for your e-mail account."

Page threw himself back and forth in his chair, trying futilely to prevent the makeshift noose from being slipped around his neck. Unable to watch, Flannary fixed his gaze on Laura Hagarty, but the terror etched on her face was just as bad.

He hadn't realized how numb he'd become over the years. How easy it was for him to detach himself from the violence and misery around him. Maybe Annika was right about there being a God. And now He had decided to show Flannary the difference between being a spectator and being a participant.

The sound of Page trying to scream through the tape over his mouth finally pulled Flannary back into the present, and he looked back at his old friend. Fedorov was standing with one hand on the rope and the other on Page's shoulder. "The password, JB. Give me the password."

"What's in it for me?" he said, his voice barely a whisper.

"What's in it for you?" Fedorov's brow furrowed. "You make me curious. What do you want?"

There was no point in asking for anything unreasonable—his bargaining position wasn't that strong, and his ability to enforce any agreement between them was nonexistent. "Kill them quick."

Tracy's head fell forward, her young body convulsing as she finally began to sob. Even after all this, she'd thought he would save her. That he'd be the shining hero.

"Let me think about that," Fedorov said and then threw his weight into the rope, hoisting Page up by the neck.

There were any number of cranes running across the warehouse's ceiling, but Fedorov didn't use one, instead fighting personally with the rope, trying to get the chair entirely off the floor.

Page's eyes bulged and his face turned red as he tried to fight, lacking the leverage to do much more than rock his shoulders. It took only a few moments before his body went slack, but Aleksei held him for much longer than that, his knuckles turning white around the rope and his eyes flashing with sadistic joy.

Finally he let go. The chair's legs slammed back to the floor and Page's body slumped forward against its bonds.

Fedorov removed the noose and put it around Tracy's neck. She didn't bother to resist, instead fixing her gaze on Flannary as he tried to push himself into a sitting position.

"If you do that to her, you'll never get my password. You hear me, Aleksei? Never."

"I still have Hagarty's sister."

"You can't kill her until he gives up Annika. And . . ." His voice lost its strength, and for a moment he wasn't sure it was going to come back. ". . . I'm not going to last that long."

Fedorov pulled a handgun from his waistband and pointed it at Tracy's head. Flannary expected some kind of discussion: a "who goes first" negotiation, a few threats. But it didn't happen that way. She was still looking right at him when the bullet penetrated her skull.

He was having a hard time breathing, and he let his head sink back to the floor. For the first time in twenty years, he wanted to cry. But it was too late for that.

"We made a deal," Fedorov said.

And a deal was a deal.

"Mtiti," Flannary said. The body of the woman next to him had cooled to the point that it could no longer provide the heat he needed. God, how he hated the cold.

"That's it," he heard the man with the laptop say. "I'm in."

A moment later, Fedorov's face was hovering over him, silhouetted by the lights above. He pressed the barrel of his gun against Flannary's forehead. "What does it feel like, JB? What does it feel like to watch every friend you've ever had die because you decided to save a bunch of niggers who don't want to be saved? Do you really believe that any of this would have made a difference?"

Fedorov's voice was becoming increasingly distant, but his question still made it through. Something for Flannary to ponder on his way to hell.

38

Josh Hagarty was surprised when they pulled up to Stephen Trent's bougainvillea-entangled gate, though he wasn't sure why. In America, driving through the high-rent district with a dead body and a kidnap victim was frowned upon, but here it was just business as usual. Who was going to stop them and complain? The cops? Soldiers? A concerned citizen? Not likely.

He had briefly considered trying to get the back hatch open and running for it, but quickly dismissed the idea. He was trapped in a universe created and presided over by the all-powerful Umboto Mtiti. There was nowhere to go.

Gideon parked and came around back, yanking the door open and dragging Josh out by the hair. What fight was left in him disappeared when he noticed the flag-decorated black Mercedes near Trent's front door. He'd seen it many times on the blurry black-and-white televisions that populated the country, and he knew exactly who it belonged to. Everybody did.

Gideon gave him a shove that sent him stumbling forward, interrupting his effort to get control of the fear that was making it hard to think. There was something about unfamiliar danger—danger not normally part of your world—that was so much more potent. In America, drunk drivers and fatty foods were the most likely candidates to kill you, but everyone worried about terrorists and sharks. Mtiti seemed to embody everything dark, everything that had hidden in Josh's closet when he was a kid.

And yet the maid smiled politely as she opened the door for them, the spotless hallway was decorated with fresh flowers, and the soothing sound of classical music hung in the conditioned air.

Mtiti didn't rise from his chair as they entered Trent's office. Josh only looked at him for a moment before turning away. While he was certain that Gideon was responsible for the actual killing, all he could see in Mtiti's face was the dirt-filled eyes of that old woman in the jungle. Hers and thousands of others.

"Please have a seat," Trent said, pointing to a chair.

Josh did as he was told, trying to ignore the fact that the president of the country seemed to be trying to bore a hole in the side of his skull with his stare.

"I want to explain some things to you," Trent started. "I know that you don't have much experience in Africa, but I do. And I can tell you that this is one of the best-run and most peaceful places on the continent. Is it perfect by European or American standards? No. But it's also not Somalia. Or Rwanda, or Liberia, or Sudan. You have no idea what President Mtiti has to deal with: tribal animosity that goes back a thousand years, massive illiteracy, cultural barriers to advancement that are virtually insurmountable, a thirty percent AIDS rate. . . . Do you understand what I'm saying, Josh?"

Honestly, he didn't understand why they were talking at all. Particularly about the general social ills of Africa. The smart money was to just say yes, but at this point he knew his fate was already determined.

"And how does that gravesite fit into your philosophy, Stephen? Was that caused by the illiteracy or the cultural barriers to advancement?"

Mtiti started to laugh, a deep rumble that seemed to have genuine humor tainted by only a hint of homicidal mania. "You're like all the others aren't you? Just another pampered little boy who comes to my country—to the place where my ancestors were born—to tell us the right way to live."

Josh stayed focused on Trent but heard the creak of the chair as Mtiti leaned forward. "We don't *want* to live like you. We don't want to cower in our homes, afraid of everything, doing what everyone else tells us. Because of me, my country, my people are free. They have what they need."

Strangely, he understood Mtiti's point. In a way, Orwell had been right. Freedom really could be slavery. In the United States, most people didn't question the thousands of rules that made the West's complicated machine function. If a neighbor pissed them off, they couldn't cut off his head and put it on a fence post. They had to just grin and bear it, or maybe hire a lawyer. The Africans had no such constraints. As long as you were on top, you were free in a way that the average American would never understand.

"Mr. President . . ." Trent cautioned, and Mtiti leaned back in his chair again. Obviously, they had agreed to let Trent handle whatever it was they were trying to handle.

"Josh, there are realities here. You've seen them. The Yvimbo rebels have to be kept down. If not, this country is going to slide into a genocidal civil war that'll last for the next twenty years. Unfortunately, there's an unpleasant side to keeping things under control."

"An unpleasant side? Are you kidding me?"

"Don't start getting indignant, Josh. You're not stupid. What if the president let those guerrillas in the South get strong enough to rise up? What do *you* think would happen?"

"Those weren't rebels, Stephen. They were farmers. And you can just get off your high horse—we both know that this isn't about helping the locals."

"They're *all* rebels," Mtiti growled. "All of them."

"He's right, Josh. The tribal divisions aren't going anywhere. One tribe or the other has to be in charge. You think things would be better if it was the Yvimbo? You think they'd be enlightened rulers?"

It was a particularly uncomfortable subject in light of the fact that he and Annika had been arguing over this same point only two days ago. And, as he recalled, he'd taken Trent's side.

"So we created this arrangement," Trent continued, gesturing respectfully toward Mtiti. "The country remains stable, its image around the world is raised, and we all benefit financially. How is that worse than the other charities? You think they don't enrich themselves? Who do you think lives in the mansions in this neighborhood? The directors of charities. Men who destabilize African countries with foreign ideas and money while they live like kings."

"There's a difference," Josh started, but Mtiti leapt to his feet.

"There is no difference!" he screamed. "This isn't about helping to you people. It's about telling the savages how to live. It's about your European superiority. It's about you stripping our natural resources to make money so you can build weapons and make even more money by selling them to us!"

"Excellency," Trent said, holding his hands out in a plea for calm, "please . . ."

Josh felt as though every muscle in his body had completely locked, and they didn't start to relax again until Mtiti sat.

"Josh, the reason we hired you is because we think you can understand what you've heard tonight. Because you can be a valuable part of this organization."

"You're offering me a job?"

"You've already got the job," Trent pointed out. "I'm offering you a promotion."

Josh actually smiled at that. "A promotion?"

"Remember what I said earlier? About your sister driving a Mercedes around the Harvard campus? We can still make that happen."

"My sister."

"We don't want to hurt her, Josh. And frankly, we don't want to lose you. I'm offering you a win-win situation. I hope you see that."

It seemed incredibly unlikely. They needed something from him, and the minute they got it, they'd kill everyone who posed even a remote threat to them. There was no way in hell that Umboto Mtiti and the man in the article he'd been sent were going to jeopardize a megamillion-dollar enterprise for an overeducated twenty-six-year-old ex-con.

"Can I have some time to think about it?"

Trent shook his head sadly. "And wait for the article to come out?"

Josh felt a burst of adrenaline course through him but tried not to let it show. "What do you mean?"

"JB Flannary is dead, Josh. And so are his editor and assistant. All their files have been destroyed."

Josh was forced to wipe the sweat from his forehead before it ran into his eyes and blinded him.

"We're holding all the cards, Josh. There's no reason for this to be difficult. Take the deal I'm offering—"

"Why are we still talking?" Mtiti cut in, his patience obviously at its end. "Who were those people at the project to you? You didn't know them. They were nobody. But your family. Your sister. Is she not important to you?"

He clearly expected an answer, and Josh cleared his throat in an effort to keep his voice from shaking. "Yes, she's important."

"You'd like her to live? Is that right?"

"Yes."

"Then we have an understanding."

Mtiti rose and strode across the office to the hallway.

"Thank you, Mr. President," Trent called after him, but Mtiti gave no indication of hearing as Gideon ran after him.

Trent waited until he was sure they were gone before he spoke again. "You've caused me quite a bit of trouble, Josh."

"More than Dan did?"

"Don't be so ungrateful. I can tell you that a friendly conversation in my office isn't what Mtiti had in mind. If I hadn't intervened, you'd be hanging by your balls while his people burned you with acetylene torches."

"Then I guess I should thank you."

"It's time for you to start thinking about yourself and your sister, Josh. Trust me when I say that you don't want to leave her to what Aleksei has planned. No one should die like that. Particularly not a young girl."

"What do you want?"

"I want to tie up the last loose end."

"Annika."

Trent nodded. "Where is she?"

He didn't answer.

"I know this is difficult, Josh. But the president is going to do whatever's necessary to make sure she never leaves this country. It's better for everyone—including her—to end this now."

"I don't really have much of a choice, do I?"

"You don't have any choice at all. Now, answer my question."

The sweat had formed at his hairline again, and he wiped it away with his sleeve. "I don't know exactly. I dropped her off on the road, and she said she was going to find a place where she could stay off Mtiti's radar. She could be a hundred miles from there by now."

The serene mask that Trent wore barely flickered. "Do you have a way to contact her?"

"She has my phone. I was going to try to get it turned back on."

"If we did that, if we reactivated it, you could call her? Set up a meeting?"

Josh stared at the window behind Trent, trying to penetrate the darkness outside. "Like I said. I don't have much of a choice."

39

The farther south they drove, the more the leafy branches on either side of the shattered road closed in overhead. They deflected the sun but also trapped the humidity and created a sense of claustrophobia that Stephen Trent found unbearable.

He shouldn't have been there. They'd passed into Yvimbo rebel territory two hours ago, an area made uncontrollable by its steep, jungle-covered mountains and plunging valleys. The best Mtiti could do was blockade the area and try to keep its inhabitants too hungry and poorly armed to rise up.

Gideon was driving, and a young man holding a machine gun was sprawled over the passenger seat. Trent was in the back, staring out the open window for any sign of danger, while Josh sat wedged between him and another armed young man. The smell of sweat was overwhelming, but Trent knew that he was responsible for much of it.

He glanced back over his shoulder and saw a matching white Land Cruiser trailing only a few feet behind, this one containing five of Mtiti's men posing as aid workers, their weapons just out of sight. A proper armored escort was impossible. Word of it would spread like wildfire through the region, likely tipping off Annika

Gritdal and even more likely causing them to become the victims of an ambush. This was the best they could do—a delicate balancing act between camouflage and firepower.

"This is close enough," Trent said. "The village she's hiding in is only a few more miles."

He grabbed the seat in front of him as Gideon pulled onto the edge of the dirt road. Their chase car skidded to a stop behind, and the men jumped out to patrol the edges of the jungle with machine guns held tightly in front of them. So much for subtlety.

Trent grabbed Josh's arm and pulled him from the vehicle. Gideon was already standing in the road, one hand on the pistol shoved haphazardly into his pants.

"Give him the keys," Trent ordered.

Gideon held them out, but when Josh reached for them, he closed his fist. "If you run, we'll find you. And we'll find her. What I did to Dan will be nothing—"

"That's enough, Gideon!" Trent said. "Just give him the goddamn keys and let's get this over with."

Josh accepted them, his expression impossible to read. "You're not going with me?"

Trent put an arm around his shoulders and led him out of earshot of the men around them.

"If Annika sees me or Gideon, she'll know what's going on, and it's hard to say what the villagers might do. None of the locals have to get hurt. You just need to go in there, get her, and bring her to us. Then we can get back to our lives. Our *good* lives."

Josh nodded numbly.

"You read that article about Aleksei, right?"

Another almost imperceptible nod.

"I know from personal experience that it doesn't even come close to capturing what he's capable of. He's the most evil, sadistic son of a bitch that I've ever had the misfortune to meet. I don't even want to think about what he'll do to your sister if this doesn't go exactly as planned. Am I being clear?"

"What about Annika?"

It was one of the rare occasions that Trent didn't intuitively know how to respond, and he looked up at the angle of the sun for a moment before speaking. "We can't have her running around with what she knows, Josh. You're not stupid. I don't have to tell you that."

"She can't prove anything, Stephen. I'll deny everything she says. We—"

"Josh, please. Don't make this any harder than it has to be. I don't want to scare her, and I don't want her to feel any pain. We're going to do this quick and easy. Tomorrow it'll all be a bad memory, and your sister will be home filling out her Ivy League applications."

"Quick and easy," Josh mumbled.

"I just want this situation to go away. I'm not Aleksei."

"No? Then who are you?"

Trent actually managed to smile at that. "I'm nobody. I'm a fucking con man from Ohio. Funny, isn't it? How things work out?"

"Yeah. Funny."

They walked to the Land Cruiser, and Trent slammed the door closed after Josh climbed into the driver's seat. "Think about your sister, Josh. You're all she's got."

He stepped back, and Josh accelerated the Land Cruiser up the road, keeping the speed low enough that it was obvious he never wanted to reach his destination.

Gideon had his pistol out now and was trying to keep his men vigilant. While the color of Trent's skin might offer him some protection from the rebels, Gideon and his Xhisa soldiers had no such hope. The Yvimbo would offer very little in the way of mercy to their age-old enemies.

Trent dialed his sat phone, retreating to the second Land Cruiser and sitting in the backseat with his feet dangling from the open door.

"Do you have her?" Fedorov said by way of a greeting.

"Josh is bringing her back."

"You sent him alone?"

Trent didn't allow himself to be baited by the question. Fedorov had agreed to the plan but was now distancing himself from it so that he could more easily place blame if things went wrong. It was a scenario that had played out many times before.

"He understands the situation with his sister, Aleksei. We haven't left him any choice. He'll be back, and he'll have Annika with him."

"When they get there, turn them over to the Africans."

Trent had anticipated the order but wasn't sure what to do about it. Watching Annika Gritdal being repeatedly raped by Gideon and his men before they beat her and Josh to death wasn't something he was looking forward to.

"We need to get out of here, Aleksei. This is unstable territory. We just don't have time to—"

"Shut the fuck up! You're going to do exactly what I tell you. This is your fault, and you're going to sit there and watch the consequences. And I'm going to be on the phone the whole time, Stephen. The whole time, I'm going to be listening to them scream while you describe every detail. Do you understand me?"

Trent wiped the sweat from his upper lip. "I understand. And Josh's sister?"

"Oh, I'm going to enjoy doing her. Maybe I'll take a video and send it to you. Would you like that?"

"The battery in my phone is getting low," Trent lied. "I'll call you back when we've got them."

He propped his elbows on his knees, staring down at the dirt and thinking of home. The cold wind whipping through the New York streets, the tiny fireplace he'd rescued during the renovation of his apartment. But those images had lost their power to calm him. They no longer seemed real.

40

Stephen Trent walked toward the edge of the road, stopping in the narrow band of shade that wasn't yet soaked in the still humidity of the jungle. It was undoubtedly cooler, but it wasn't long before the bugs forced him back into the grueling sun. Gideon's men didn't seem to notice the insects clinging to them like bloodthirsty tendrils of smoke, and they sat silently in the shadows, guns lying next to them in the dust.

It had been almost two hours since Josh had driven away, and the initial diligence of his guard detail had faded into drowsy boredom. Even the periodic barking from Gideon elicited only brief stirs in the stupor of the African afternoon.

Trent paced in the center of the road, attempting to create an artificial breeze against his sweat-soaked face. His skin was burning to a deep red, but he barely noticed. Two hours was too long. The village was only a few miles away, and it wasn't as though Annika would have had any possessions to gather. How long could it take to say good-bye to people she'd only just met? He had no choice but to start considering the possibility that they had run.

No. Where would they go?

Unknown to Josh, there was a car full of Mtiti's men blocking the only other road out of there. Besides, there was just no way he would do anything to jeopardize his sister. Annika was a beautiful woman, but not beautiful enough for him to doom his own flesh and blood to a slow, horrifying death at the hands of Aleksei Fedorov.

He glanced at his watch for what must have been the hundredth time and licked the salt from his lips. It was going to be okay. Josh was completely, irretrievably trapped. The villagers had probably insisted that he and Annika stay for a meal or some ceremony. The Africans had a lengthy and pointless ceremony for everything.

A dust plume became visible in the distance, moving in their direction. Trent took up a position next to Gideon and watched it approach, feeling the tension in his neck and shoulders loosen a bit. It was them. Thank God.

"When they get here, you can do what you want with them," he said, aware that his voice was barely a whisper. For some reason, he didn't want to be heard by the men around them. As though they might judge him. "We don't have much time, though. We need to be out of here before dark."

Gideon gazed down at him through his ever-present sunglasses, a vague smile playing at his lips. Trent wasn't sure he had ever seen the man smile before and frankly would be happy to never see it again. There was no humor in it, only a sadistic delight uncontrolled by the conventions of the world Trent had grown up in. The world he hoped someday to return to.

The vehicle was close enough now to make out two figures in the front, and Trent took a few hesitant steps forward. It continued to approach, though its trajectory was becoming increasingly erratic.

She'd spotted them.

Through the dirty windshield, Trent could see that Josh was holding her by the hair, trying to keep control of the wheel as she clawed desperately at him.

The soldiers were on their feet now, and Gideon said something to them that replaced their malaise with excitement—perhaps a description of their role in Josh and Annika's last hour.

The Land Cruiser slowed abruptly about fifty yards away, nearly plunging into a ditch when Annika managed to get hold of the wheel. The guards laughed and joked with each other as Josh fought to regain control, the drama playing out in front of them heightening their anticipation.

A young man standing at the edge of the jungle suddenly let out a scream and began desperately trying to pull his rifle from his shoulder. It got caught on his elbow and he was still trying to free it when the left side of his neck exploded, creating a crimson cloud in the humid air as he sank to the ground.

Trent froze, unable to fully process what was happening as no less than thirty men rushed from the jungle armed with a mix of machine guns, machetes, and spears. Shouts and gunshots filled the air as his guards either succumbed to those weapons or dropped their guns and raised their hands in the air. One broke and ran but made it only a few yards before a spear hit him just below the right shoulder blade. He fell forward, the spear point jutting from his chest hitting the ground first and leaving his twitching body suspended a foot from the ground.

They were all around him now, and Trent was hit from behind, the force of the blow making the landscape around him spin as he dropped to his knees. He looked toward the approaching Land Cruiser and saw that it was going straight now, rolling unhurriedly toward them as the hot barrel of a machine gun was pressed to the back of his head.

Gideon hadn't surrendered, but he also hadn't been summarily executed like the other resisters. He blocked a blow from a man holding a stick the size of a baseball bat and slammed an elbow into his face. Another man jumped on his back, only to land on his dazed compatriot when Gideon flipped him over his shoulder.

But it was useless. There were too many of them, and Gideon

was driven to the ground by the sheer weight of his attackers, absorbing blows from fists, rocks, and pistol butts as he fell.

The rest of Trent's men were facedown in the road with their hands clasped behind their necks, each guarded by no fewer than three Yvimbo men dressed in everything from Western street clothes to traditional costumes of war.

The Land Cruiser glided to a stop a few feet away, and Trent was pulled to his feet by the man behind him. From this distance, he could see that there were actually three people in the vehicle: Josh and Annika in front and an African man in the back. Trent didn't recognize him immediately, but when he stepped out, he saw that it was Tfmena Llengambi. Gideon saw him, too, and his thrashing increased in violence, ceasing only when a knife was pressed to his throat.

"What are you doing?" Trent heard himself stammer as Josh stepped out. "We . . . we have your sister."

━━━

Josh slammed the door behind him and surveyed the scene. Tfmena's people had everything under control, with Gideon on the ground bleeding badly from a head wound and the other men either dead or subdued. Trent was staring at him with understandable confusion.

Annika had done better than he'd dared hope. Apparently news of the white woman on the run from Mtiti had spread quickly through the region, and it hadn't been long before word reached Tfmena, who had taken her in. While he'd certainly had the respect of the people working on NewAfrica's agricultural project, here, away from the dominance of Mtiti's Xhisa, Tfmena was a man of genuine power.

"If they don't hear from me, they'll kill your sister," Trent said, obviously still unable to understand exactly what was happening.

"You don't have my sister," Josh said as Annika came up alongside him.

"What?" Trent said.

"You kidnapped a woman named Fawn Mardsen. She's not actually related to me."

"But she was there," Trent whined. "She was the one you told us . . ." His voice trailed off as Tfmena began shouting orders and Gideon was dragged off to lie with his men at the jungle's edge.

Hearing Fawn's voice over Trent's phone may have been the happiest moment of Josh's life. His plan had been so desperate and hastily constructed that he'd never really believed it would work.

He had told Laura to take Fawn's wallet and leave her own out on the table, full of what cash and credit cards she had, before running to the tree house they'd built when they were kids.

Predictably, Fawn had taken the wallet, and given her resemblance to Laura, Fedorov's men would have had no reason to doubt that they'd found the girl they were looking for. Of course there had been a thousand things that could have gone wrong, but, for the first time in his life, they hadn't. Maybe he had Annika to thank for that. Maybe he was finally taking a few unsteady steps toward getting right with God.

Trent's eyes had cleared a bit as his mind began to process what he'd heard and the hopelessness of his situation. "What are you going to do with us?"

"I'm not going to do anything, Stephen. Annika and I are leaving."

Josh reached for her hand but then though better of it and instead pointed in the direction of the Land Cruiser. Trent grabbed his arm.

"Wait! You can't leave me like this. You can't leave me to what they're going to do."

Josh tried to pull away but couldn't so easily escape. Annika's expression had settled into an odd combination of panic and resignation. The realization that there was no way out was hard for her to deal with. Even with all her years in Africa, she couldn't shake the European concept of having choices.

"Josh," Trent pleaded, glancing back at the ecstatic men whose care he was about to be remanded to, "remember what I said about Annika? Remember that I said it would be quick for her?"

"But was it true, Stephen? Was she really going to get a bullet between the eyes? Was I really going to get a quarter-of-a-million-dollar-a-year job and a sister at Harvard?"

Trent's slick facade had completely crumbled. "This wasn't my doing. I swear it wasn't."

Josh looked down at the bright feathers decorating the spear that had impaled one of Gideon's men and then at the others lined up in the dirt. He was a participant in all this—not an outsider, not a spectator. These people were going to die, and he was the cause of it. The question was how cowardly and hypocritical he was going to be in dealing with that fact.

He glanced at Annika but found no help there. He was on his own.

Gideon's pistol was still lying where he had fallen, and Josh picked it up, trying to ignore the weight of Tfmena's eyes on him. He hoped someone would stop him, but no one moved.

Trent seemed to be struggling just to remain standing as Josh aimed the gun. The man guarding him moved to a safe distance, but Josh wasn't sure it was necessary. He wasn't going to be able to do it. He wasn't going to be able to shoot an unarmed man in cold blood.

Trent sensed his hesitation and smiled. A clear drop ran down his right cheek, but it was impossible to tell if it was a tear or just sweat.

"I always knew this is how I would end up," he said. "But I'm still kind of scared."

The sound of his voice was strangely calming. "I am, too," Josh said. And then he pulled the trigger.

41

The outskirts of the capital city were quiet, matching the silence that had prevailed in the car for the last five hours. To her credit, Annika had tried to open a dialogue, but she'd gotten nothing more than one-word answers. She was now motionless in the passenger seat, staring out at the firelight leaking from the shacks lining the road.

What was there to say? He'd killed a man. The proof was all around him: in the leather-trimmed interior of the Land Cruiser, in the phone and wallet lying on the dashboard, in the diamond ring rattling inside the cup holder. All stolen from Stephen Trent. Or more precisely taken from the dead body of the human being whose life he had ended. Josh's gaze wandered to Gideon's pistol gleaming on the dark floorboard, and he wondered if the African was dead yet. And if not, what he and his men were going through.

"What did you want me to do?" he said finally, his voice impossibly loud in the confines of the car.

Annika turned away from the window. "I don't understand what you're asking."

"They were going to kill Stephen. I . . . I saved him from that. You understand, don't you?"

"Understand?" She let out a bitter laugh. "For everything he's done—for the way he's preyed on the most defenseless people in the world. On women and children . . . I would have left him to the Yvimbo."

She'd actually approached Gideon as he was being dragged away and asked him what had happened to her village. The answer was a string of threats, but in them was the clear implication that nothing had been done yet. Publicity and logistics had to be dealt with before the genocide could start.

"Annika . . ."

"I mean it, Josh. Isn't that strange? I didn't know I could feel this way. If Mtiti was standing in front of me right now, I'd kill him. And I wouldn't regret it. I think I'd enjoy it."

The memory of the buck of the gun and the sound of Trent's last breaths made his stomach roll. "Doing it is different than talking about it."

"Is it? How would it feel to kill Mtiti? How would it feel to know I'd saved the people who have been my family for most of my adult life?"

He stared through the windshield for a few moments, straining to see the dark outline of the capital city ahead. "I want to help you, Annika. And I want to help the people here. But my first priority is keeping us alive and making sure my sister is okay. I can't save Africa. Only the Africans can."

Annika went back to looking out the window. A good five minutes passed before she spoke again. "I used to see God everywhere. But more and more I wonder if He's forgotten this place."

Ahead, an armored personnel carrier parked across the road became visible through the darkness and smoke, forcing Josh to swerve down a side street to avoid being spotted.

"Shit! That's the third one."

He'd hoped that Mtiti would have called off the men blocking access to the consulates and that they'd be able to slip in and get help. But you didn't become president of an African country by being careless. Power, phones, and Internet were still down, making communication with the outside world impossible. Trent's sat phone was charged and tempting, but it would be impossible to know who might be listening and whether it could be tracked.

Josh eased the car to a stop in the unusually quiet road and turned the headlights off. "Mtiti and Fedorov probably already figure something went wrong."

She leaned back in the seat and let out a long breath. "They won't stop until they find us, Josh. They'll do whatever they have to."

"Back in the States, we have an old saying: A good offense is the best defense."

He could just make out her silhouette as she turned toward him. "Did you have something in mind?"

42

The well-maintained asphalt felt strangely exotic beneath Josh's feet as he hurried up the steep road. Around him, rare electric lights were reflecting off walls strung with bougainvillea and razor wire.

He continued to the end of the cul-de-sac, watched by the man policing the gate to Stephen Trent's home. It was the same guard who had been there the first time Josh had visited, and despite the recognition in his eyes, he hadn't yet fulfilled Annika's prediction and started shooting.

"Hi. I'm Josh Hagarty. I'm here to meet with Mr. Trent."

"No one told me," the man said, his accented English barely decipherable.

Josh shrugged disinterestedly, trying to emulate the attitude of the wealthy whites he'd seen in Africa.

"He not here."

"I know he's not here," Josh said, affecting irritation and hoping it would mask the fear eating away at him. "He called me from the road. He's on his way."

Josh was counting on the fact that the guard had no real authority or big-picture knowledge of the workings of NewAfrica.

His job was to dissuade the local riffraff from looting the place. Nothing more, nothing less.

Apparently he saw it the same way, because a moment later Josh found himself strolling through the open gate, trying to shake the feeling that he was breaking *into* prison instead of out.

The maid who answered the front door was even less inquisitive, taking Josh at his word that Trent was on his way and that Josh had been instructed to wait in his office. After he declined her offer of coffee, she wandered off. When her footsteps had completely faded, Josh pushed the office door closed and hurried to the filing cabinets lined up against the wall. He ignored the standard ones and went straight for the safe-like units in the corner. The laser-cut key he'd taken off Trent's body slid easily into the lock, and Josh tried to turn it. Nothing. He tried again with the same result.

Just as panic was starting to set in, he noticed that blood had dried in a few of the indentations on the key. Using a paper clip, he gently dug it out, trying not to replay what it had felt like to root around in the blood-and-sweat-dampened pockets of a corpse.

This time when he turned the key, a green light flashed and the drawer slid open.

After a quick overview of the files, he knew he'd found the records that Flannary had told him about—the ones that never made it back to the United States. There were payments from Mtiti for ambiguously defined services, profits from the sale of food aid, statements from foreign banks, and documents for countless offshore corporations and partnerships.

He began pulling out the most incriminating of them, creating a neat stack on the floor.

Every once in a while footsteps would become audible in the hallway and he'd have to slam the cabinet closed and take a seat in front of Trent's desk. But other than the maid, who was very concerned about his fluid intake, no one seemed to even know he was there.

Josh had been at it for almost twenty minutes when the sound of a powerful engine reached him from the front of the house. He froze, listening to it grow in volume, and then went into panicked motion when it was overpowered by the screech of tires.

Shouts and running feet in the entryway were already audible when he picked up the nearly foot-tall stack of documents and looked desperately around the room. There was nowhere to run. He dumped the papers into the trash can by Trent's desk as someone in the hallway began shouting what sounded like orders. It took a couple of seconds for him to place the voice, but when he did, he started moving even faster.

Mtiti.

Josh closed the cabinet drawer and locked it, dropping to the floor behind the desk just as the office door burst open. He squeezed past the chair and crammed himself into the small space once occupied by Stephen Trent's legs, listening to Mtiti's men fan out into the room. He could hear his own jerky breathing, too loud in the confined space he was contorted into. Adrenaline was causing him to shake, and he tried to keep from banging audibly into the polished wood surrounding him. The chair was pulled back, replaced by the lower half of a fatigue-clad soldier. Josh's breath caught in his chest as the man started to crouch, but a face never appeared. Instead two hands began removing the drawers and stacking them on Trent's blotter.

The center drawer was locked, and after a brief discussion, a pistol appeared. Josh covered his face just as a bullet tore through the lock, sending wooden shrapnel into his sweat-soaked forearm. A couple of kicks from a military boot and the drawer was free.

Mtiti's orders were partially drowned out by the scraping of metal on tile as the file cabinets were dragged toward the hallway. Josh remained completely still, concentrating on keeping his breathing as even as possible. It was all he could do to control his panic, to fight off a feeling of claustrophobia he'd never experienced before, to quell the urge to break and run.

Then it was over. The sound of voices and dragging furniture became distant as Mtiti and his men made their way to the front door. Five minutes later, the engine outside roared to life again and then faded away.

He didn't move, thankful that he hadn't taken up the maid's offer of coffee. Caffeine and a full bladder would not have served him well in this particular situation. Finally, as the silence continued to stretch out, he dared a look at his watch.

Eight thirty-two.

He leaned forward and took a quick peek over the desk. The room had been almost entirely emptied: file cabinets, bookshelves, desk drawers. Even the liquor cabinet and in/out box were gone.

The door was open, but no one was in the hallway, so Josh stood and dabbed sweat from his face. He was trying to regain enough composure to walk casually out of there when he froze, staring down in amazement.

The trash can was still there. And still full of the papers he'd put in it.

43

Aleksei Fedorov's phone rang, and he snatched it from his pocket. "Stephen! Where have you been?"

"This isn't Stephen."

Fedorov stopped pacing at the sound of Umboto Mtiti's voice. Around him, everything in the warehouse was still. The blood had run from JB Flannary's body into a drain in the floor, and for the last hour the soft drip of it had been the only thing moving the cold air. Josh Hagarty's sister had stopped struggling after seeing what had happened to the others and now just stared blankly at the bodies of Robert Page and Flannary's young assistant, still slouched in their chairs.

It was an atmosphere that Fedorov always found calming. Dead bodies represented problems permanently solved: a continuation of his power and a warning to anyone who might decide to try to move in on him. But there were still people unaccounted for, and Mtiti's voice on the other end of the line wasn't the one he'd hoped to hear.

"Excellency. I'm honored by your call."

"But not expecting it, I see. Can I assume that you've lost Stephen Trent?"

Fedorov tried to calculate the most beneficial spin, but there was no way to be sure what Mtiti knew. He was an animal, but not one to be underestimated when playing on his home field.

"My understanding is that they went to retrieve Annika Gritdal so that we can resolve this . . . problem."

"That was twenty hours ago, Aleksei. *Twenty hours*. I want to know where they are, and I want to know now."

"They took some of your people along, didn't they, Excellency? Have you contacted them?"

Mtiti's voice came back loud enough to distort over the marginal connection. "If I could contact them, would I be calling you?"

"No," Fedorov said, unaccustomed to being yelled at but managing to keep his anger hidden. "I suppose you wouldn't."

The area that Annika had chosen to hide in was beyond Mtiti's reach—a rebel-controlled black hole to his government. At this point, it seemed likely that Trent's motorcade had been attacked. But with what outcome? Certainly Mtiti's men were dead, but would the rebels kill Trent and Hagarty? It seemed that there would be better uses for two white men.

"Then what's happened?" Mtiti demanded.

"I can't be expected to know what goes on in your country hour by hour, Mr. President. I'm thousands of miles away."

"Are you suggesting that I don't have control? That I'm weak—"

"I'm suggesting nothing," Fedorov interrupted, letting some of his anger and frustration creep into his voice, "other than the possibility that something has happened to our people and—"

"I wonder."

"What?"

"I'm starting to question your commitment to our charitable activities, Aleksei. Suddenly every employee you send is less competent than the last. And the one man you have who has proven to be even somewhat reliable has suddenly disappeared. I have to wonder if your priorities have changed."

The wording was careful, implying that Mtiti thought someone might be listening—that NewAfrica's real purpose had been discovered and Fedorov was now working with the American authorities.

"This has been a very profitable situation for both of us, Mr. President. I wouldn't do anything to jeopardize that."

There was a brief silence. "In the interests of my people, I am shutting down all of NewAfrica's projects and nationalizing all of its interests in my country—"

"You can't do that!" Fedorov shouted. "We've spent years building this business. I've done—"

"Then perhaps you would be willing to show me that you're taking our relationship seriously?"

Fedorov pulled out his pistol and aimed it at Hagarty's sister, the only living thing left in the room. She came out of her stupor and began trying to scream through her gag as his finger hovered over the trigger. For everything her pissant brother had done, for everything his bullshit had cost, she deserved to die. She deserved the worst he could dream up. . . .

His finger relaxed, and he reluctantly tucked the gun back into his waistband. Not yet.

"What did you have in mind?"

"I think I could be persuaded to let NewAfrica continue its work if you were to come here personally and oversee the efforts to fix the problems you've caused."

Fedorov began pacing again. His African operations had become so profitable that he'd dedicated virtually all his resources to them. There was no denying that he was now completely dependent on Mtiti for the flow of money that kept him stronger than his enemies. If Mtiti were to throw NewAfrica out of his country, USAID and the UN would pull the contracts NewAfrica was managing, and the profits from drugs, weapons, and the resale of food aid would cease. His power would disintegrate almost overnight.

"Aleksei?"

The only option was to stall. In Africa he would be entirely at the mercy of Mtiti's wild mood swings and paranoia. At some point the risk might be necessary, but the situation hadn't degenerated that far yet.

"Thank you for the invitation, Excellency. Of course I'd be honored to come."

"And when can I expect you?"

When hell freezes over.

"Let me look into travel arrangements, and I'll get back to you."

44

T here was no way I could have just walked out with them," Josh said. "There were people everywhere, and I didn't know if the guards were still there."

It was hard to see Annika's face in the darkness created by the blanket he'd thrown over them, but when he moved to dislodge the vehicle's jack from his back, a flash of light illuminated an uncertain expression.

"I guess what I'm trying to tell you is that I'm sorry, Annika."

"For what?"

"I appreciate the sentiment, but come on. For a million things."

"Oh, I know. I meant which one of those things in particular?"

He was shocked when he saw the dim outline of her mouth turn up for a moment.

Even pissed off, she continued to be the most amazing person he'd ever met. Her ability to maneuver through a country that would stop at nothing to kill them was not only fascinating to watch but also the reason he was still breathing. She'd managed to find a Yvimbo store owner who was willing to hide them and who had sent his children to watch Trent's neighborhood for the arrival of the truck that picked up the trash. And now their new accomplice was cheerfully tailing that truck in Trent's Land Cruiser.

"Soldiers," the man said in Yvimbo. It was one of ten or so words Josh understood, and he peeked out from beneath the blanket, glimpsing a rusting Jeep as it passed. Mtiti's men gave their vehicle a quick look and continued on.

Josh had used white house paint to cover the NewAfrica logo on the Land Cruiser's door and then spent a sweaty two hours kicking dents in it and dousing it with mud. So far the impromptu camouflage job was working.

"I should have gone back," he said, retreating back beneath the blanket. "When there weren't any guards, I should have gone back for the papers."

"I'm grateful you made it out at all, Josh."

He wanted to believe she was right, but the truth was that he'd made the decision based entirely on fear. Once he'd escaped through the front gate, nothing was going to get him to go back.

"Let's see if you still feel the same way after spending the day digging around in an African garbage dump," he said, trying to lighten the mood and failing miserably.

She rolled on top of him, creating a quiet sucking sound as their sweaty bodies stuck together. "I'm sorry, too."

"For what?" he said, trying not to show his surprise at the sudden collapse of the distance that had seemed to grow between them since their escape from her village.

"I've been unfair to you."

"Are you kidding? I—"

"Let me finish. I've judged you because I believed that everything you were doing was to save yourself. And I believe it's intentions, and not so much actions, that define us."

"Annika, you have to under—"

"You're not letting me finish!"

"Sorry."

"I let myself forget that you could have sat by your pool and left the project to Gideon while you waited for a plane to take you home. There was no reason for you to get involved in this when JB asked you. But you did."

"And now a lot of people are dead. Including us, maybe."

"Yes, maybe. But when you're finally judged, I think you won't have as much explaining to do."

"The pearly gates? I don't think so. I'm alive now, and I'd like to keep it that way."

"Best to not put all your chickens in one basket."

"Eggs."

"What?"

Despite the heat, he wrapped his arms around her. It felt good to have her back. "Never mind."

They drove for another hour, her sleeping with her face buried in his neck and him thinking of home, of Laura, and of the old woman with dirt in her eyes.

"We here!" the man driving suddenly announced.

Annika's head jerked up and the blanket slid from them, letting in the blinding midmorning sun. Josh pushed himself up on his elbows and squinted through the windows, perplexed by what he saw. The garbage truck—actually just an open dump truck—was there, but instead of a lonely, rotting landfill, he saw a dusty plain crowded with people.

As usual, Annika seemed neither surprised nor particularly concerned. She flopped over the seat and got out through the back door, poking her head back in a moment later. "Are you coming?"

"Where the hell are we?"

She held out a hand and he took it, following her out into the heat as the crowd waited for the garbage truck to be unloaded. The man who had chauffeured them there came around the car and held out a hand. "I wish you luck."

Josh shook off his confusion long enough to reach out and take it. "You really saved us, man. I can't tell you how grateful we are."

He obviously didn't understand, but his eyes widened when Josh proffered the ring he'd taken from Stephen Trent's finger. To his surprise, the man just shook his head and started walking back toward the city.

"It's a market," Annika said, tugging him toward what he estimated to be at least a hundred people. "What wealthy people throw away still has value to the poor."

He didn't move. "I thought nobody'd be here, Annika. What are the chances nobody here knows Mtiti's looking for us?"

"Pretty small," she said, pulling harder on his arm. "But there's no point in worrying about things that we can't control."

Most of the people there were focused on the men throwing garbage bags from the truck, but he and Annika were receiving an increasing amount of attention as she barged through the crowd with him in tow.

"You go that way," she said pointing to the right. "I'll look over here."

"We should stay together," he said nervously.

"No, it's better if we find what we're looking for quickly and leave here."

He watched reluctantly as the bemused Africans moved aside to let her examine and occasionally rifle through the neat rows of refuse on display.

He did the same, pushing his way down the line of people negotiating unintelligibly for things that even his family wouldn't have thought twice about throwing away.

Paper was pretty common, but he seemed to be the only person interested in that particular class of rubbish. Most of it was shredded—valuable perhaps to get a cooking fire going, but not for much else. After ten minutes of wrestling with the mob, the closest he'd come to finding what he was looking for was a stack of old recipes written in Dutch.

He was nearly to the end of the row when angry shouts became audible to his left. A few people who weren't having much
luck shopping perked up at the possibility of a fight over a broken
lamp or leaking car battery, but he ignored the noise and continued his search. A moment later a man standing on the bumper of
the garbage truck started pointing at him and then in the direction
of the yelling.

Annika.

He shoved his way desperately through the people but slowed
when he got closer, crouching slightly to try to stay as hidden as his
skin tone would allow. The crowd seemed inclined to help him,
and people moved quietly out of his way as he pressed forward.

He stopped about five feet from the edge of a large circle that
had opened in the crowd. Annika was at the center of it, arguing
loudly with yet another well-armed child. He was probably fifteen, wearing a typical uniform of tattered fatigue pants and a
dirty T-shirt that read, "Don't Worry, Be Happy." The machine
gun in his hands was aimed at Annika, but when he spoke he
seemed to be addressing the crowd—undoubtedly explaining that
she was wanted by the government and listing whatever charges
Mtiti had manufactured.

Josh maneuvered until he was directly behind the boy, but he
wasn't certain what to do. What he was sure of, though, was that
the more Annika protested, the madder the kid got. He seemed to
want the people around him to do something—grab her? Kill
her? Call Mtiti? There was no way to know. So far everyone
seemed content to just watch. It wouldn't last, though. Eventually
something was going to give.

With no other options to consider, Josh slipped out of the crowd
and walked as calmly as he could toward the boy. All eyes were
suddenly on him, but the boy was too focused on Annika to immediately notice. When he finally spun, Josh was only a few feet away.

He lunged and grabbed the barrel of the gun, pushing it sky-
ward as the boy pulled the trigger. He could feel the heat of it as it

jerked in his hand, drowning out the sudden panicked shouts of the people around them.

With his free hand, Josh pulled Gideon's pistol from his waistband and slammed it into the top of the kid's head. He sank to the ground, and Josh just stood there, heart pounding in his chest and machine gun burning in his palm. The crowd that had partially scattered reassembled, and he looked at the individual faces, wondering what to do. He'd nearly decided on firing the machine gun into the air and making a break for the Land Cruiser when a man emerged and pointed to the stack of NewAfrica documents at Annika's feet.

Whatever he said was met with a smirk and roll of her eyes. He spoke again, and a noisy argument broke out between them. Despite this, and the fact that Josh was still standing there with a gun in each hand and an unconscious soldier at his feet, the people around them quickly lost interest. They began talking among themselves and went back to their shopping as though this kind of thing happened every day.

Annika waved a dismissive hand in the air and started back toward the Land Cruiser.

"Annika! What's going on?"

"He wants ten euros."

"Are you nuts? Give it to him."

"I'm not paying ten euros for a bunch of papers no one wants."

Josh dropped the machine gun and fished around in his pocket for the money, but by the time he found it, the man had run up behind Annika and put a hand on her shoulder. After another few seconds of discussion, a triumphant smile spread across her face and she peeled two one-dollar bills off the wad in her hand.

45

Josh penetrated deeper into the cave, trying to ignore a stench that he'd decided was a leopard lying in wait. Only when it became too dark to safely continue did he turn on Stephen Trent's sat phone, confirm that there was no signal, and disable the GPS function. Satisfied that the phone couldn't be tracked, he walked back out into the sunshine, where Annika was organizing the supplies they'd purchased: a water purifier, food in bags emblazoned with *A Gift from the American People*, a tent, a solar stove.

"How long do we have?" he asked.

Annika slid out of the vehicle's backseat and chewed her lower lip for a few seconds. "Three weeks. Maybe a month if we don't eat much."

It was longer than they needed. If they were in the same situation in a month, their chances of survival would have shrunk to about zero. Mtiti would be closing in to finish off whatever the sweltering bush and malarial mosquitoes had left.

"Five messages," he said, holding up the phone.

"Can you play them?"

He shook his head. "Password. But they've all come in the last few hours, and they're all from the same New York number."

"Aleksei Fedorov wondering what happened?"

When he glanced down at the phone again, the number of messages had increased to six. "Seems like he's getting pretty agitated."

Despite the heat, Annika wrapped her arms around her torso and looked off into the distance. They were on a high knoll that afforded them a view of the lone dirt road winding in and out of the jungle below. So far it seemed all but abandoned—traveled only by a handful of people on foot and the occasional animal-drawn cart.

"What's wrong?" he said. "This is what we wanted. For them to—"

"Is this what we should be doing?"

"What are you talking about? Mtiti is wiping out the Yvimbo right under the noses of the rest of the world. As soon as he can figure out how to cover it up, he's going to burn your village to the ground with everyone in it. We're trying to stop that."

"And to save ourselves."

"What's wrong with that?"

"What happens after? If Mtiti loses power, is my village really saved?"

Of course she was right. The universe abhorred a vacuum, and the one that Mtiti's implosion would leave had the potential to throw the country into complete chaos. Many of her friends would die in the ensuing violence—or in the disease and starvation that followed.

"If this isn't what you want, now's the time to say it."

She continued to stare out over the landscape. "All I asked God for was a little piece of Africa. Something small enough that I could make a difference. A place where I could see people's lives getting better and know I had a part in it. If you try to do any more than that—if you pull back and see too much at once—it looks hopeless."

Below them a dust plume became visible, moving toward them at a speed that only a four-wheel-drive could sustain. Josh pulled a pair of binoculars from the car and peered through them, thankful for the interruption. This was no time to get paralyzed by philosophical questions.

———

Katie eased the Land Cruiser to a stop, eying the machine gun hanging across Josh's back and the pistol tucked into his shorts. The young boy in the passenger seat, who was more accustomed to such accessories, jumped out and headed straight for Annika. She patted him on the head and said something in Yvimbo before handing him five euros. He examined the bills for a moment and then ran off at a speed that suggested he thought she might change her mind.

Josh had initially resisted Annika's plan to hire the boy to courier a message to Katie at the compound, but in the end he couldn't come up with a better plan. Phone service and power were still intermittent all over the country, and he wasn't sure if Fedorov had the ability to listen to or trace calls made over Trent's sat phone. So hiring a disinterested ten-year-old had made sense— by African standards, anyway.

"So what the hell's going on?" Katie said, stepping from the vehicle but keeping the hood between her and them. "Where've you been, Josh? And what's with the guns?"

"Maybe you should sit down," he said. "It's kind of a long story."

———

"I'm not sure what to believe," Katie said after an hour sitting beneath a tree listening to Josh's account of his time in Africa. She had her fatigue-clad knees pulled to her chest and kept glancing back at the road. Her increasing nervousness made it clear that she knew exactly what to believe. The question was whether or not she wanted to get involved.

"We've told you everything as accurately as we can," Josh said. "We want you to know exactly what you're doing if you decide to help us."

He'd chosen her and not one of the other people he knew from the compound because of her personality: idealistic and a little angry. But now he was wondering if it was enough. As he'd listened to himself talk, he'd started to think that anyone in their right mind would run screaming from this.

Annika obviously had the same feeling. "Katie, we'll both understand if you get back in your car and just drive away. If I was in your place, I know I might."

"But all those people," Katie said quietly, the indignation she always displayed lost now. "All those dead people . . ."

She was right. There were already a lot of people dead, and they had no right to make her next on the list.

"I'm sorry, Katie. We should have never contacted you. We've already screwed you just by getting in touch. Go back to the compound, get your things, and get out of—"

"No!" she blurted suddenly, showing some of the passion that Josh remembered in her. "Fuck Umboto Mtiti. And fuck New-Africa. All I ever wanted to do was go to work for an NGO and come to Africa. My whole life. And now they've twisted it into something evil. They can't get away with that."

"Are you sure?" Annika said. "Even if you're careful, there's no guaranteeing that someone won't find out you're helping us. And if they do, there won't be anywhere to hide from them. JB was—"

"I *liked* JB Flannary," Katie said. "He was a cynical asshole, but I liked him. And I think in his way he cared about Africa. Hell, maybe he cared more than any of us. They can't just murder him. It's not right."

Josh picked up the documents he'd taken from Trent's files and held them out.

Katie hesitated, clearly aware that once she started down this path there would be no turning back.

———

"Do you think she'll do it?" Josh asked as Katie's vehicle disappeared into the jungle.

"I don't know. It's a long drive back. A long time to think about what could happen to her and her family."

"That actually wasn't an honest question. I was hoping for a little reassurance."

She came up behind him, wrapping her arms around his waist. "In that case, yes. I'm certain she will."

"I feel so much better now."

"And what about you? Are you going to do what you said?"

"I suppose we're committed."

She released him, and he turned on Trent's phone, dialing the number of the person who had now left nine messages. It rang only once before being picked up.

"Where the fuck have you been, Stephen? Didn't you get my messages?" The voice was slightly accented and full of rage. Exactly the way he'd imagined Aleksei Fedorov would sound.

"Stephen's dead. I killed him."

There was a brief silence. "Who is this?"

"Josh Hagarty," he responded, trying to keep his voice completely emotionless. Fedorov would undoubtedly see him for what he was—a twenty-something American kid way out of his league. He needed to change that image.

When the Russian spoke again, a hint of uncertainty was audible. "I have your fucking sister, you piece of shit. You start playing games with me and I'll mail her to you in pieces."

"I understand, Aleksei. But I have a foot-high stack of documents from Stephen Trent's office that I think you'd prefer not to have out on the street."

"Bullshit. How would you get those?"

"I'd stroll past the guy guarding his house, wipe Trent's blood off the key to his filing cabinet, and walk out with them. Have you even been here? The security's a little half-assed, you know?"

Annika gave an impressed nod. His badass act must have been coming off better than he'd expected. Who would ever have thought that the things he'd learned in prison would be so much more valuable than the things he'd learned in school?

"Do you have any idea who you're fucking with—" Fedorov started, but Josh cut him off.

"I don't have time to go back and forth with dumbass threats. You're thousands of miles away, and you can't do dick, so just shut up and listen."

Annika actually looked a little surprised at the ferocity of his outburst but then shrugged and gave him a thumbs-up.

"Let's get this all out on the table, Aleksei. I don't give a shit about you, Mtiti, or the Africans. I just want my sister back, and I never want to set foot on this godforsaken continent again."

"So what's that mean to me?" Fedorov said.

"I propose a trade. You give me my sister, I give you your documents, and then we forget we ever heard of each other."

"How do I know you haven't made copies?"

"Are you kidding? There aren't exactly Kinko's on every corner here. And Mtiti's cut off power to the entire country."

The ensuing silence was broken only by Aleksei's strained breathing. There was something in the uncontrolled rhythm of it that made Josh sweat even more.

"Okay. Have it your way. Where and when?"

46

Aleksei Fedorov leaned toward the window as the plane began to descend, examining the dirt runway cut from dense jungle. Josh Hagarty's sister showed no such interest, slumped in her chair across from him, spit running from the corner of her mouth. It had been hard to gauge how many tranquilizers to give her, and he'd erred on the side of caution.

The trip had taken more than forty hours on three very expensive private planes. And now he was about to land in Africa, a dangerous, unpredictable shithole in which he had no real power base—less now that Stephen Trent was dead.

The wheels touched down, and the plane bounced to a stop next to a building that wasn't much more than a shed.

"Wake up," Fedorov said as he unbuckled the girl's seat belt. Her eyes fluttered open as he jerked her to her feet. The pilot appeared in the cockpit door, smiling politely as he opened the hatch in the side of the plane. And why wouldn't he be smiling? For the amount of money he was being paid, he could afford to be cheerful.

"How's your daughter doing?" he asked as Fedorov made a show of carefully helping her up the aisle. Explanations had been tricky. He'd had to convince three different flight crews that she had an intense fear of flying and had taken sedatives prescribed by her doctor. And while they'd taken him at his word, he was painfully aware of the loss of anonymity he'd suffered. Stumbling, drooling girls being ferried to the middle-of-nowhere Africa tended to stick in people's minds.

"She'll be fine," Fedorov said, forcing a grin. "It's not the first time we've done this, and it won't be the last. I swear I don't know why she doesn't just stay home."

The pilot nodded sympathetically and helped him get her out of the plane before carrying their bags to the shed.

"Where's my car?" Fedorov asked a young man sitting in the shade provided by the structure. No response other than a confused stare.

"I've got some things to take care of before we lift off again," the pilot said. "Don't worry, though. I won't leave until you've got everything straightened out."

Fedorov ignored him and grabbed the seated man by the arm, pulling him to his feet. "I arranged for a car," he said, enunciating slowly. "A four-wheel-drive. Where is it?"

"Car?" the man responded in almost incomprehensible English. "They come."

God, how he hated this fucking continent. The same stupidity, dishonesty, and laziness that made Africans easy to exploit also made them almost impossible to deal with.

He released the girl and shoved the man back against the building as she sank to the ground. "When? When is my car going to get here? If you think I'm going to—"

The sound of an approaching engine made him fall silent. As it got closer, though, it became clear that it wasn't just one engine. It was many. He stepped out from behind the shed and looked up the dirt road, spotting a long line of vehicles as it appeared from the trees. Two uniformed men led the motorcade on motorcycles, and at its center was a black limousine with flags flying on the fenders.

"Fuck!" Fedorov said, grabbing the girl and pulling her to her feet as the motorcade continued to close. He'd kept this trip quiet, using one of his many aliases, paying in cash, and flying into this remote airstrip well away from the country's capital. His plan had been to meet a group of South African mercenaries he'd worked with in the past, deal with Hagarty and Annika Gritdal, then be gone before Mtiti knew he was there.

Behind him the pilot slammed the plane's hatch closed, and a moment later the props started to turn.

Fedorov tried to calmly reevaluate his position and run through the available options. He could make a break for the plane and hope the pilot would open up for him, but that was an all-or-nothing strategy with almost no chance of success. Instead he raised a hand in greeting as the motorcycles passed by. The limousine pulled up a few seconds later, and a man jumped out, opening the rear door in what appeared to be an invitation to get inside.

He put one of the girl's arms over his shoulders and dragged her to the limo, pushing her into a seat and then following her inside.

"I wonder," Umboto Mtiti said as the door was slammed shut and Fedorov's pupils struggled to adjust to the interior gloom, "why you wouldn't have informed me you were coming to my country?"

"You asked me to come, Excellency, and I chartered the soonest available plane. I was going to call you as soon as I got to the house."

Mtiti just stared at him, and he used the time to refine his story. Mtiti was a monkey, but he was a smarter monkey than most.

"Who is this woman?"

Fedorov glanced over at her and saw that she'd slipped fully into unconsciousness again. "Josh Hagarty's sister, sir."

"And what is it you intend to do with her?"

"I plan to flush out Josh Hagarty and kill him."

Mtiti nodded. "With your South African mercenaries?"

Fedorov tried not to let the sudden surge of adrenaline coursing through him show. In the United States he was surrounded by guards at all times, he had informants keeping an eye on his competition, and he killed anyone who was a threat to him well before they could become dangerous. But this wasn't the States. Here Mtiti dominated everything. Soft leather and air conditioning notwithstanding, Fedorov knew he had become a prisoner the moment he'd passed through the limousine's door.

"I can only assume that you feel my people aren't good enough?"

"Excellency, you made it clear on the phone that it was my responsibility to deal with this problem. So now I'm here personally with a team of men to resolve this issue and prove my loyalty."

Mtiti smiled, but it was impossible to tell if it was because he believed what he was hearing or merely admired Fedorov's skill at lying. "Unfortunately, things have changed in a way that will make your plan impossible."

The implication was clear. The South Africans were all dead.

Mtiti leaned forward and patted Fedorov's knee. "I appreciate your commitment, Aleksei. And to show that mine is equal, I want to make you a guest at my palace. And to offer you the use of my best people."

"I wouldn't want to impose on your hospitality," Fedorov said. "I'm happy to stay at Stephen Trent's house."

"I insist."

Fedorov forced a smile. "Then I accept. Thank you."

"And where is Stephen, Aleksei?"

It was impossible to know whether Mtiti was genuinely looking for information or if he already knew the answers to his questions and was testing. Lies had to be considered carefully. The wrong one could be fatal.

"He's dead, Excellency. And I suspect Gideon is, too. I'm sorry. I know he was a relation to you."

Mtiti didn't react other than to reach beneath his seat and hand

Fedorov a stack of file folders. They were all empty, but their prior contents were noted on labels relating to various NewAfrica bank accounts, bogus projects, and payoffs.

"We found these in the secure file cabinets in Stephen's office. Would you happen to know where the documents are?"

Fedorov's stomach tightened, and he was forced to wipe the sweat from his face before it began dripping from his chin. "Josh Hagarty has them."

"And why wasn't I told about this?" Mtiti said, his voice filling the back of the enormous car.

"Because I just found out," Fedorov replied. "And there wasn't a secure way for me to get in touch with you while I was in transit."

The girl started to mumble incoherently, and Mtiti looked down at her. His face twisted with rage, and without warning he slammed the heel of his boot into the side of her head.

Fedorov slid in front of the now silent girl, holding his hands up. "We need her alive. Not for much longer, but—"

"The world is lining up against me," Mtiti shouted. "I can no longer count on you—on the people who were supposed to be my friends. The Europeans came here and enslaved the black man for a hundred years, stripping our homelands of everything of value before they turned their backs and walked away. The Americans bomb anyone who might cost them money and develop weapons that can destroy all life. But who lives beneath the world's microscope? I do. I am the man everyone wants to call a war criminal. I am the brutal dictator. And do you know why?"

"Excellency, I—"

"Because my country is poor. We don't have the oil that allows the Saudis to do whatever they want with the blessing of America. We don't have a billion future customers for American products, like the Chinese. And so while their much greater crimes are ignored, I am criticized for doing nothing but trying to keep my country at peace."

"Excellency, I understand your situation, but—"

"Do you? Do you understand that my future—the future of my people—is hanging by a thread? Do you understand that your failures, your incompetence, could be enough to destroy everything I've built?"

"It won't come to that, sir. I guarantee it."

Mtiti sat back again, the storm suddenly over. "I hope you're right, Aleksei. Because if you're not, I don't know what will happen."

47

I'm here," Aleksei Fedorov said into the phone while keeping his eye on Umboto Mtiti across the desk. The president was leaning back in a chair that looked vaguely like a throne, listening in on another handset.

"In Africa?" Josh Hagarty responded. Despite the fact that he was undoubtedly within a few hundred miles, his voice echoed with a slight delay.

"Where the fuck do you think I mean?"

"And you've got my sister?"

"Yes. Do you have my documents?"

"Yeah, I have them."

"Then we don't have much more to talk about, do we? Where are we meeting, and when?"

"Did Stephen tell you about the village where Annika was hiding out?"

"Yes."

"Let's meet on that road. Say, five miles before the village turnoff."

"Is that where you killed him?"

"It is, actually."

There was a nonchalance to his voice that Fedorov found vaguely disconcerting. In an effort to avoid hiring another over-educated do-gooder, they seemed to have gone too far in the other direction. It was difficult to tell if his attitude was just a bluff or if he'd learned more in prison than they'd anticipated.

"From what I heard, he had five or ten guys with him. Did you kill all of them?"

No response.

"That's what I thought. You're in rebel country, and it sounds like you made some friends there. Fuck you, we do this some-where neutral."

"There is nowhere neutral. We do it there, or we don't do it at all."

"Well, why don't we ask your sister—" Fedorov started but then fell silent when Mtiti held up a hand and nodded. "Okay, fine. When?"

"Five days from now. An hour before sunset."

"Five days? No way. Tomorrow."

"It's a little hard for me to travel right now, Aleksei. I've got a price on my head, and Mtiti's got people everywhere. It'll take me five days just to get there."

"How do I know you aren't trying to get the documents out of the country?"

"Because you have my sister, remember?"

Fedorov glanced at Mtiti, and again the president nodded.

"Five days, then. And you'd better not be screwing with me. Because you can be sure that while I'm tearing your sister apart, I'll tell her exactly whose fault it is."

"I want this over with, Aleksei. Just like you."

The line went dead, and Fedorov replaced the handset as Um-boto Mtiti looked on.

"I don't believe that bullshit about them being five days away from the meeting place," Fedorov said. "Is there any way they could make copies?"

"No," Mtiti said. "There are very few copiers in this country, and I have people watching all of them. I also still have the power and phones cut off in most of the country."

"What about the borders? They could be running."

The muscles in Mtiti's jaw started to bulge as though he were chewing something. In the short time he'd been there, Fedorov had come to recognize this as one of the warning signs that the man was about to lose it.

"Just because you can't control your people and your business, Aleksei, doesn't mean I can't. If they show their faces anywhere—*anywhere*—I'll know it."

Fedorov looked around him—at the guards by the door, at the dilapidated city on the other side of the bulletproof glass that framed Mtiti. All he could think about was cutting Josh Hagarty's heart out for forcing him to come here. For making him a prisoner of this ape that passed for a dictator.

"How much intelligence do you have on the terrorists in that area?" Fedorov said, being more careful of his phrasing this time.

Mtiti's expression turned to one of disgust. "I've left that land to the Yvimbo for now—there's nothing of value on it. But if your young friend thinks I'm powerless there, he's going to be very surprised."

48

The sun was starting to get low on the horizon, and Aleksei Fedorov dared a quick glance at his watch before going back to scanning the jungle on either side of the road. Nothing. He was alone except for Josh Hagarty's sister, who was handcuffed to the bumper of the Land Cruiser he'd driven there.

She was no longer drugged, but it was hard to tell. Mtiti's people had taken charge of her the day they'd arrived and apparently thrown her into the local prison. She was bruised, battered, and filthy enough that he'd had to drive with the windows open to take the edge off the smell. Alive, yes. But completely broken.

Hagarty was now half an hour late. Mtiti was watching and would be getting impatient. Fedorov considered calling him to make sure he stayed put, but it would do more harm than good. Mtiti did what he wanted when he wanted—most often with no thought at all for anything beyond that moment.

Instead he dialed the number for Stephen Trent's sat phone. Hagarty picked up on the first ring.

"Yeah?"

"Where the fuck are you?"

"I'm not coming."

"What? What the—"

"I told you to come alone, and you're not alone, are you? You were followed."

Fedorov looked around him for signs of Mtiti's men. He'd tried every argument he could think of to get Mtiti to use outside professionals, but the man had insisted on troops loyal to him—by all measures a bunch of poorly trained, drunk assholes. And now one of them had let himself be spotted.

"This is bullshit, Josh. I'm here with your sister, alone. Just like you said. You—"

"Do you think I'm an idiot, Aleksei? I know what I saw. When you—"

Fedorov cut off the connection and dialed another number. "He's got us. Go!"

At first there was nothing. Then, less than a minute later, small dots in the sky became visible in every direction.

The helicopters arrived first. Nine in all, they'd been brought in four nights ago, full of troops who were now blocking the only road in and out of the area. The planes would be next, flying in from an airstrip fifty miles north. Most were rickety, '60s-era warplanes, but there was one important exception: a state-of-the-art spy plane full of sensors and high-definition cameras designed specifically to find ground targets. The Russian pilot said he could track a rat through the Siberian forest in a snowstorm.

If Josh and Annika were close enough to have seen Mtiti's men, there was no way they could avoid being spotted or get through the net that was now closing around the area. It was only a matter of time before they were caught.

Fedorov walked back to the car, removing the handcuffs from one of the girl's limp wrists and shoving her back into the vehicle. He'd heard talk of a method of execution that was uniquely

African: They slid a tire over you, pinning your arms to your sides, and then set it on fire.

With a little luck, all this would be over by sundown. The documents would be destroyed, and Hagarty, his sister, and Annika Gritdal would be burning.

49

O h, my God . . ."
Annika was lying on her stomach in the dirt peering
through a pair of binoculars. Josh knelt next to her, and she held
them out to let him have a look.

Even with the magnification, he couldn't make out much more
than dark specks against the sky. Their speed and pattern of
movement made an educated guess possible, though. "Maybe
seven or eight helicopters and probably double that many planes.
Looks like a few are jets."

"I think it's the entire air force, Josh. I can't believe it. Mtiti
sent the entire air force."

They were many miles from the place where they were supposed to meet Fedorov and, until the aircraft appeared, hadn't
known if he'd kept his word and shown up alone. Clearly deceit-
fulness ran deep on both sides of the table. While everyone talked
about an honest exchange, Fedorov's real agenda was to see them
dead, while theirs was to stall and hope Katie hadn't gotten cold
feet.

"Kind of makes you think, doesn't it?" Annika said as Josh
rolled onto his back and stared into the empty sky.

"What?"

"What do you mean, what? Mtiti shut down the country's entire power grid, and now he's sent the entire air force after us."

"Good thing we're not down there."

"This time. But what about next time? Or the time after that?"

"I don't know what to say, Annika. We talked about this, and it was the best thing we could come up with. If you have any other ideas, I'm listening."

She shook her head, her frustrated expression seeming foreign to her face. "I've spent my entire life doing things myself—never counting on anyone else for anything. And now we've given the only things that can save us to a woman I barely know, so she can deliver them to someone I've never heard of, so that maybe he can do something that will stop Mtiti before he decides to set the entire southern half of his country on fire to kill us."

She was right. Their lives were hanging from an extremely long chain made up entirely of weak links. "I know it's starting to seem hopeless, Annika. I'm sorry—"

She clamped a hand over his mouth, silencing him. "I'm not blaming you, Josh. I knew what I was getting into. Well, that's not entirely true. I was hoping it might go a little better than this."

He motioned around them at the empty knoll and pulled her hand from his mouth. "What do you want? A butler?"

That elicited a smile, and for some reason it made him feel better about their situation.

"My idea of luxury is running cold water," she said. "I used to think that made me a cheap date."

"Me, too."

She looked through the binoculars again and watched Mtiti's pilots continue their futile search. "So what now?"

He wanted to call Katie, to find out what was happening. To get some idea of how long they'd have to keep ducking Mtiti or if they should try to get over a border. But there was no way. Fedorov would be able to see what numbers had been called from Trent's phone, and Katie would be dead in an hour.

"I guess we set up another meeting."

"Now? Maybe you should wait until he's in a better mood."

"Nah," he said, dialing Fedorov's number. "Let's see if we can make it worse."

"Where the fuck are you, you little son of a bitch?"

"Somewhere you're not going to find me. Don't get me wrong, though. I applaud the effort. Annika and I have been wondering— is that the whole air force?"

The tirade that followed was mostly in Russian, with a few choice English words for emphasis. Poking a wild animal with a stick was a dangerous game, but he and Annika had decided it made sense in this situation. The more they could keep Fedorov focused on homicidal fantasies, the less he'd be able to think straight. The problem was that the strategy had the potential to backfire badly if he ever got his hands on them.

"Aleksei! You're wasting my time again. We—"

"Wasting your time?" he shot back. "You want me to use your time better? How about you listening while I cut your sister's finger off?"

"Aleksei! Don't—"

The sound of Fedorov's phone dropping to the ground was followed quickly by Fawn's screams. At first they were just fear, but then they became the gurgling screeches of pain and horror. And then, just as suddenly as they had started, they stopped.

"Aleksei!" Josh shouted. "Aleksei! What—"

"The little bitch passed out," Fedorov said when he returned to the phone. "Ruining all our fun, huh, kid? Tell you what. I'll just leave her finger here for you. You can come and pick it up later. A souvenir of your trip to Africa."

Josh's mouth went dry, and he had to make a concentrated effort to conjure enough spit to speak. Aleksei was trying to rattle him, and he couldn't let that happen. Not with the odds stacked so high against him.

"That's fine, Aleksei. If I'm not getting my whole sister back, you're not getting all your documents back. I just peeled ten pages right off the top."

"You little son of a bitch! If I don't get every page back, I'm going to—"

"Shut the fuck up!" Josh screamed into the phone. "You want the documents, and I want my sister. Now, if you quit fucking around, we can get this done. But every time something happens to my sister, some of these pages are going to disappear. And I wouldn't want to be the one explaining why that happened to Umboto Mtiti."

"If you think you're going to—"

"Three days from now, Aleksei. Same place. And this time, leave the troops at home. I have spies everywhere. There are a lot of people in this country who hate Mtiti, and they're falling all over themselves to help me. If my people don't tell me that all those aircraft are sitting on the base outside the capital, I'm not coming."

"I wouldn't wait too long, Josh. You know where we're keeping her? The prison. Doesn't look like she's been gang-raped yet, but three days from now . . . Let's just say I can't make any guarantees."

"Another five pages of your documents just disappeared, Aleksei."

Fedorov exploded into another Russian diatribe, and Josh turned off the phone. When he did, though, it suddenly became hard to breathe.

"Josh? Are you all right? What happened?"

He walked toward the edge of the knoll, feeling increasingly dizzy despite the cool of the approaching darkness. Fawn Mardsen was an evil bitch. A white-trash con woman who took advantage of the goodwill of others. Maybe even a half-assed murderer. But she hadn't deserved that.

"Josh?" Annika said, putting a hand on his shoulder.

"He cut her finger off."

It was a few seconds before she responded. "It's not your fault, Josh. You had no way of knowing—"

"I had *every* way of knowing. I wrapped her up and delivered her right into the hands of a homicidal psychopath. What did I think was going to happen? The answer is, I didn't care. As long as it wasn't Laura, I didn't care."

50

Aleksei Fedorov rolled over in bed, awakened by the crack of gunfire outside. He'd become accustomed to the sound over the days he'd been confined in Mtiti's palace, but today it seemed closer. More urgent.

He went to his open window, squinting against the sun reflecting off the razor-wire-topped walls protecting the compound. The fortifications were better-manned than before, and there were two armored personnel carriers coming through the heavy steel gate. The soldiers crammed inside jumped out before the vehicles had come to a full stop, taking up positions on the wall with their machine guns at the ready.

The meeting with Hagarty was scheduled for that afternoon, and by that night Fedorov hoped to be on a plane out of this shithole. He'd managed to get Mtiti to agree to let him bring in another group of mercenaries, and they were already in position near the meeting site—dug in with sniper rifles that would finally put an end to Hagarty and the Norwegian bitch who was helping him. They deserved something so much slower than a bullet for the trouble they'd caused, but it was better to resolve the situation quickly. Before Mtiti's paranoia became any more dangerous.

The sound of men running in the hallway prompted him to start toward the robe hanging on the bathroom door. He was supposed to meet Mtiti in an hour to go over the plans for dealing with Hagarty. It was the fifth such meeting, and each time the man displayed an uncanny ability to ask the same questions over and over again.

Fedorov was just reaching for the robe when the door to his room burst open and armed soldiers flooded in.

"What the fuck—"

The lead man slammed a rifle butt into his stomach, driving him to his knees. Another kicked him in the side, knocking him to the floor and leaving him to try to protect his head from the blows that followed.

Were they Yvimbo rebels? Was this a coup? No. Mtiti's soldiers wouldn't have gone down without a fight. And he recognized some of the men from his time there.

The hard toe of a boot hit him in the small of his back and he grunted in pain as he tried to crawl away from the now laughing men.

"I'm here as Mtiti's guest!" Fedorov said. "I want to talk to him. Take me—"

An arm snaked around his throat, and he heard the thickly accented words of the man choking him. "You want to see Mtiti? Yes, we take you there."

He was dragged naked through the halls, passing soldiers, maids, and servants, all of whom stopped and stared dully. The door to Mtiti's office was partially ajar, and the men holding him slammed his head into it as they passed through. His vision blurred and the room rocked sickeningly as he was shoved to his knees in front of the president's desk.

"Did you know, Aleksei, that JB Flannary has a brother?" Mtiti said, rising from his chair. "And that his brother is a reporter for the *New York Times*?"

"I don't understand, Excellency. I—"

Someone behind grabbed him by the hair and yanked his head back, forcing him to meet Mtiti's stare.

"Answer my question, Aleksei. Did you know this?"

"No, I—"

"No?" Mtiti said, his anger building in a way that was well-known in the country. "Why would you not know, Aleksei? You killed Flannary, didn't you? And you killed his assistant and the man he worked for. Is that not correct?" He was shouting now, the sweat on his face glistening in the sunlight streaming through the windows. "Why would you not know his brother was a reporter? Why wouldn't your people be watching him?"

Fedorov tried to answer, but the words became trapped in his throat. He was completely alone here. Even the police and court system that he so despised weren't here to keep the situation from flying out of control. There was no law other than Mtiti.

"I don't understand," he finally managed to get out. "Excellency, I have—"

"Well, then, let me help you understand," Mtiti said, throwing a thin stack of paper on the floor in front of Fedorov.

The grip on his hair eased, allowing him to examine the poorly copied newspaper article. It was from that morning's *Times*. The headline was "U.S. Charity Connected to Organized Crime."

He shuffled through the pages, feeling the grip of panic tighten on his chest. It was all there. Pictures of both him and Mtiti, quotes from Josh Hagarty, including the exact location of the mass grave he'd found, background on Stephen Trent's criminal past, a list of bogus projects. Even estimates of the money siphoned from American taxpayers through USAID.

"He smuggled the documents out of the country!" Mtiti said. "He sent them to the media!"

"No. He wouldn't. . . . We have his sister."

"Keep reading, Aleksei."

He went to the next page, which implicated Fedorov in the deaths of JB Flannary and his colleagues as well as the disappearance of a Kentucky woman named Fawn Mardsen.

"You don't have his sister, Aleksei. Your people took the daughter of a man his mother divorced years ago. *You have the wrong woman!*"

"No," Fedorov stammered. "I . . . She was—"

"I've already had calls this morning from the U.S. government and the United Nations," Mtiti said. "I have power shut down everywhere, but this article is still getting in. By tomorrow everyone in my country will know about it. The mining companies won't take my calls, and I have reports that they're starting to evacuate their people, Aleksei!"

"No," Fedorov said. "We can fix this. We can."

Mtiti pointed, and an arm slid around Fedorov's neck again. He was dragged to his feet and led outside with Mtiti close behind.

"I understand that you've been inquiring about one of our methods of execution," Mtiti said, walking to the center of the courtyard as soldiers hurried to get out of his way. "I'm glad you're interested in learning about us and our culture."

When Fedorov saw the tire lying in the dust, he began to fight, but the arm around his neck constricted, cutting off the blood flow to his brain. He had nearly lost consciousness by the time the man behind him released his neck and pinned his arms to his sides.

The two soldiers lifting the tire in front of him gave him a burst of energy, but it wasn't the first time they'd done this, and they anticipated his every move. A moment later the tire was over his head and shoved down tightly over his arms. He desperately gulped the rubber-and-gasoline-scented air, managing to clear his mind and regain enough strength to pull free of the man holding him.

He only made it a few feet before he fell, the weight of the tire throwing off his already impaired balance. The courtyard had gone silent, and everyone stopped to watch as he rolled back and forth, struggling to free himself.

"You can't do this!" he shouted. "We've worked together for years! I've made you millions of dollars!"

A soldier grabbed the tire and used it to pull him back to his feet as Mtiti retrieved a gold lighter from his pocket.

"Excellency, I can fix this. I swear I can. Don't do this. I'm begging you—"

"And just how would you fix this, Aleksei? How would you stop the investigations of the Americans and Europeans? How would you get back the support I need to keep the Yvimbo from rising up against me? How would you convince the mining companies to keep operating?"

"We just need to talk. You need to give me a little time."

Machine-gun fire erupted somewhere beyond the wall. It was getting closer.

"But there is no more time, Aleksei." Mtiti flicked a thumb against the lighter, and a flame sprang to life.

The soldier holding the tire suddenly released it, and Fedorov ran, careful to maintain his balance this time. He'd made it only ten feet before he realized he hadn't been fast enough. The ring of flame rose up around his head, blinding him and drowning out the sound of cheering. He screamed when his hair caught fire, the smell of it mingling with the black smoke blinding him and burning his lungs. He closed his eyes tightly against the heat, but they were burning, too, boiling inside their sockets as he fell to the ground.

51

Josh slammed on the brakes and skidded to a stop as a vehicle-mounted machine gun swiveled in their direction. There was a short pause while he stared down the barrel of a weapon that could undoubtedly cut the Land Cruiser into pieces, and then the soldier turned his attention back to the crowd that had started throwing rocks.

"Jesus," Josh said weakly. "How many lives do we have left?"

"Don't worry. We're going to be okay," Annika said.

"How do you know?"

"I have a feeling."

"Great," Josh muttered as he slammed the accelerator to the floor again, charging up the city street as people broke for the edges to avoid being run over. The glint of flame in a man's hand outshone the sun for a moment, and Josh jerked the wheel hard, nearly plowing into a storefront before realizing the Molotov cocktail wasn't meant for them.

"This is crazy," he said. "Let me get you out of here, and then I'll come back—"

"You'd have been dead twenty times over if it wasn't for me," she said indignantly. "What makes you think you'd do any better now?"

Of course she was right. Just in the last few hours, her language skills had gotten them through two very hairy roadblocks, and it had been her idea to roll down the windows and break out the front windshield of Trent's Land Cruiser. Their white faces, which had been such a liability only a few days ago, now seemed to make them almost invisible in the chaos gripping the country.

Word of the *New York Times* article had swept through the population at a velocity that he still couldn't comprehend. Despite a literacy rate barely in the double digits, an almost complete lack of English speakers, and a failed power grid, it seemed that everyone knew about it. And now the Yvimbo rebels were using the unrest it had created to escalate their guerrilla war into a civil one.

Aid workers, mining employees, and representatives of foreign governments were fleeing like rats from a sinking ship, and the Africans knew it. Whites had once again become irrelevant, and that kept them from becoming a target. Unfortunately, it also stripped them of any protection they'd once enjoyed. So far that day, they owed their survival to the fact that no one wanted to waste a precious bullet on them.

"Let me take to you the airstrip, Annika. Get you on a plane . . ."

"Who would translate for you?"

"I'll be the only white guy there. What else would I want?"

She pointed through the hole where the windshield had been. "Turn left here."

Despite everything that was happening, Annika seemed to have found her moral compass again. Or maybe she'd never lost it and was just happy he'd found his. Whatever it was, the darkness that had descended on her was gone. They were embarking on what was almost certainly a futile and probably fatal attempt to save someone else. She was once again in her element.

The people thinned out, but he still wasn't able to maintain a speed much over thirty miles per hour. Smoke from the fires burning across the city blew through the open vehicle, burning his eyes and obscuring his vision.

A burst of machine-gun fire became audible behind them, and he thought of the crowd they'd just passed through. This wasn't a world of empty threats and warning shots. He wondered how many people had just died. Ten? Fifteen?

Annika twisted around in her seat, looking into the smoke behind them. "This was coming," she said, almost as though she were responding to his thoughts. "Without us, it wouldn't have been today. But it would have been tomorrow. Or next month, or next year."

He wanted to believe that because it absolved him in the deaths of those people in the crowd. And of all the others who would die as the violence inevitably escalated.

"Maybe something better will come out of it," she said. "Maybe they'll find a way to find some balance—"

A pickup overflowing with soldiers appeared from a side street and skidded to a stop, blocking the road.

"Keep going!" Annika said.

He pulled the Land Cruiser as far left as he could, grinding its side against the shacks lining the road. Annika ducked, scooting away from the open window and throwing an arm up against the chunks of wood flying through it.

The soldiers were piling out of the truck, hurrying to retrieve their rifles as Josh sped toward them.

"We're not going to make it!" he said. "They're in the way!"

"Keep going!"

She hadn't been wrong yet, and he pressed the accelerator to the floor. Instead of trying to avoid the men in the road, he headed right for them, forcing them to forget their guns and dive out of the way.

A few shots rang out after they'd passed, but none hit their mark. In the rearview mirror, all Josh could see was smoke.

The prison was at the edge of town—an old European factory that looked vaguely like the set of a horror movie. Through the rusting iron gate, Josh could see a mob of no fewer than a hundred men packed into the courtyard shouting at the soldiers looking down on them from perimeter towers. Apparently word of the *Times* article had found its way into the prison, too.

Josh let his foot off the accelerator, and the vehicle began to coast. The image of the enraged crowd brought a reality to what he was doing that the roadblocks for some reason hadn't. It was something he had to do to be able to live with himself, but it had nothing to do with Annika. It wasn't her crime.

She once again demonstrated her uncanny ability to read his mind. "It's going to be okay, Josh. I promise."

She put a hand on the wheel and kept him steady as they eased to a stop in front of the prison's main gate. A soldier stepped in front of the Land Cruiser and aimed his gun at them, shouting at them to get out. Josh started to comply, but Annika grabbed his wrist and shouted back at the soldier in Xhisa.

He moved forward, never taking his gun off them, but looking increasingly uncertain. Annika leaned out the broken windshield and held out twenty euros. A few more words between them and he took the money and opened the gate.

"Go ahead," Annika said, and Josh crept forward, feeling the Land Cruiser bounce as the soldier jumped onto the rear bumper.

Josh kept as far from the prisoners as possible, staying in the no-man's-land between them and the guards as the man on the bumper leaned in the broken rear window and offered incomprehensible directions.

"He says to go to the building in the middle," Annika said. "Get as close as you can."

Josh parked parallel to a heavy wooden door, leaving just enough room for him and Annika to slip out the passenger side.

The guard pounded on the door with his rifle butt, and a moment later another guard opened it. Instead of letting them in, though, the two men started what seemed to be a serious and intricate conversation that was nearly drowned out by the prisoners as they whipped themselves into a frenzy that would soon make their captors' weapons useless.

"What the hell's going on?"

"They're negotiating," Annika said.

"For what?"

"I had to offer the guy who came in with us everything we had. Twenty euros to get us through the gate and the rest when we're safely out. Any expenses in between come out of his pocket."

The man guarding the door pointed at Josh and Annika, the volume of his voice rising. The argument went on, with Annika quietly translating in his ear. The bottom line was that the soldiers were less concerned with the vagaries of political breakdown than with how they could turn a profit on it. After what seemed like an hour but was probably really only a few minutes, they came to an agreement, and Josh and Annika were led inside.

At first all he could see was the guards' backs, but as his eyes adjusted, the cells lining the walls emerged. They were uniformly filthy, with dirt floors and bars fashioned from the same construction debris that the rest of the country had been built with.

Most of the cells were empty, and the ones that weren't were occupied by what appeared to be corpses. The heat became overwhelming, and Annika slid an arm through his as they penetrated deeper into what seemed to be a good approximation of hell.

They found Fawn Mardsen at the end of the corridor, pressed into the back corner of her tiny cell. The mud spattered across her ragged dress smelled of death and excrement, and her right hand was wrapped in a bloody rag. Her head rose, the matted hair falling from her face as she peered in their direction.

"Josh?" she said, the single syllable nearly choked off in her throat. "Oh, my God. Is that really you?"

The soldier unwound the rope holding the cell door shut, and Josh pulled away from Annika. "Stay out here."

"Josh?" Fawn said again, taking an unsteady step in his direction. He'd expected her to scream at him, maybe even try to strangle him. God knew he deserved it. Instead she started to cry. "Please, Josh. Don't leave me here. Please help me."

"It's okay," he said, lifting her arm over his shoulder and supporting her weight. "We're going home."

EPILOGUE

The cold of the Kentucky air and the heatless sun above seemed strangely foreign to him. As though his many years there had been wiped away by his short time in Africa.

"Laura!"

Again there was no response, and he picked up his pace, breathing hard as he scrambled up a steep slope tangled with underbrush.

They'd gotten on one of the last UN evacuation planes three sleepless nights ago. Fawn needed medical attention for her gangrenous hand, and he'd left Annika to look after her at a hospital in Belgium while he caught the first available flight home.

Reports from Africa were sporadic and less than reliable at this point. Mtiti's forces were on the run in what was now a full-scale civil war, and the president was trying to escape his country by any means possible. So far every government he'd approached had turned down his request for asylum, and many of the assets he'd managed to expatriate were being frozen. The general consensus in the South African press was that he wouldn't survive the week.

"Laura!"

He'd phoned her from every plane and every airport he'd been in, with no luck. Of course that was to be expected—there was no cell reception in the mountains behind his family's property, and she'd have no way to charge a battery even if there was. But that didn't prevent him from using the endless flights to create elaborate scenarios for her demise. He doubted he'd left a single possibility unexplored in the hours he'd spent staring at the back of the seat in front of him—everything from Fedorov's people coming after her for revenge to Ernie Bruce attacking her when Fawn had disappeared to her falling out of the rickety tree house and dying a slow, lonely death in the woods.

He couldn't shake the feeling that he'd used up a lifetime's worth of luck escaping Africa and that this was where it was going to run out.

The tree house came into view, and he actually slowed, unsure if he could handle what he'd convinced himself he was going to find. What would he do? Walk back to town, get a job, get married, and eventually die of old age? How much blood could a person live with on his hands? How much *should* a person live with?

He didn't recognize the figure that burst from the trees and charged him—the heavy hunting jacket, the plaid hat, the rifle held in one hand. He raised his arms reflexively but was driven backward by the impact. The rifle hit the ground first, bouncing away as he landed on his back and felt the air go out of him.

"Josh!"

Laura threw her arms around him and squeezed harder than her thin frame would suggest she could. "The radio says there's a war going on! I thought you'd gotten trapped. I thought you were never coming back."

The muscles that had been knotted for so long that he barely noticed anymore suddenly relaxed, and he found himself unable to do anything but stare up at the dirty, tear-streaked face hovering above him.

Third chances didn't come along every day. This time he'd be grateful for everything he had. This time he'd do everything right.